Murder of Innocents

A Redmond and Haze Mystery

Book 14

By Irina Shapiro

Copyright

© 2024 by Irina Shapiro

All rights reserved. No part of this book may be reproduced in any form, except for quotations in printed reviews, without permission in writing from the author.

All characters are fictional. Any resemblances to actual people (except those who are actual historical figures) are purely coincidental.

Cover created by MiblArt.

Table of Contents

Prologue 5
Chapter 1 7
Chapter 2 11
Chapter 3 16
Chapter 4 23
Chapter 5 28
Chapter 6 33
Chapter 7 40
Chapter 8 46
Chapter 9 51
Chapter 10 55
Chapter 11 59
Chapter 12 64
Chapter 13 72
Chapter 14 82
Chapter 15 87
Chapter 16 95
Chapter 17 101
Chapter 18 106
Chapter 19 115
Chapter 20 122
Chapter 21 125
Chapter 22 128
Chapter 23 135
Chapter 24 139
Chapter 25 144
Chapter 26 146

Chapter 27	150
Chapter 28	158
Chapter 29	164
Chapter 30	167
Chapter 31	175
Chapter 32	181
Chapter 33	190
Chapter 34	192
Chapter 35	196
Chapter 36	205
Chapter 37	210
Chapter 38	213
Chapter 39	216
Chapter 40	221
Chapter 41	225
Chapter 42	231
Chapter 43	237
Chapter 44	249
Epilogue	255
Prologue	258
Chapter 1	260
Chapter 2	266
Chapter 3	268

Prologue

The house was silent and dark, the gallery, hung with portraits of long-dead baronets and their pasty-faced ladies, lost in shadow. The wooden staircase creaked as Amy warily trudged up the stairs, the flame of her candle wavering in the drafty emptiness. She hated her first chore of the day, partly because the task was disgusting and demeaning and partly because the gloomy, empty corridors frightened her. There was something malevolent about the ancient house, its low ceilings and narrow passageways making her feel trapped, and the snooty ancestors' painted eyes following her every move.

Eager to get the unpleasant task over with, Amy crept into the baronet's bedroom and slid the chamber pot from beneath the bed. She needn't have bothered to be quiet. He was out cold, his breath reeking of spirits and the chamber redolent with the odors of a man with healthy appetites, both for food and self-pleasure. Amy stepped outside, emptied the nightsoil into her bucket, then returned the chamber pot to the room and shut the door.

Her lady's bedroom was next, followed by the rooms of the upstairs servants whose nightsoil fell under the upstairs maid's remit. Amy was passing one of the unused bedchambers when she became aware of a strange odor. Putting her apron over her nose to keep out the noxious smell, she pushed the door open and peered inside.

The sun was just coming up and pale pink light streamed through the leaded windows, dispelling the murky darkness within. The room was empty, the massive tester bed hulking above her like some ancient ship, its curtain sails limp in the stagnant stillness. Amy lowered her apron and sniffed. The malodorous smell appeared to be coming from the carved sea chest at the foot of the bed. Inching forward, she gingerly lifted the lid. The smell assaulted her senses, but she forgot about her own discomfort as her hand flew to her mouth and tears spilled down her cheeks.

A sob tearing from her chest, Amy dropped the heavy lid and hurried from the room, her shoes making a terrible clatter on the stairs as she ran for help. She prayed there was still something to be done, but deep inside she knew. Death had come to Fox Hollow.

Chapter 1

Saturday, March 27

Even with the windows closed, Jason noticed the change in the air. It smelled of loamy earth, new grass, and pungent manure. The sky was clear, the ever-present coal soot that hovered over London replaced by puffy white clouds. It had rained earlier, but now the sky was a brilliant blue, the blossoming blackthorn and cherry plum buoyant against the backdrop of cobalt. On any other day, Jason would have enjoyed an outing to the country, but not today. For one, the brougham was trundling toward Fox Hollow, where two young children had died in suspicious circumstances. For another, he desperately wanted to be at home with his family.

Jason longed to see Micah, who had just arrived in London to spend Easter with the Redmonds, and talk with Mary. Mary Donovan, now O'Connell, and her son Liam had unexpectedly appeared on his doorstep that very morning, nothing short of an Easter miracle since the ship they'd reportedly sailed on from America had gone down off the coast of Ireland, all souls aboard lost. Mary had boarded another ship, narrowly avoiding certain death, but Jason would have liked to welcome her properly and hear more about the troubles that had forced Mary to flee Boston. Still, he could hardly complain. His family was safe and under the same roof once again and would spend Easter together as they had done before Mary decamped to America.

As he and Daniel neared their destination, Jason's thoughts turned to the grief-stricken parents who'd just lost both their children. Nothing would bring back the deceased, and Jason wasn't at all sure it would be a comfort to the family to learn how the boys had died. Regardless of whether they had been murdered or had died accidentally and might have been saved had they been discovered in time, they were gone. The knowledge would only give the parents reason to blame themselves and question their every decision leading up to the tragedy, wondering again and again if they might have done something differently that would have prevented the deaths of their babies. But if the children had been murdered, the killer could hardly be allowed to evade capture, so Jason supposed it was a moot point. His job was to determine the cause of death, while Daniel's job was to bring the culprit to justice.

Given Daniel's daughter Charlotte's recent abduction, Jason wished someone else had been tasked with investigating the deaths of the children. Daniel still felt the aftershocks of those few days and was particularly sensitive to anything involving small children. He would have gladly declined the assignment, but it seemed that Daniel and Jason had been requested by name, a state of affairs Superintendent Ransome both welcomed and resented. The summons had come from a noble personage, which always guaranteed a high-profile case, but the baronet's country seat happened to fall outside the jurisdiction of Scotland Yard, and the investigation would infringe on the territory of the Essex Constabulary and take up resources that would otherwise be allocated to inquiries that took place in London. Jason was paid a nominal fee for his involvement, which he donated to a charity for fallen women, but Daniel, being one of Ransome's most trusted detectives, was more difficult to spare when the Yard was snowed under with cases of varying importance.

Jason glanced at Daniel, who sat staring out the window, his gaze fixed on the fields and forests of his native Essex, his shoulders squared, his jaw tight with tension. Daniel turned to face Jason, his expression one of dismay since it seemed that his thoughts were running along the same line as Jason's.

"I just don't understand why Lady Foxley requested us by name," he grumbled. "That woman always did treat everyone as if they were her flunkeys and should jump to attention when she so much as graced them with her presence."

Daniel had good reason to resent Lucinda Foxley and didn't think any interaction with her would go any better than their previous encounters in Birch Hill. Just because Lucinda was now married didn't mean she had changed or had come to see the error of her ways. Lucinda Foxley's understanding of right and wrong was fluid at best, and her privileged upbringing and autocratic father had damaged her beyond repair, a happenstance that wasn't her fault but still made her extremely difficult to deal with. The Lucinda they had known was impulsive, callous, and utterly devoid of compassion, even toward those close to her.

Jason had no wish to belittle Daniel's feelings, since his irritation was perfectly justified, but thought he could defuse whatever residual anger Daniel felt at being ripped away from London to do Lucinda's bidding by focusing on the positive aspects of the summons.

"Presumably we were asked for by name because Lucinda Foxley trusts us to conduct a thorough investigation," he said.

"But why is she even involved?" Daniel countered. "The children can't be hers, since she married quite recently."

"No, but perhaps she's worried about her reputation and standing in the village."

Daniel hmphed. "As well she should be. Wherever Lucinda Foxley goes, death follows."

Lucinda Chadwick, as she was then, had been a suspect in two previous investigations. She had managed to avoid the repercussions and a stain on her name, but that didn't mean she was wholly innocent or even remotely sorry. Daniel had written her off as a bad seed, but Jason was prepared to give Lucinda the benefit of the doubt since she had been very young at the time of the investigations. He hoped marriage had had a positive effect and she was now content with her lot, but Daniel doubted that a wild and unrepentant nature like Lucinda's could ever be fully tamed. Perhaps Sir Lawrence had found a way to calm his tempestuous bride, or perhaps he'd given her leave to do as she would, and the result had proved tragic.

"Daniel, our duty is to two little boys. We will either rule the deaths accidental or open an investigation. Either way, we're here to do a job and should leave our personal feelings about Lucinda Foxley at the door."

Looking chastised, Daniel nodded. "You're right, and I will do my best to forget the beating I received at the hands of that woman or the role she played in the death of the poor young man who only wanted to discover the truth about his family. You have my word that I will try to remain neutral and objective."

"You always are," Jason reassured him, even though that wasn't strictly true.

It was difficult to remain objective when one's feelings and family were involved, but Jason trusted Daniel to do the right thing and knew that whatever the outcome, Daniel would remain courteous and professional.

Chapter 2

When it finally came into view, the house wasn't at all what Jason had expected. With a name like Fox Hollow, he had thought it might be quaint, but the sprawling Tudor manor that sat solid and proud amid the greening lawns put him in mind of the Dark Ages. When this house had been built, England had been a place of unfathomable ignorance, ruthless political maneuvering, and merciless religious persecution. It was also a time when America, the country of his birth, had been nothing but rivers and forests, the people that inhabited the land living without fear of extinction. A time no one cared to remember.

The house boasted four timber-framed sections, each one with its own steeply pitched roof and a jettied upper floor. Two massive brick chimneys were positioned on either side, and the mullioned windows were divided into ten panes, the diamond-shaped segments of glass reflecting the afternoon sun. Jason couldn't see the grounds beyond, but he was sure there was a kitchen garden, an herb garden, and probably a walled rose garden, where the ladies sat in the shade of the arbors on warm days or took the air when the weather turned cold. There was a well-tended herbaceous border that must be stunning in the summer, potted plants, and flowers that had yet to bloom planted beneath the ground floor windows. There was probably a number of outbuildings discreetly tucked away behind the hulking structure, each with its own purpose and designated staff. The house appeared untouched by time, a haunting relic of centuries gone by, and lives lived in isolated splendor.

The carriage rolled through the open gates and continued down the drive until it came to a stop before the black-painted door studded with iron nails. The door promptly opened to reveal a woman in her forties, presumably the housekeeper. She was dressed in black bombazine, and an intricate silver chatelaine, the sort Jason had never seen up close, hung from her waist, five household appendages affixed to stylized chains glinting in the early afternoon light. There was a thimble, sewing scissors in an engraved sheath, a tiny notebook, what appeared to be a pen, and a heart-shaped container the size of a walnut that probably contained smelling salts. The woman's dark hair was covered by a black lace cap, and her pale blue eyes seemed to radiate relief when Daniel stepped from the brougham and tipped his bowler.

"Are you the gentlemen from Scotland Yard?" the housekeeper asked, her gaze sweeping over Jason and Daniel. "Inspector Haze and Dr. Redmond?"

The form of address wasn't lost on Jason, and he didn't correct her. He and Daniel often downplayed Jason's rank for the sake of an investigation since it made Jason seem more approachable, particularly to working people.

"I'm Inspector Haze," Daniel said, and held up his warrant card for the woman's inspection. "And you are?"

"Mrs. Buckley, the housekeeper. Do come inside. My lord," she added deferentially, and inclined her head to Jason as a sign of respect.

The foyer smelled of musty wood and beeswax and was dominated by a wide dark-wood staircase that was handsomely carved and soared majestically toward the upper floor. The overhanging gallery overshadowed the outer parts of the foyer, and the light filtering through the windows was so distorted by the panes as to seem almost otherworldly. No gas lamps were in evidence, and the tall candles in iron holders were not lit so early in the day. The interior was so outmoded as to make one feel as if they'd time-traveled into the distant past.

"Is Lady Foxley expecting us?" Daniel asked as he took in his surroundings, his nose twitching with distaste. Not from a noble family himself, Daniel had little appreciation for country seats and dusty relics, particularly when they were achieved through marriage rather than birth.

"I'm afraid my lady felt unwell and needed to rest. I'll tell Sir Lawrence you're here," Mrs. Buckley replied.

She instructed a young parlormaid to take their coats and hats and invited them to wait in the parlor, which was dominated by an arched stone fireplace that was big enough for Jason and Daniel to stand in side by side. The fire had not been lit and the room was chilly, damp, and unpleasantly gloomy, the light seemingly leached by the coffered ceiling made of dark wooden squares, each adorned with a five-petaled flower. Several faded tapestries hung on the walls, and a framed document, written in Old English and dated October 2, 1563, was on display, the missive written in flowing script and embellished with the wax seal of Elizabeth I, the wax yellowed with age. It appeared to be a pardon bestowed on some long-dead Foxley who had probably come dangerously close to losing his head.

Jason and Daniel settled into the hardback chairs that resembled thrones and were extremely uncomfortable since the cushions were so threadbare, they barely padded the seats. The same parlormaid that had taken their things brought two cups of mulled wine, the spiced drink filling the room with the pleasant aromas of honey and cloves. After taking a sip, Jason set the cup aside. He liked the idea of mulled wine a lot more than he enjoyed the taste. Daniel drained his cup, glad of a hot drink after the long drive.

Creaking came from somewhere above, and then the unmistakable sound of a heavy tread as the master of the house descended the stairs and approached the parlor. Jason had not seen Lawrence Foxley in nearly two years. Outwardly, Sir Lawrence had not changed. He was still in fine physical form, his bearing erect, and his clothes fashionable and expensive. The cabochon ring on his pinky reflected the afternoon light, his watch chain gleamed, and his buttons shone with polish. The fair hair that he'd worn artfully tousled while courting Lucinda Chadwick was now longer, the sideburns edged sharply just beneath Sir Lawrence's fleshy cheekbones, the points angled toward a sensual mouth. There were no obvious signs of ill health, but Jason got the impression that Sir Lawrence overindulged in spirits and had grown slightly thicker around the middle.

The baronet smiled, and Jason saw genuine grief in his blue eyes. "Lord Redmond, Inspector Haze, I thank you for coming. Would you care for some tea? Or perhaps something a little stronger?"

"Thank you, no," Daniel said. "We quite enjoyed the mulled wine. Sir Lawrence, if you would be so kind as to tell us why we were sent for?"

Sir Lawrence nodded and sank onto the plush red settee that showed considerable signs of wear, particularly in the center. "I was going to send word to the Brentwood Constabulary, but Lucinda begged me to send a message to Scotland Yard. She's quite distraught."

"Can you tell us what happened?" Jason asked.

Sir Lawrence's mouth dipped, and he sighed heavily, his shoulders dropping. "Our cook, Mrs. Powers, has—had," he amended, his expression pained, "two boys. John was six, and Bertie was four. The boys had the run of the estate and spent hours playing outside in all weather. When they didn't come home for supper last night, Mrs. Powers became worried, so we organized a search party. We looked for hours but found no sign of the children. The boys' father and I even followed the path along the river, in case the children had fallen in and been pulled along by the current."

Sir Lawrence sighed again, even more audibly this time. "This morning, the upstairs maid, Amy, smelled something foul coming from one of the unused chambers. The odor was coming from an old sea chest. When she opened the chest, she found the children. They were dead and had probably been for hours."

"Might it have been an accident?" Daniel asked. "Could the children have become trapped in the chest and suffocated?"

Sir Lawrence shook his tawny head. "I don't believe so, Inspector Haze. The trunk was not locked when Amy entered the room, so the children could have climbed out at any time if they were playing a game. And someone would have heard them if they had called for help. There's always someone about. It would seem that the boys became ill and passed before they could call out. Mrs. Powers is convinced that her children were murdered."

"Who would want to murder two little boys?" Jason asked.

"I don't know," Sir Lawrence said, his voice quavering and his eyes misting with tears. Jason hadn't taken Sir Lawrence for an emotional man, especially when it came to those who served him, but he appeared sincere in his grief.

"Has anything been moved since the maidservant discovered the children?" Jason asked.

Sir Lawrence shook his head. "Mrs. Powers wanted to take the children home and lay them out, but I explained how important it is for the police to see the deceased as they were found. I locked the room, so no one has been inside since the boys' parents saw them this morning."

"Then you had better show us," Daniel said.

He looked grim, and Jason shared his apprehension. Accustomed as he was to handling the dead, he found it difficult to remain emotionally detached when the deceased were children.

"I hope you will forgive my presumption," Sir Lawrence said before taking them upstairs, "but I thought it best not to mention your noble title to anyone except Mrs. Buckley, my lord. It would prevent the servants from speaking frankly in your presence, and I need to know who did this."

"There's no need to apologize," Jason said. "You made the right decision. And now I need to see the deceased."

Chapter 3

The ceiling upstairs was even lower than on the ground floor, and since most of the doors were shut, the narrow passageway was almost completely dark, the only source of light the candle Sir Lawrence had thought to bring. He led the way, his face set in grim lines and his shoulders stooped with either genuine sorrow or the very real worry that he might be on the verge of a massive scandal that would haunt his family for generations.

The smell permeated the corridor despite the closed door and instantly put Daniel in mind of cholera. It was a noxious combination of feces and vomit that he associated with the illness and would know anywhere, even though he'd been exposed to it only once, when he was twelve. His grandfather, who'd lived with Daniel's family when he was a child, had contracted cholera while visiting the London docks. He'd accompanied a friend who'd gone to inspect a shipment of tea from India, and days later, they were both ill. Oscar Haze had died in agony, his final moments spent lying in his own waste since their one servant had been too afraid to approach the dying man, and with good reason.

It was only years later that cholera had been proven to be catching, the rapid spread of the illness finally curtailed by periods of quarantine to minimize contagion. Had it not been for Daniel's father's quick thinking, they would all have perished. Daniel and his mother had been sent to the seaside to stay at a modest beachfront hotel while his father remained at the house to ensure that his father was looked after, taking every precaution not to become ill. The smell had lingered long after Oscar Haze's remains had been taken away, the room fetid and haunted by the spirit of the man who'd been brought so low.

Even now, Daniel was tempted to put a handkerchief over his face to block out the noxious odor, but Jason didn't look concerned, so Daniel followed him down the corridor, his gaze on Sir Lawrence's broad back. When he unlocked the door, Sir Lawrence didn't go in but remained outside by the door. It was obvious from his expression that he couldn't bear to see the children's remains again but intended to stay near enough to hear what Jason had to say. Jason paused on the threshold, taking a moment to take in the room before striding toward the window and throwing open one of the casements. Daniel followed him inside.

The room could only be described as a medieval bedchamber since it clearly hadn't been updated in centuries. The walls were paneled in dark wood, and the bed that dominated the space was so ornately carved and brightly painted that Daniel was hard-pressed to find an inch of wood that wasn't adorned with some sort of image or symbol. The bed hangings were made of mustard-colored fabric that matched the pillow covers and counterpane. There was a filigreed bronze brazier in the corner, a painted cabinet with four square drawers, and a heavy carved chest at the foot of the bed. The brass latch was down, locking the chest from without.

Although eager to examine the chest more closely, Daniel stood back, allowing Jason to open the lid. Jason relied heavily on first impressions, and if Daniel were honest, he dreaded the thought of seeing what lay within. Like Jason, he came in contact with death nearly every day and had seen his share of children who'd died of disease, hunger, and neglect. Seeing the tiny corpses broke his heart and chipped away at his faith, all the more so when the child had no one to claim their body or see to a proper funeral and the remains were sent to the dead house and eventually tossed into a pauper's grave. Daniel wanted to believe that God loved all His children and had a plan for each man, woman, and child He'd allowed to grace the earth, but seeing the emaciated, rag-covered remains of urchins who had died in doorways and alleyways and the bloated, half-eaten faces of children who had been pulled from the river would make even the most ardent believer question God's plan.

Jason undid the latch and slowly opened the lid. The stench instantly grew stronger, the odor of human waste combined with the acrid smell of vomit. The children snuggled inside the trunk looked nothing like the sad creatures Daniel had seen in London. They were clean, well fed, and neatly dressed. Both boys wore short pants, woolen hose, and sturdy leather shoes. Their shirts were made of fine linen, and their coats were made of good-quality wool. They lay face to face, their snub noses almost touching, their eyes closed as if in sleep. The older boy had his arm around his brother, the younger boy's chubby fingers holding on to the lapel of his brother's coat. Death had yet to start about its ugly work, and the children looked as cherubic as if they had been painted by a loving hand.

Jason stood silently next to the chest, his gaze firmly fixed on the children's faces. After a few moments, he leaned down and sniffed experimentally, then moved away.

"Might this have been a tragic accident?" Daniel asked. He saw no signs of violence or any obvious wounds.

"I don't know," Jason replied. "I will need to take a closer look."

"Will you not perform a postmortem?"

"I would like to examine the children first, and then the trunk. Then I will decide."

"I don't want them mutilated," Sir Lawrence said from the doorway. "They must return to God as He made them."

Sir Lawrence didn't strike Daniel as a God-fearing man, but death affected everyone differently, especially when it was sudden and tragic. And Sir Lawrence had obviously cared for the boys.

"Sir Lawrence, if you wouldn't mind waiting downstairs," Jason said, and shut the door in the man's face. "Help me, Daniel."

Jason pulled back the counterpane, then lifted one of the children from the trunk and laid him on the bed. Daniel followed suit and arranged the second body next to his brother. The boys' limbs offered no resistance, and they were able to lay them flat.

"Rigor has passed," Jason observed, "so they have been dead for at least eight hours, probably longer. Help me undress them."

They worked in silence as they removed the soiled clothes. Jason carefully looked at every item before he set it aside. Once fully undressed, the children looked even more vulnerable. Their skin was chalk-white after the winter months, and their cheeks and bellies were still rounded with babyhood, their eyelids almost translucent. Light brown hair curled over delicate ears, and the boys' chubby hands, little toes, and a healing scab on Bertie's knee brought tears to Daniel's eyes. They were so small, so perfect, and they would have had so much living left to do. Instead, they would be put in the ground, their features never maturing and their bodies never growing into adolescence and then manhood.

Jason didn't say a word, but Daniel could see the emotion in his face. John and Bertie were only a few years older than Jason's daughter Lily and Daniel's daughter Charlotte. Little boys that had been full of life yesterday were now nothing but empty husks, their laughter silenced forever.

"What a dreadful waste," Daniel said, unable to contain his dismay any longer. "How did they die?"

"There are no obvious signs of violence," Jason said. "The vomiting and diarrhea suggest that the children ingested something highly toxic."

"Such as?"

Jason shook his head. "I don't know yet."

Daniel watched as Jason examined the children. He looked deep into their eyes, peered into their mouths and noses, palpated their bellies, and examined their bottoms. He looked carefully at their hands and feet and took a cursory look at their genitals. Jason touched the boys gently as if they were still alive and could feel discomfort or embarrassment, and covered the lower halves of their bodies with a sheet once he was finished.

"What do you think, Jason? Could they have become trapped and suffocated?" Daniel asked.

"On the face of it, yes, but I don't think that's what happened."

"Based on what?"

"As Sir Lawrence pointed out, there are enough people in this house that someone would have heard their cries and the noise they would have made as they tried to free themselves. The hands show no evidence of trauma, the kind that would occur if they had tried to pry open the lid or beat at the wood." Jason reached for Bertie's hands and showed them to Daniel. "No bruising, no broken nails, not even bits of wood beneath the fingernails, but there's a bluish cast to the skin at the fingertips." He replaced the child's arms by his side and reached for his brother's hands, which were unblemished. "Likewise, their lips are bluish, as are their toes." He nodded to himself as if something had been confirmed in his mind.

"Some might say the diarrhea and vomiting were brought on by fear, but there's a musty smell beneath the other odors," Jason mused. "And something else that I can't quite identify."

Jason walked to the foot of the bed and sniffed again, then peered into the trunk, staring at the pools of semi-dried vomit and shit. Finding a clean towel next to the pitcher and ewer on the washstand, Jason reached inside and scooped up a bit of vomit. He then walked over to the window and studied the sample. Daniel stood next to him, trying valiantly not to breathe too deeply. The vomit was mostly green, but there were flecks of pink, and beneath the acrid smell there was a sickly sweetness that seemed entirely out of place.

Jason didn't seem bothered by the odor or the sight of the noxious sample, but given what he usually worked with, this was nothing out of the ordinary for him. He looked at the towel for a few long minutes, then brought it to his nose and sniffed it again before setting it aside.

"What do you smell?" Daniel asked.

"Mustiness, digestive juices, and something else. Cocoa, maybe."

"The mustiness could be from the trunk. It must have been used to hold clothes and blankets for centuries, and I suppose the children might have had a pudding with their midday meal. But what are those pink flecks? Could it be the poison?"

"I can't say just by looking at it, but the flecks appear grainy. The only pink poison I can think of is foxgloves, but it's not in bloom yet. If someone had some on hand from last year, the petals would be moist and limp."

"So, what do you reckon?" Daniel asked.

Jason looked pensive. "By themselves, the symptoms don't add up to much, but taken together…"

"What are you thinking?"

"I recently attended a lecture at the Horticultural Society on the properties of common poisonous plants and how to identify the culprit in a case of accidental poisoning. Bluish lips, fingertips, and toes are attributed to hemlock poisoning. Had the children ingested hemlock, they would have felt weak, disoriented, and sick to their stomachs. Vomiting might have saved their lives by ejecting the poison, but if they had taken a large amount, they would have experienced acute respiratory failure and died before anyone had a chance to go for help."

"They may have consumed the poison by accident," Daniel pointed out. "Hemlock resembles Queen Anne's lace, although neither plant would have blossomed so early in the year."

Jason shook his head, clearly dubious. "If they had eaten something while out in the grounds, they would have become ill long before coming inside the house and hiding in a trunk. Poison acts quickly, especially in children. And why would they eat hemlock or Queen Anne's lace? Any child that grows up in the country knows which plants to avoid. Besides, hemlock has an unpleasant odor and a terrible taste. They would have to have eaten enough to kill them, and I highly doubt they would keep eating something that tasted and smelled awful."

"You have a point there," Daniel agreed. "So, you think someone gave it to them?"

"That's the more likely possibility. The leaves are highly toxic. If they were mashed and mixed into something edible, the children would ingest enough poison to kill them before they realized something wasn't quite right."

"Jason, are you certain the children were murdered?"

"With no obvious wounds and no way to test the toxicity of the blood, it's impossible to say for certain. In a case like this, I have to trust my gut reaction, and I believe that these children were deliberately poisoned."

"How long would you say they have they been dead?" Daniel asked.

"Twelve to twenty-four hours."

"We will need to interview everyone who was at the house yesterday, starting with Lucinda Foxley."

"I'd like to have a word with the upstairs maid before we speak to Lucinda," Jason said. "I need to clarify a few points."

"Yes, of course," Daniel replied. Given that Amy had been the one to find the children, it made sense to interview her first.

Chapter 4

They found Amy in the laundry room, her hands and face red from the steam and her apron damp from handling the wet garments. She was bent over the tub but immediately straightened when Daniel and Jason entered the room, her eyes opening wide with apprehension to see two strangers entering her steamy domain.

"Are you the gentlemen from Scotland Yard, then?" Amy asked as she took a step back, clearly frightened.

"I'm Inspector Haze, and this is my associate, Dr. Redmond," Daniel said, smiling at Amy in what he thought was a reassuring manner. "If we might ask you a few questions, Amy."

Amy looked uncertain, but she could hardly refuse, so she nodded and clasped her reddened hands before her, like a schoolgirl.

"Perhaps we can talk outside," Daniel suggested. His forehead was already beaded with sweat, and he was terribly warm in his tweeds.

Amy obediently followed them outside and breathed deeply of the fragrant spring air as she leaned against the wall, possibly for support. She was a little older than Daniel had first thought, maybe thirty, and had a short, stocky body and blunt features, her face dominated by a too-wide mouth and eyes as dark as blackberries.

"I was given to understand that you are the upstairs maid," Daniel said. He was grateful to be outside after the stifling heat of the laundry room and thought that Amy was just as glad of the reprieve from her chores.

Amy scoffed. "There is only a handful of servants, Inspector Haze, so we do whatever we're told."

A house the size of Fox Hollow would normally have a well-established hierarchy of servants that would include head housemaid, parlormaid, chamber maid, and laundry maid, as well as several kitchen maids, a scullion, and a pair of footmen, but it seemed that the manor was woefully understaffed, each person expected to perform several jobs.

"That must be difficult," Jason said. He smiled at Amy, and she couldn't help but smile back, even though she was clearly nervous. "So, what are your duties, Amy?"

Amy sighed. "I'm in charge of the upstairs rooms, including the servants' quarters, which are in the attics. I'm also expected to light the fires, bring hot water, take out night soil, and see to the laundry."

"How often do you do the laundry?" Daniel asked. With so many people and only one laundry maid, Amy had to spend a lot of time in the laundry.

"Twice a week," Amy replied miserably. "And it takes most of the day."

"That must be tiring," Jason remarked.

"I barely have time to sit," Amy complained. "The mistress likes the sheets changed every week, and there's everyone's hose, and undergarments, and shirts. And I have to do a separate wash for the towels."

Daniel was eager to hear Amy's unguarded comments. She clearly felt put upon, and although it was unusual for a servant to vent their grievances to complete strangers, her frustration helped him to understand something of the running of the household without having to question Mrs. Buckley, who wouldn't be likely to admit to a shortage of staff or any lingering dissatisfaction on the part of the maids.

"Can you tell us what happened this morning, Amy?" Jason asked.

Now that Amy felt more at ease, she would be more likely to share the details without worrying how she might be affected by her testimony.

"The mistress likes me to empty the chamber pots first thing in the morning, so she can piss into a nice clean pot when she gets up," Amy said bitterly. "Sir Lawrence is not as fussy; he'll piss out the window and not give a toss if someone's standing beneath, or lift up his shirt and do his business even if I'm standing right there." Amy wrinkled her nose in disgust. "That's an experience I'd rather avoid, so I'm usually the first one up, well before sunup. I do Sir Lawrence's room first, while he's dead to the world and not likely to go waving his prick about, then I go to her ladyship's chamber. Afterward, I head upstairs to do the servants' rooms. Most of them are up by that time, so they don't mind me coming in."

Amy's face creased with sadness as she recalled how that morning had been different. "Anyway, I was just passing the guestroom when I smelled something foul, so I went inside to check, since I would be blamed if something died in there."

Having realized what she had just said, Amy blanched, and her eyes filled with tears. "I couldn't have known, could I?" she moaned. "I knew the boys had gone missing, but I figured they must have found their way home and were snug in their beds. How could I have guessed?" Amy was crying softly now, the tip of her nose turning red.

"It's all right, Amy. No one is blaming you," Jason said. "Please, go on."

"Well, the smell was coming from the trunk, so I opened it. I thought maybe a rat had got in and or maybe it was Polly."

"Who's Polly?" Daniel and Jason asked in unison.

Amy sniffed. "Polly is the cat. She disappeared a few days ago. Probably went off somewhere to die. She was old," Amy explained. "Well, imagine my horror when I saw the boys. If not for the awful smell, I'd have thought they were sleeping, but then I knew," Amy said shakily. "I knew."

"Amy, I need you to think very carefully before you answer," Jason said. "Take your time. Was the latch up or down when you approached the trunk?"

"The latch was up," Amy replied without a moment's hesitation. "I am certain."

"And what about the door?" Daniel asked. "Was the door to the room firmly shut?"

"It was. I had to push it open," Amy said. "Sometimes it jams."

"Did you see anything else inside the room? Anything that was out of place?" Jason pressed.

Amy shook her head. "No, nothing. Except that the doorknob and the latch on the trunk were tacky when I touched them," she added.

"Tacky?" Daniel asked.

"Like someone had touched them with grubby hands."

"And who would do that?" Jason asked.

Amy smiled sadly. "John and Bertie. They must have had something on their hands when they opened the trunk. Mrs. Powers was always telling them to wash their hands after they'd eaten."

"Was anyone else upstairs yesterday afternoon?"

"Just me, her ladyship, and Miss Carlin, her maid. Mr. Wylie—that's Sir Lawrence's valet—had gone into Brentwood to collect Sir Lawrence's new coat and didn't return until later. It doesn't take hours to collect a parcel, but I reckon he and Clegg, the coachman, made the most of it. They joined the search as soon as they came back. Everyone else was downstairs." Amy looked

26

from Jason to Daniel. "If that's all, Inspector Haze, I really must get back or the water will get cold."

"Go on," Daniel said, and watched as Amy hurried back inside, her relief at being set free evident.

"Let's have a word with Lucinda," Jason said, and followed Amy into the house.

Chapter 5

Lady Foxley was still resting, so Jason and Daniel were invited to attend on her in her sitting room. It was a feminine room, the décor quite at odds with the rest of the house. There was a rather modern chaise upholstered in mauve velvet, an inlaid rosewood desk and chair, and a thick carpet in shades of pale pink and cream. Pastel wallpaper and light damask curtains with gold tassels gave an impression of air and light despite the small mullioned windows that even on the brightest day would filter out most of the sunlight. It was the sort of room one might find in Belgravia or Park Row, not this ancient manor house that had barely changed since the Middle Ages and instantly made one feel oppressed with its dark wood paneling and low ceilings.

Lucinda Foxley was not yet twenty, but just then she had the look of a much older woman. Her face was blotchy, her eyes puffy, and her stomach so grotesquely swollen as to make Daniel wonder if she were expecting a baby elephant. Her dark hair was loosely braided into a thick plait that hung over one shoulder, and she wore a shapeless garment in dark blue satin. The baroness lay back on the chaise, her legs covered by a woven throw. She sat up gingerly, as if anticipating a stab of pain, but an expression of relief flitted across her face when she looked at Jason, and she tried to smile, but it came out as more of a grimace than an expression of welcome.

"Lord Redmond, I thank you for coming," Lucinda said, then nodded to Daniel. "Inspector Haze."

"Lady Foxley."

"Why did you send for us, Lucinda?" Jason asked, surprising Daniel with the use of her Christian name. Perhaps he wanted to remind her that he had known her when she was plain Miss Chadwick, or perhaps he wished to establish a rapport and show Lucinda that he was her friend rather than a near-stranger who was there in his professional capacity.

"Because I'm afraid," Lucinda said, her face crumpling and her eyes filling with tears. "Mrs. Powers all but accused me of murdering her children."

"And why would she think that?" Jason pulled up a chair and sat next to the chaise.

Lucinda took a deep breath and tried to compose herself. "Because I'm the only person on this estate who bore them a grudge," she whispered.

"I think you had better explain, my lady," Daniel said. He remained standing and moved closer to the chaise to hear Lucinda's explanation. "What possible reason would you have to bear a grudge against two little boys?"

Lucinda nodded in understanding. "I see he didn't tell you. Not that I'm surprised. My husband is not one to give anything away unless it's absolutely necessary."

"It would seem that in this case, it is," Daniel replied, but Lucinda's meaning was becoming obvious.

"John and Bertie were my husband's sons by *the cook*." Lucinda put undue accent on the final two words, making her feelings crystal clear.

"Were you aware of the children's paternity before you married Sir Lawrence?" Jason asked.

"Of course not. I didn't know they existed."

"And when did you discover the truth?"

"Quite recently."

"Who told you?" Daniel asked.

"Lawrence. After I confronted him."

"What made you suspect the children were his?" Jason asked.

Lucinda sighed. "Lawrence is not a patient man, nor a master who pays much mind to his servants. People are there to look after his needs, and he likes them best when they keep out of his way, but he always had a smile and a kind word for those boys. He gave them the run of the house, and on his last trip to Brentwood, he purchased them a rocking horse each."

"Did he readily admit to fathering the children?" Daniel asked.

"He denied it at first. Said I was being ridiculous. But when pressed, he finally admitted it. He said it was a youthful indiscretion and he can't help but feel affection toward the children."

"And how did you respond?" Daniel inquired politely.

"I felt angry and betrayed and asked him to keep the boys from the house. Their parents have a perfectly adequate cottage on the estate, and there are extensive grounds to play in. There was no need for them to come into the house and taunt me with their presence, especially in my condition."

Lucinda's hand went to her belly, and her eyes brimmed again. "I know these things are quite common and should be overlooked. I hardly thought that Lawrence had led the life of a monk before we married." Lucinda's voice quavered with emotion. "Mother warned me that men have their needs and will satisfy them with anyone they have to hand, but to be confronted with the result of such careless behavior and know that one's husband has feelings for his bastard children was surprisingly painful."

Tears slid down Lucinda's cheeks, and she fixed Jason with an expression of mute pleading. "I know what you must think of me, given our past interaction, Lord Redmond. I have no right to ask you for anything, nor you, Inspector Haze, but I did not murder those boys. I would never harm an innocent child." Her hand was still on her bulging belly, and she shuddered with either chill or extreme emotion. "The children were no threat to me," she said quietly. "Or to my child."

"Who's looking after you, Lucinda?" Jason asked. "Is there a midwife, or are you attended by a physician?"

"There's a midwife in the village. Mrs. Grimsby. She's delivered most of the children in the parish."

"I would like to examine you, if you have no objection."

"Why?" Lucinda asked tearfully.

"Because you don't look at all well."

Lucinda nodded. "I don't feel well. I haven't felt myself in ages."

"Has anyone visited you? Your mother or sister?"

Lucinda had been close with her sister Arabella, but marriage had a way of straining the bonds of sisterly love, particularly when the older sister remained unmarried. It was unorthodox to allow the younger daughter to marry first, but Caroline Chadwick had not been about to pass up an opportunity to marry her daughter off to a baronet, Arabella's feelings be damned. Perhaps the sisters were estranged.

"I haven't seen Mother and Arabella since Christmas," Lucinda admitted sullenly.

"Have you quarreled?" Daniel asked. He couldn't imagine Caroline Chadwick forgoing the chance to visit her titled daughter, especially when Chadwick Manor wasn't so very far away, and Lucinda clearly needed her mother.

"No, but Mother is busy. Arabella has just become engaged to a man Mother wholeheartedly approves of, and the two of them are in London to order Arabella's trousseau. They are due to visit next week. Harry was here, though. He stayed with us for two days and left yesterday, in the afternoon." Lucinda fixed her tearful gaze on Jason. "Will you help me prove my innocence, my lord?"

Jason tilted his head to the side and studied Lucinda, as if asking *Are you innocent?* He must have seen something in her face because he gave a reluctant nod. "I will do what I can."

"Thank you," Lucinda exclaimed. She tried to smile, but the tears came for real this time, and a sob tore from her chest, making her shudder with misery.

"Let me help you to bed, and we'll see how your baby is doing," Jason said soothingly.

"I'm going to have a word with Sir Lawrence before I start on the staff interviews," Daniel said, and left Jason to it.

Chapter 6

Lucinda's bedroom was lovely, a delicate confection of pale pink and gold that was both modern and functional. There was a painted silk screen depicting a peaceful oriental scene that hid a brass tub from view, and a pitcher and ewer painted with a pattern of blossoming cherry trees sat on the washstand. The bed was high and wide, the headboard and posts carved with climbing vines and ripe fruit, a non-too-subtle symbol of female fertility. Jason couldn't help but wonder if Sir Lawrence had been a frequent visitor before Lucinda had grown large with child and if he had been a gentle and caring lover to his young bride.

Lucinda looked small and pale next to the huge bed, but even though she was clearly frightened, she was the sort of person who channeled her fear and uncertainty into defiance rather than permitting herself to show vulnerability.

"The child is fine," she said dismissively. "It doesn't allow me to get any peace. Much like its father."

"Let me have a look," Jason cajoled. Lucinda looked distinctly unwell, and Jason didn't think it was because of the deaths of the children.

Lucinda hefted herself onto the bed using a painted footstool and lay flat, her belly swelling above her like a rising hot air balloon. Jason took hold of her wrist and measured her pulse, then opened his gladstone bag and took out the stethoscope. He pressed the tube to her chest and listened to her heart before moving the apparatus to her stomach. Lucinda shut her eyes and would have looked peaceful, but her breathing was ragged, and she was trembling, possibly with nerves.

Jason set aside the stethoscope and placed his hands on Lucinda's belly, gently pressing on the distended flesh as he moved from spot to spot, feeling the child within and gauging its size. Having finished, Jason lifted Lucinda's skirts and examined her ankles, which were swollen and pushing against the shafts of her low-heeled kid boots.

"I'm going to die. I know it," Lucinda whispered, having abandoned all pretense of indifference. Tears slid down her temples and into her hair, and her lower lip quivered as she tried to hold back the flood.

"Why do you think you're going to die?" Jason asked gently.

"The child is so large. Sometimes I feel like I can't breathe, and at other times it feels as if my very bones are shifting. And my head hurts nearly all the time, making it difficult to see clearly. It's as if there's unbearable pressure building within, and my skull is going to split open." Lucinda fixed Jason with a desperate stare. "God is punishing me for the things I've done. I know it. I want to go home," she cried. "I don't want to die here. I hate this place. And I hate Lawrence. I want Arabella, and my mother," she wailed. "Please, take me to Chadwick Manor. I want to be buried at St. Catherine's, next to Father. I want to know that someone will visit my grave. Please, take me home."

"I'm afraid you're in no condition to travel," Jason replied. "You need peace and plenty of rest."

"Well, I'm not likely to get that here, am I?"

"I will see that you do." Jason replaced the stethoscope in his bag and snapped it shut.

"Please," Lucinda tried again.

She began to sob and gasp for breath, her hand flying to her bosom as she wheezed. Jason slid his arm beneath the struggling woman and lifted her upper body, using his other hand to slide pillows behind her back. He allowed her to recline and gave her a few moments to catch her breath. Lucinda looked pale and terrified, and an image of her galloping through the woods dressed in breeches and a man's shirt flashed through Jason's mind. He could still see the sparkle in Lucinda's eyes and the flush of excitement on her cheeks, her lips curled into a smile that was part amusement and part cruelty. That was only two years ago, but it may as well have been a lifetime ago.

"How far along are you, Lucinda?"

"Close to eight months."

"That's what I thought," Jason said. "Why don't you rest a while. I need to speak to Sir Lawrence."

"To tell him I'm going to die?"

"Of course not," Jason replied, smiling down at her. "You're not going to die. Not if I can help it."

"*Can* you help it?" she asked, a spark of hope lighting in her eyes.

It was only then that Jason realized she had been preparing herself for certain death and her outburst wasn't simply a moment of hysteria brought on by the unexpected tragedy of the boys' deaths and her obvious discomfort. All women were frightened as their time approached, and with good reason, but Lucinda had harbored no hope of living beyond the birth.

"I'm not going to leave you to face this on your own," Jason replied, and laid his hand over hers. "I will be with you every step of the way."

"You promise?" Lucinda pleaded.

"I promise. Now, close your eyes and try to sleep. I will be here when you wake."

"Thank you, Lord Remond." Lucinda's smile stretched into something reminiscent of her old sardonic smile. "Jason," she added softly.

"Sleep now," Jason instructed, and let himself out of the room.

When he returned downstairs, Jason called out to Mrs. Buckley. "Where can I find Sir Lawrence?"

"He's in the study. Just there." Mrs. Buckley pointed to a closed door some way down the corridor.

"Mrs. Buckley, kindly prepare a fillet of beef with potatoes and vegetables for your mistress."

"Yes, doctor," Mrs. Buckley replied, but she looked quite scandalized by the request.

"And I would like a word when you have a moment," Jason added.

"Can it wait, my lord? With Mrs. Powers unable to perform her duties, I'm afraid it's up to me to see to the meals."

"Of course," Jason replied. "Whenever is convenient."

Mrs. Buckley bustled off to the kitchen, while Jason strode toward the study. Sir Lawrence was sprawled in a chair by the hearth, a nearly empty tumbler in his hand. He stared desolately into the flames, his mouth slack, his hand trembling slightly. Upon seeing Jason, he instantly sat up, set the glass on the occasional table at his elbow, and squared his shoulders, as if bracing himself for the worst possible news.

"May I sit down?" Jason asked when Sir Lawrence failed to speak.

"Of course. I'm sorry. I'm just…" His voice trailed off, his chest deflating like a punctured balloon.

"Sir Lawrence, I need to speak to you about your wife."

"Lucinda hasn't been well," Sir Lawrence rushed to explain. "She's weak and distracted and can barely hold a conversation. And she has been so melancholy," he added miserably. "She cries and begs me to take her home. I don't know what to do."

His fear for Lucinda seemed heartfelt, and Jason felt a twinge of sympathy for the young man, who was clearly in the midst of one of the worst days of his life.

"I have examined Lady Foxley, and I believe her life is in danger."

"What?" Sir Lawrence cried in alarm. "From whom?"

"From your children," Jason replied.

"My children are dead," Sir Lawrence muttered. Jason wasn't sure if he had meant to admit to the children's paternity or was too distraught to know what he was saying.

"Lucinda is carrying twins, and I believe her health has been deteriorating rapidly these past few weeks."

Sir Lawrence stared at Jason in disbelief. "Twins?" he echoed. "The midwife never said."

"She might not have realized if the babies' hearts beat in unison. What did the midwife suggest when she was last here?" Jason asked, wondering if the woman had even noticed that her patient was far from well.

"She said Lucinda should be bled, but Lucinda flat-out refused. I couldn't very well hold her down, could I?"

"Lucinda should absolutely not be bled," Jason replied, his anger mounting. "Why have you not called in a physician?"

"I have. I brought in Dr. Hollis from Brentwood. He said much the same thing. He also said that Lucinda should have nothing but bone broth, tea, and toast to keep her weight down."

"Cretin," Jason said under his breath.

"Is Lucinda going to die?" Sir Lawrence cried. "I know she thinks I don't love her, but I can't lose her, Lord Redmond. Or my children. I just…" The thought of losing four children in the space of a few weeks left Sir Lawrence speechless, and for a moment

Jason saw the little boy he must have been and tasted the fear that seemed to possess him. "Doris Powers is convinced that Lucinda killed the boys. She's threatening to report her to the Essex police. She'll see her hang for murder."

"Leave the investigation to Inspector Haze and the care of your wife to me. Lucinda has dangerously high blood pressure. If we do nothing, she will die."

Sir Lawrence's face went slack with fear. "What is there to do?"

"The babies are near to term, and I will deliver them within the next few days. But first, Lucinda must regain some strength. Otherwise, she won't survive the birth. She needs to eat meat, vegetables, and eggs. Several small meals throughout the day would be best."

"Please, save them," Sir Lawrence pleaded. "I can't lose them all."

"I will do everything in my power, but you must help me."

"I will do whatever it takes."

"You must make sure no one leaves Fox Hollow."

Sir Lawrence nodded. "Whatever you say."

Having issued his instructions, Jason went in search of Daniel, who was in the kitchen, seated across from what could only be Doris Powers. Mrs. Powers looked mutinous, Daniel appeared exasperated, and the scullery maid, who was standing with her back to the two, was clearly listening.

"Daniel, a word in private," Jason said, and waited for Daniel to follow him into the corridor. Jason led him further away from the kitchen, where they wouldn't be overheard.

"Lucinda Foxley is hanging on by a thread," Jason said. "I think the only reason she's made it this far is because of her innate stubbornness. I need to give her a few days to regain her strength, then I will operate. In the meantime, we need to conduct our investigation from within. Whoever poisoned those boys is here, in this house."

Daniel nodded. "We can always rely on assistance from the Brentwood Constabulary. DI Coleridge will send reinforcements if we require help."

"We might require assistance down the line, but for now, we need to make certain no one is allowed to leave. Have you learned anything from Mrs. Powers?"

"She hasn't been very forthcoming."

"Let's speak to Mrs. Powers together, shall we?"

"She might be more impressed with you than she is with me," Daniel agreed. "And she seems in awe of Sir Lawrence."

"Let's find an empty room we can use. Mrs. Powers will not reveal anything as long as she can be overheard by members of Sir Lawrence's staff."

Daniel shot Jason a questioning look. "Do you think she's hiding something?"

"No, but I expect there are things she'd prefer to keep to herself."

"I think you're right. We can use the parlor. It's currently unoccupied," Daniel said.

Jason nodded. "I'll meet you there."

Chapter 7

Doris Powers was about twenty-five, at least six years closer to Sir Lawrence's age than his teenage bride. Her eyes were red-rimmed, her skin blotchy, and her hair had come loose from its pins and stuck out like chicken feathers, but beneath the ravages of grief and pain, it was clear that she was a handsome woman. Mrs. Powers stared balefully at Daniel, but her expression changed to one of admiration and respect when she turned to Jason.

"She killed my babies," she said, speaking directly to Jason. "She hated them, and she killed them."

"Why would Lady Foxley want to murder your children?" Jason asked.

"Because she knew they were Larry's," Doris Powers replied without a moment's hesitation.

"Your children were no threat to Lady Foxley," Daniel pointed out. "Her son would be the legitimate heir to the baronetcy."

"Larry loved our boys," Mrs. Powers cried. "It infuriated her that he didn't act as if they didn't exist. He played with them and brought them presents."

"That's hardly reason to kill them."

"She's a vicious, evil shrew," Doris Powers cried. "She kills everything she touches."

"Mrs. Powers, Lady Foxley is very ill. Even if she wanted to murder two little boys, she wouldn't have the strength to do it," Jason said gently.

"You don't need strength. All you need is cunning, and she has that in spades."

"And how would she murder them?" Daniel asked. "She barely leaves her bed these days."

"John and Bertie liked to play hide-and-go-seek with Mrs. Buckley's granddaughter, Daisy. They probably ran upstairs to hide in the chest, and that witch locked them in."

"The children did not suffocate," Jason said.

Mrs. Powers looked shocked, her every assumption about the deaths of her children obviously shattered. "Then what happened?"

"They were poisoned."

"Has anyone spoken to Daisy?" Daniel asked.

"She says they weren't playing at that time," Mrs. Powers said. "She was helping her mother in the dairy."

"When was the last time you saw the children?"

"I fed them their dinner in the kitchen, and they ran off to play. It must have been just gone one in the afternoon."

"What did they eat?" Jason asked.

Mrs. Powers seemed surprised by the question. "Pea soup and buttered bread."

"Any pudding?" Daniel asked.

"Pudding?"

"Did they have anything for dessert?" Jason reiterated.

"Why are you asking?" Doris countered.

"There was a sweet odor I couldn't account for," Jason replied, and saw Mrs. Powers wince. "And tiny pink bits."

"Pink bits?"

"They were almost like crushed eggshells," Jason explained. "Did the children consume anything like that?"

"No."

"What about anything that might contain cocoa?"

Mrs. Powers shook her head. "I made custard yesterday." She looked down at her hands, then started violently, as if she had just realized something.

"What is it?" Daniel asked.

"Lady Foxley's maid, Miss Carlin, makes a pot of chocolate for her ladyship every afternoon. She normally drinks tea, but she's been feeling weak and said the chocolate makes her feel stronger."

"Does Lady Foxley drink the entire pot?" Jason asked.

He could see how the sugar and caffeine in the chocolate would give Lucinda a boost of energy, but an entire pot of chocolate every afternoon could cause other problems, like high blood sugar.

Mrs. Powers sounded wary. "No. There's usually some left."

"What happens to the leftover chocolate?"

"Amy brings the tray to the kitchen, and Dorothy washes out the pot," Mrs. Powers said.

"What time does Lady Foxley normally take her chocolate?" Jason asked.

"At three o'clock."

"Did anyone else see the children after three?"

"I don't know," Mrs. Powers admitted. She seemed lost in thought, her head bowed as she stared at her folded hands.

"Mrs. Powers, how long have you and Sir Lawrence been lovers?" Daniel asked, startling her out of her reverie.

"We're not lovers," Doris Powers snapped. "We are parents."

"When did you first become lovers?" Jason asked, rephrasing the question.

Doris Powers smiled sadly, as if recalling a bittersweet memory. "When I was fourteen. I was the scullery maid then, and my mother was the cook. Larry was sixteen, and we used to sneak out to the woods. I loved him, and he loved me. Those were the happiest years of my life."

"But then you got with child," Jason prompted.

Doris nodded. "I lost the first baby, but then I got with child again a year later. My late husband, Donald, was courting me then, so I lay with him and told him the child was his."

"Did he ever find out the truth?" Daniel asked.

Doris Powers shook her head. "He was a bit thick, my Donald. Believed whatever I told him."

"And you resumed your affair with Sir Lawrence once you married?" Jason asked.

"Larry and I never really stopped, not then. When I got with child again, I knew it was his, and I was glad of it. I didn't love Donald."

"And does Mr. Powers know that your children were sired by Sir Lawrence?" Daniel asked.

"I never told him outright, but Richard guessed, and he didn't mind. All he asked of me was that I remain faithful to him, and I have been. I thought we might have a child of our own, but it hasn't happened for us," Mrs. Powers admitted. Her face crumpled with misery, and she began to cry, burying her face in her apron.

"So, you and Sir Lawrence have not had relations since you married Richard Powers?" Jason asked once the sobs had subsided.

"That's right. But what does that have to do with the death of my boys?"

"If you believe that their paternity was the reason your children were murdered, then plenty," Daniel replied.

Doris Powers fixed Daniel with a tearful stare. "Please, find whoever did this, Inspector. I know it won't bring my babies back, but I'll sleep better knowing that a child killer is no longer walking this earth."

"We will do everything in our power to see justice done, Mrs. Powers," Daniel promised.

Mrs. Powers nodded and stood. "I'll be off home, then."

Before she left, she fixed Jason with a look of naked pleading. "Please, can I take my boys home now? They wouldn't want to be up there all by themselves, not after they spent the night alone and in the dark. I need to see to them, Doctor."

"Of course," Jason said softly. "You can take them home. That's where they belong."

Mrs. Powers smiled sadly. "They'll want to sleep in their own bed once they're clean and tidy."

"Do you need assistance getting the children back to your cottage?" Jason asked.

Mrs. Powers shook her head. "I'll ask Clegg to help me. He'll bring the cart around."

With that, she bowed her head and hurried from the parlor.

"I think we should speak to the lady's maid next," Jason said once the door closed behind Mrs. Powers.

"I'll ask Mrs. Buckley to send her in," Daniel said, and stepped outside. He returned momentarily.

"Lucinda sent Miss Carlin to the village. It seems she had ordered something from a catalogue and wanted Miss Carlin to check with the postmistress if it had arrived. She should be back within the hour. I propose we have a visit with Richard Powers," Daniel suggested.

Jason pushed to his feet. "I for one will be interested to hear how Mr. Powers felt about his wife's relationship with Sir Lawrence."

Chapter 8

The estate manager's office was located in a squat brick building near the stable block. The area smelled strongly of horses and hay, as did the teenage boy who gave them a wave and disappeared inside. The green-painted door was closed, so Daniel knocked and pushed it open without waiting for an invitation. A man in his thirties sat behind a desk, a ledger open before him. He had been making an entry but looked up when the door opened, visibly surprised by the appearance of two unexpected visitors.

"Mr. Powers?" Daniel asked.

"Yes. And you are?"

"Inspector Haze of Scotland Yard, and this is my associate, Dr. Redmond."

"Gentlemen," Richard Powers replied gruffly. He looked wary as he set down his pen and gestured toward the cane guest chairs before his desk.

The first thing that struck Jason about Richard Powers, immediately after the fact that he was at work mere hours after his stepsons had been found dead, was that he resembled Sir Lawrence to such a degree as to imply that there was a close familial connection. Perhaps siring children on their servants was a long-honored Foxley tradition and everyone accepted it without question.

"I didn't realize that Sir Lawrence had called in Scotland Yard," Richard Powers said as he leaned back in his chair. "Not really on your patch."

"We met Sir Lawrence during an earlier investigation," Daniel explained. "He knows he can trust us to get to the truth."

Powers sighed heavily. "The truth won't bring John and Bertie back."

"No, but it might help your wife to make peace with their passing."

"Will it? What's easier to accept, Inspector, a tragic accident, or the intentional murder of innocents? Doris is beside herself with grief. The truth will not diminish her pain, nor will it absolve her of guilt."

"Guilt?" Daniel probed.

"Yes, guilt. The boys were always running wild. I told Doris they should have a routine, and daily chores, but she was always too busy up at the house to be a proper mother to them. 'Let them have a carefree childhood,' she said. 'There will be time aplenty for them to work once they're older. They're happy,' she said," Richard Powers choked out. "She should have kept a closer eye on them instead of pandering to that spoiled, ungrateful harpy."

"Are we to understand that the harpy in question is Lady Foxley?" Jason asked.

"Who else would it be?" Powers snapped.

"Mr. Powers, your stepsons are dead, yet here you are, working instead of supporting your wife through what has to be the worst day of her life," Jason pointed out.

Richard Powers shot him a filthy look. "You think that because those boys weren't mine, I didn't love them?"

"Did you?"

"I'm the only father they ever knew." Powers fixed his clear blue gaze on Jason. "How did they die, Doctor?"

"They were poisoned."

"Did they suffer?" Richard Powers asked softly, the pain in his eyes a testament to his feeling for the boys. "They were terribly sick."

"It would have been quick," Jason replied. "No more than a few minutes."

"Thank the Lord for small mercies."

"When was the last time you saw the children?" Daniel asked.

"Yesterday, around two o'clock. They came by the stables to pet Dusty." Richard's eyes misted with tears. "Sir Lawrence bought the pony so they could learn to ride. They loved him, and Mr. Clegg took special care of him and always kept a few apples on hand so the boys could give Dusty a treat."

"And then?"

"And then they went back to the big house. Sir Lawrence allowed them to play in the library on rainy days. They liked to move the pieces around on the chessboard and pretend they were waging an epic battle, and there were some picture books that Sir Lawrence kept on the lower shelves, to make them easily accessible."

"That's kind of him," Daniel said.

"He's a kind man."

"Did the boys know who their natural father was?" Jason asked.

Powers balked. "Of course not. And they never would. As far as they were concerned, their father was Donald Morse."

"Did you not think they would begin to question Sir Lawrence's involvement in their lives as they grew older?" Daniel asked.

"They would have accepted him as a benevolent benefactor. Much as Sir Lawrence's father was to me," Powers added, his meaning crystal clear.

"Sir Lawrence's father had a legitimate son to inherit the title and the estate," Jason pointed out. "If Sir Lawrence never produced a male heir, he might have looked to John to take on the estate. It is possible to legitimize a child through the courts."

Richard Powers had the look of someone who had never entertained the possibility. "Sir Lawrence is expecting a child of his own and will likely have more children in the future. John and Bertie would have never found themselves in that position, so they were no threat to anyone."

"Your wife seems to think that Lady Foxley is responsible for the deaths of her children," Daniel said.

"Doris is grieving," Powers said.

"So you think Lady Foxley is innocent?" Jason asked.

The manager shrugged. "No woman wants to see her husband's by-blows every day of her life, nor does she want to have to explain their place in the household to her own children."

"Sounds to me like you agree with your wife."

"I didn't say that, but Lady Foxley does have rather a colorful past. That family's transgressions are not the secret she believes them to be."

"What are you suggesting, Mr. Powers?" Daniel asked.

"A person born of sin, who's committed sin, will see nothing wrong with sinning again."

"A person doesn't choose the circumstances of their birth," Jason said.

Richard Powers shot Jason an angry look. "You're quite correct, Doctor; they don't, but a person can choose how they live, and that woman is ruled by self-interest."

"Let he who's without sin cast the first stone."

"I wasn't casting stones. I was simply pointing out the obvious. Lady Foxley is the only one who was bothered by John and Bertie's presence. They were a blight on her marriage and a blow to her pride. And now they're gone."

"Where were you yesterday afternoon, Mr. Powers?" Daniel asked.

"I came here directly after breakfast and did not leave until six o'clock, at which time I went home. Once Doris and I realized the boys were missing, I went out on the estate to search for the children. Sir Lawrence can vouch for me. We were together most of the time."

There didn't seem to be anything more to say, so Daniel pushed to his feet with Jason following suit. "Thank you, Mr. Powers. We're sorry for your loss."

Richard Powers nodded in acknowledgement but did not reply.

Chapter 9

"What did you make of him?" Daniel asked once they left the manager's office. "He's clearly a relation. If I had to guess, I'd say he's the baronet's older brother."

"He implied as much," Jason replied.

"Richard Powers holds a respectable position, so Sir Lawrence must hold him in high regard."

"Or perhaps he feels a sense of obligation to a man who would have been baronet had he not been born out of wedlock."

"Sir Lawrence did not allude to the relationship when he mentioned Richard Powers earlier," Daniel pointed out.

"The fact that the mother of Sir Lawrence's children married his illegitimate brother is a tad incestuous, wouldn't you agree?" Jason said.

"It is rather close for comfort," Daniel said. "He doesn't appear to know anything."

"Doris Powers fed the children around one, and Richard Powers says he saw them at two, when they set off for the house. As of now, that's the latest known sighting of the boys."

"Someone must have seen them after that."

"That's what I was thinking," Jason said.

"At the outside, how long would it take for the poison to take effect?" Daniel asked as they strode across the newly greening lawn.

"Given that the boys had consumed enough of the substance to kill them, I would say not long."

"So the poison had to have come from the house."

"Or just outside," Jason replied. "They would have ingested it shortly before getting into the trunk."

"Both Doris and Richard Powers seem to think Lucinda is guilty. They have nothing to gain by accusing her of murder, so they must have reason to suspect her."

"I'm not ready to accept that Lucinda is guilty," Jason said. "Not without solid evidence. For one, there was no reason for her to murder the children. They may have been a source of irritation and a blow to her pride, but I can't see her poisoning two little boys, not when they weren't a genuine threat to her or her unborn children. For another, given her current state, I can't see how she could have managed it. She's not exactly inconspicuous. The parents are grieving and need someone to blame, and they clearly dislike Lucinda, probably because she upset the established balance when Sir Lawrence brought her to Fox Hollow."

"Richard Powers made sure we knew that he's aware of Lucinda's past," Daniel remarked. "All that talk of sin."

"He wants us to think that he shares a close bond with the baronet," Jason said. "But even if that's true and Sir Lawrence acknowledges Powers as his brother, I can't imagine Sir Lawrence would tell him anything that might cause a scandal if it became widely known. Sir Lawrence has a healthy sense of self-preservation, much like his wife."

"So how does he know? Or was he fishing for information?" Daniel asked.

"I don't think he was fishing. Richard Powers knows something, but it's difficult to ascertain exactly how much without revealing the truth," Jason replied. "I very much doubt that even Sir Lawrence knows that Lucinda was sired by the man the world believed to be her grandfather or that she helped him to murder his own grandson. That's not the sort of thing Caroline Chadwick would ever let slip, not when the information could destroy everything she holds dear."

"Perhaps Lucinda confided in her husband," Daniel suggested. "She was smitten with him when they first met."

"Which was all the more reason for her to keep quiet. Sir Lawrence would never have married her if he knew."

"Perhaps he knows now. His brother might have poured poison in his ear."

"That I can believe," Jason replied.

"And Lucinda is clearly not happy here," Daniel added.

"Can you blame her? She thought they would settle in London, not in this damp, outmoded Tudor crypt that was completely passed over by progress. Chadwick Manor is the beacon of modernity compared to this."

Daniel shot Jason a sidelong glance. "Jason, is it possible that Lucinda Foxley was the intended victim?"

"Who here would benefit from her death?"

"Sir Lawrence, for one. Lucinda received a sizable portion when she married, but it probably went to pay his debts and there's nothing left, if the state of this place is anything to go by. And if he found out that he was intentionally deceived, he might want to marry someone who's not only more suitable but who has a sizable fortune that can replenish his coffers," Daniel offered.

Jason shook his head. "Sir Lawrence seemed genuinely fond of John and Bertie. I find it hard to imagine that he would poison his unborn children and their mother. He might be self-serving, but he doesn't strike me as someone who's inherently evil. Besides, if he wanted to be rid of Lucinda, all he had to do was wait. She's not likely to survive the birth without medical intervention."

"Perhaps time was of the essence," Daniel suggested.

"You mean if he had a pregnant mistress waiting in the wings and wished to marry her?"

"It is possible."

"At the moment, there's nothing to suggest that Sir Lawrence is responsible, but we do need to learn more about his whereabouts."

"He won't take kindly to having to account for his movements."

"Which is why we won't ask him. Mrs. Buckley is sure to know where everyone was yesterday afternoon. But first, I'd like to have a word with the gardener. What do we know about him?"

"His name is Emmett Doyle, and he's married to Mrs. Buckley's daughter, Rose. They have a cottage on the estate. They certainly have a closely related group of people here," Daniel observed.

"I think you'll find this is quite common. It's easier to embark on a relationship with someone who lives and works in close proximity, especially when most servants have a free afternoon every other week and can't get very far on foot."

"I suppose," Daniel replied. "Still, it gives them a reason to cover for each other when the only outsider is the lady of the house."

"Which brings us right back to the beginning. Until we know where the poison came from or how it was administered, we will continue to grope in the dark," Jason said. "Perhaps the gardener can shed some light."

Chapter 10

Emmett Doyle looked young and fit from a distance, but when he turned to face them, Daniel was horrified by the terrible scars that covered the left side of his face. The skin was red and puckered, and no hair grew over the scar tissue, the skin resembling melted wax that had solidified into irregular patterns. Emmett wore a wool cap that was pulled low over his eyes and a tatty coat that was patched at the elbows. He had been on his knees, digging with a trowel, but he pushed to his feet and stood waiting, his demeanor that of a man who knows he's grotesque and is bracing himself for the shock that is sure to come.

"Mr. Doyle, I'm Inspector Haze, and this is my associate, Dr. Redmond," Daniel said.

"I know who you are. Heard you've been here asking questions," Emmett Doyle replied. His manner bordered on hostile, but he could hardly refuse to speak to them since they were there at the behest of his master.

"If we might have a moment of your time," Daniel said politely, and hoped that the gardener would relax his defensive stance.

Emmett stared at him bullishly, then gave a small nod. Daniel couldn't help but feel sympathy for the man and wondered if he had suffered the burns before or after he was married and how his wife felt about her husband's disfigurement. His misfortune bore no relevance to the investigation since it had clearly happened some time ago, and it would be unkind to inquire as to the circumstances, but it was obvious that the accident had affected the man's personality and his interaction with others.

"How long have you worked for the Foxleys, Mr. Doyle?" Jason asked.

"These seven years. I was in the army before. Took the Queen's shilling," he added bitterly. "Thought I'd get to see something of the world."

"And did you?"

"All I saw was misery, pain, and injustice."

"I was in the army myself," Jason said. "Fought in the American Civil War. Is that a souvenir of your soldiering days?" he asked conversationally, clearly alluding to the burns.

"No. That was the result of my own carelessness. An oil lamp tipped onto the bed while I was asleep and set the pillow on fire. I was so drunk, I didn't realize I was burning until half my face was gone," Emmett Doyle added shakily. "If not for my wife, I would have died that night. She beat the flames out and looked after me when all I wanted was to die."

"I'm sorry," Jason said. "You must have been in great pain."

Emmett nodded. "I can barely see out of my left eye, and my hearing is not what it was. But you don't want to hear about that. It's a terrible thing about those boys," he added, his attitude having thawed somewhat.

"Mr. Doyle, does hemlock grow on the estate?" Jason asked.

"Of course. There are all sorts of poisonous plants. Hemlock, wolfsbane, foxgloves. Why do you ask?"

"Because the children were poisoned. How close to the house do these plants grow?"

"The foxgloves grow in the garden, but the children know not to touch them. The hemlock and wolfsbane grow in the woods and near the riverbank. They like moist places, hemlock especially."

"How far is the river from the house?" Jason asked.

"Quarter mile as the crow flies," Emmett Doyle replied.

"Did you see the children out in the grounds yesterday?" Daniel asked.

"They were outside in the morning, but then it started to rain. I didn't see them after that."

"And is Daisy your daughter?" Jason asked.

Emmett nodded. "Daisy often plays with the boys, but she was with my wife for most of the day yesterday. They were in the dairy in the morning, and then they baked a cake in the afternoon. It was to be a surprise for Doris Powers. Today is her birthday."

"Oh, the poor woman," Daniel exclaimed.

Emmett nodded. "Not the gift she was expecting."

"Did you see any strangers about yesterday?"

"No."

"Can you think of anyone who might have wanted to hurt the children?" Daniel asked.

"Are you saying someone gave them the poison?" Emmett asked, his one remaining eyebrow lifting in surprise.

"It's a possibility we're exploring," Daniel replied noncommittally.

At this stage he had no idea whether the children had been the intended victims. Nothing he and Jason had learned so far pointed to anyone in particular, and the more questions they asked, the fewer answers they got. Daniel saw no reason anyone would want to murder two small children, least of all Lucinda Foxley, and he knew his theory about Lawrence Foxley was a weak one. If the baronet had wanted his wife dead, he would hardly invite Daniel and Jason into his home and beg them for help, not even if he had hoped to divert suspicion by involving Scotland Yard. Tasking

Daniel and Jason with solving the murders would be too much of a risk, even for someone as self-assured as Sir Lawrence.

Emmett shook his head. "I can't help you, Inspector. I don't go inside the big house. I do my work and go home."

"You're out in the grounds. You must see things."

"Lady Foxley is mad for horses, or was when she could still ride, and Miss Carlin likes to take walks. That's all I can tell you."

"And what about Sir Lawrence?" Jason asked.

"What about him?"

"Does he go out much?"

Emmett Doyle shook his head again. "He's been keeping close to the house these past few weeks, on account of her ladyship not being well."

"Thank you, Mr. Doyle," Daniel said. "Where might we find your wife and Daisy?"

"They're at home. Normally, Rose helps out at the house, but Daisy took to her bed when she heard about the boys. She's heartbroken, the poor love. They were her dearest friends."

Emmett's affection for his daughter was obvious, and he seemed to feel no animosity toward his employers, probably because he rarely set foot in the house.

"The poor child," Jason said as he and Daniel walked away. "She must be in shock."

"I think everyone is," Daniel replied. "The deaths of those boys came like a thunderbolt out of the blue."

"Not for everyone," Jason said quietly. "Someone was intent on murder, and the fact that the children were poisoned the day before their mother's birthday can't be a coincidence."

Chapter 11

Jason and Daniel walked along a well-trodden path toward the row of thatched-roof cottages that probably dated back to the construction of the big house. There were four cottages in total, each with a neat front garden and flagstone path. The Doyles' cottage was on the end and had the most well-tended garden, even though most of the flowers had yet to bloom.

Rose Doyle was a buxom, fair-haired woman in her mid-twenties. The swell of a new pregnancy was clearly visible beneath her apron, as were bruises that encircled her wrists and a purpling contusion on her left cheek.

"Mrs. Doyle, if we might have a moment of your time," Daniel asked once the introductions were made, and hoped the woman wouldn't turn them away. "We've just met your husband."

"Come in," Rose said, and stepped back from the door to allow them to enter. She tried to hide it, but she was obviously in pain, and her hand went to her side when she accidentally brushed past a chair.

Although small, the cottage looked cozy and bright, the furniture well used and comfortable. The scent of baking hung in the air, and a perfect Victoria sponge sat beneath a glass dome on the kitchen table, the cake untouched.

"I made that for Doris," Rose said when she noticed the direction of Daniel's gaze. "Today is her birthday." She sounded very tired and sad, as if she had no more energy for grief. "The kettle's just boiled. Can I offer you gentlemen some tea and a slice of cake? Shame for it to go to waste. Daisy wouldn't like that. She helped me to make it."

"Thank you. That's very kind," Daniel said.

It had been hours since he'd eaten, and he thought Jason should eat something as well. Jason had to eat at regular intervals to keep dizziness and fatigue at bay. Cake wasn't his nourishment of choice, but since no one had offered them anything else, it would have to serve until they got a proper meal.

They took a seat at the table and waited while Rose made the tea and cut the cake. She sat down heavily, exhaling with relief to be off her feet.

"Are you all right, Mrs. Doyle?" Jason asked, watching her closely.

"I am. Thank you for asking, Doctor. It's just that I hardly slept at all, and this baby seems to take more out of me than Daisy did." She laid a hand on her belly and patted it affectionately. "Maybe it's a boy this time."

Rose poured out the tea, then served Jason and Daniel slices of cake but didn't take any for herself. "I don't think I can eat," she explained. "My stomach is all in knots."

It seemed wrong to eat a birthday cake meant for someone else, but Doris Powers wouldn't be celebrating her birthday this year, and neither would anyone else. Perhaps Daisy would manage a slice of cake, or perhaps, like her mother, she wouldn't be able to stomach the cake when her friends were lying dead only a few doors down.

"Is Daisy all right?" Jason asked, his gaze straying toward the corridor. The house was awfully quiet, the silence somehow tense and watchful.

"She's finally fallen asleep, and thank the good Lord for that, or she would have seen Mr. Clegg unloading the bodies from his cart not an hour ago." Rose sighed heavily. "She was up crying all night. She's heartbroken." Rose looked from Daniel to Jason. "How do I explain this to her? How do I tell a five-year-old girl that her friends were murdered?"

"Perhaps you can tell her it was a terrible accident," Daniel suggested. "That might be easier to understand."

"But she'll still find out the truth. Someone will say something, and then she'll know I lied."

"At this age, Daisy will believe anything you say. Spare her this awful knowledge," Jason said.

Tears slid down Rose's pale cheeks and plopped into her teacup. "I keep thinking I could have lost her," she whispered. "She was always running around with the boys. She could have…" She couldn't finish the sentence and buried her face in a tea towel that had been within easy reach. "I can't believe they're dead," Rose moaned. "Just like that. Here one day, gone the next."

Jason and Daniel drank their tea in silence, giving Rose time to calm down. She finally set the towel aside and took a gulp of tea, sucking in a shaky breath once she set the cup back down.

"Mrs. Doyle, would it be all right if I asked Daisy a few questions?" Jason asked. "I will be very gentle."

"You want to question my Daisy?" Rose looked outraged by the very suggestion.

"I won't ask her anything upsetting. Just some general things about her friends and the games they used to play."

"No," Rose snapped, shaking her head for emphasis. "I won't have her upset. She already thinks she will be next."

"Why would she think that?" Daniel asked.

"She's five. Reason doesn't come into it."

"Mrs. Doyle, can you think of anyone who might have wanted to harm the boys?" Daniel asked.

"Who would want to harm two innocent children?" Rose replied.

She seemed to have regained control and with it some of her impatience. It was clear she wanted Jason and Daniel gone, but they couldn't leave until she'd answered their questions.

"What about Mrs. Powers? Would someone want to get at her?" Daniel asked.

Rose shook her head. "Doris is a good sort. She's always kind to everyone and helped me look after my Emmett after his accident. She was a great comfort to me."

"What about your mother? Did she not help you?" Jason asked.

"Mother lives at the big house, but Doris and I have lived next door to each other since I married Emmett. We support each other, as women do."

"And Mr. Powers?"

Rose looked blank. "What about him?"

"Is he a good sort as well?"

Rose shrugged. "I don't have much to do with Richard Powers. He's a busy man."

"Does he get on with your husband?" Jason pressed.

"Richard Powers doesn't have a very high opinion of Emmett, but he's a good neighbor."

"In what way?" Jason asked. Daniel noticed that he was looking at Rose's bruises and knew he wouldn't just let it go. It wasn't in Jason's nature to ignore abuse, not even when the abuse was sanctioned by the law and probably overlooked by anyone in the Doyles' sphere.

"Mr. Powers allocated funds for the repair of the cottage after the fire, and found us a new bedstead and carpet, since ours were ruined."

"Was that all he did?" Jason asked.

Rose looked nonplussed. "What else would he do?"

"Intervene when your husband loses his temper."

Rose's face crumpled once again. "I couldn't bear that. The shame of it. Emmett is a good man. He was so lovely when we were courting, but since the fire, he hasn't been himself. He…" She let the sentence trail, but her meaning was clear. Emmett flew into rages and took out his anger and frustration on his wife.

"Does he hit Daisy as well?" Jason asked.

"No, he dotes on Daisy. She's the one person who can bring a smile to his face and make him forget how he looks. And he's excited about the new baby. He so wants a boy." Rose choked up. "I thought our boy would have John and Bertie to look after him, but now there'll be no one, except Daisy."

"You should allow Daisy to attend the funeral," Jason said. "Sometimes saying goodbye is the only closure we get in life. Don't take that away from her."

Rose nodded but didn't commit herself either way. Instead, she pushed to her feet and began to tidy away the tea things, a clear sign that she wanted them to leave.

"Please, look after yourself, Mrs. Doyle," Jason said. "And if your husband gets rough with you, you can always go to Sir Lawrence for help. He will intervene."

"I know he will. Sir Lawrence is a good master, and has always looked after us."

There didn't seem to be anything left to say, so the two men returned to the house.

"We need to speak to Mrs. Buckley," Jason said. "I know she's short-handed without Mrs. Powers, but surely she can spare us a few minutes."

Daniel nodded. "As the housekeeper, she knows more about what goes on in that house than anyone else."

"That's what I was thinking," Jason said.

Chapter 12

Mrs. Buckley was in her office, which was hardly more than an alcove with a door and a narrow leaded window. There was a small desk with a hardback chair, a cabinet for housekeeping ledgers, and a tiny brazier that glowed warmly and made the room feel stuffy. The housekeeper looked exhausted, dark smudges beneath her eyes and a downward cast to her mouth. There was an empty teacup and a small plate where a teacake or a small sandwich might have rested before Mrs. Buckley had consumed it.

She looked up, the spark of hope in her eyes quickly dying out.

"Nothing, then?" she asked.

"Not yet," Daniel replied. "We need to ask you a few questions, Mrs. Buckley."

"I must get started on dinner," she said. "Dorothy can't manage anything more complicated than boiled eggs on her own, and Rose didn't come today."

"We just spoke to Rose, and to Emmett," Jason said.

Mrs. Buckley nodded. "They have enough of their own troubles."

"So it would seem."

"Did you see Daisy?" Mrs. Buckley asked.

"She was sleeping."

The housekeeper nodded. "The poor little mite. She's been on my mind all day, but I haven't been able to nip to the cottage, what with everything that needed doing."

There wasn't anywhere for Jason and Daniel to sit, so Daniel asked Mrs. Buckley if they might speak somewhere else, and the three of them adjourned to the parlor. It was now late afternoon, and the shadows were lengthening outside, the house sinking even deeper into gloom. No fire had been laid in the parlor and no one had bothered to light the candles, leaving the room nearly devoid of light and too cold for comfort.

Mrs. Buckley took out a box of lucifer matches from a drawer and lit the brace of candles before sinking onto the settee. Her day was nowhere near over, and she looked like she could use a solid meal and a hot water bottle.

"Where is everyone?" Daniel asked.

The house seemed strangely empty, as if no one was about, not even the servants. Perhaps everyone had retreated to their private quarters, unnerved not only by the deaths of the children but by the presence of strangers.

"Sir Lawrence is with her ladyship. Has been for most of the afternoon. I don't believe Miss Carlin is back yet. Mrs. Powers left shortly after speaking with you. I expect she's laying out the boys. Amy and his lordship's valet are upstairs, and Gwen is in the kitchen with Dorothy. I asked them to start cutting up the vegetables for dinner. I really don't have much time," Mrs. Buckley reminded them.

"Of course. Let's get started, then," Daniel said, and flipped open his notebook.

He could hardly say as much to Mrs. Buckley, but he was annoyed that the housekeeper was more concerned with her domestic duties than helping them with their enquiries. Two children were dead. Surely dinner could wait a half hour, and if Sir Lawrence did not get a hot meal, he would survive. A cold supper would work just as well, but it wasn't Daniel's place to offer advice, and if he wanted Mrs. Buckley's help, he needed to flatter her into believing that her position was important, and her opinion carried weight.

"Mrs. Buckley, as the housekeeper, you know everything that goes on in this house," Daniel began. "What do you think happened? I would dearly welcome your insight."

Mrs. Buckley looked taken aback. She had probably expected to be questioned, maybe even accused of wrongdoing, but she hadn't expected to be asked for her opinion by a detective from Scotland Yard. She visibly preened, her earlier fatigue forgotten.

"Well," she began, "I initially believed that the children had become trapped, but there were at least three people within hearing distance all afternoon, and no one seems to have heard a thing."

"Who was within hearing distance?" Jason asked.

"Miss Carlin, Sir Lawrence's valet, Mr. Wiley, and Lady Foxley. She was unwell and did not come down until dinner."

"So, all three were upstairs and heard nothing?"

"I didn't ask Lady Foxley outright," Mrs. Buckley said, "but I did speak to Miss Carlin and Mr. Wiley. They both said they were in and out of their masters' bedrooms and hadn't heard any banging or cries for help. Also, Amy was attending to her chores and didn't hear a thing."

"Did anyone see them after two o'clock?" Jason asked. "Mr. Powers saw them by the stables and said the children were headed to the big house to wait out the rain."

"Yes," Mrs. Buckley replied. "I saw them around half past two. They asked if they could play in the library. If it were up to me, I wouldn't allow them in there, not with all those expensive volumes, but Sir Lawrence said it was all right as long as they didn't misplace any chess pieces."

"Did anyone see the boys leave the library?" Daniel asked.

Mrs. Buckley shook her head thoughtfully. "I don't believe so."

"Where was everyone?" Jason asked.

"Well, let me see. I had a dreadful headache and retired to my room just after four. Mrs. Powers had finished her preparations for the evening meal by a quarter to five and had nipped to her own cottage to have supper with Richard and the boys before returning in time for the dinner service. She had assumed the children had gone home. Gwen served tea to Sir Lawrence and Mr. Chadwick at four, then collected the tray at five and brought it back to the kitchen. Mr. Chadwick left directly after tea."

"Were there any visitors to the house yesterday?" Jason asked.

"Yes. The butcher's boy came at ten with our meat order, and then Mr. Plimpton called around half past three. He and Sir Lawrence were closeted in the parlor for about twenty minutes."

"And who's Mr. Plimpton?" Daniel asked.

"I don't know what his business was with the master, but I did hear raised voices when I walked past. And Sir Lawrence didn't call for refreshments," Mrs. Buckley added, "so the gentleman wasn't staying long."

"Did you hear what was said?"

"Mr. Plimpton said something about Sir Lawrence paying up or he'd see him in church. Sir Lawrence seemed preoccupied after Mr. Plimpton left."

"Why would he want to see Sir Lawrence in church?" Daniel asked.

"I'm sure I don't know, Inspector. Perhaps Mr. Plimpton wished to see the new window Sir Lawrence had paid for."

"Had Mr. Plimpton ever called at the house before?"

"I've never seen him before, but I got the impression that Mr. Plimpton and Mr. Chadwick knew one another."

"Did they converse?"

"No, but when Mr. Plimpton passed Mr. Chadwick on his way out, Mr. Chadwick appeared surprised to see him. Shocked, almost."

"And what of the men who reside on the estate? Did you see Mr. Powers at any point yesterday afternoon?" Daniel asked. "Or Mr. Doyle?"

Mrs. Buckley shook her head. "Mr. Powers usually eats his luncheon at his office, and Emmett prefers to eat at home. He's become something of a recluse since his accident and rarely comes inside the house."

"So, no one saw the boys after they entered the library?" Jason verified.

"Not as far as I know, but I heard them laughing in there around three."

"So, they must have gone in the trunk and died between three and five," Daniel said.

"I suppose so," Mrs. Buckley replied, her uncertainty evident. "The poor mites. I keep hoping it was a dreadful accident. Of course, knowing that won't bring the boys back, but it would make it easier for the rest of us to make peace with their passing. To think that someone wanted them dead…" She shook her head in dismay. "It doesn't bear thinking about." Mrs. Buckley sighed heavily. "Lord have mercy on their souls. They were such sweet boys. So full of life."

"It would appear that the children were intentionally poisoned, since they weren't likely to have eaten random plants," Daniel said. "The poison was quick-acting, which also points to it being administered once they were back at the house. However, we have yet to determine if John and Bertie were the intended victims."

Mrs. Buckley's eyes glittered with unshed tears. "I can't imagine that anyone in this house had been earmarked for death."

"Mrs. Buckley, was there anyone who didn't like the boys or begrudged their presence in the house?" Jason asked.

Mrs. Buckley squared her shoulders and jutted out her chin. "There was no one."

"It has been repeatedly mentioned that Lady Foxley resented the children."

Mrs. Buckley looked dubious. "Resented is a strong word, Dr. Redmond."

"So, how did she feel about them?" Daniel asked.

"The way one feels about a housecat."

"And how is that?"

"Like it's there."

"Mrs. Powers has accused Lady Foxley of murdering her children," Daniel pointed out.

"Poppycock," Mrs. Buckley exclaimed. "Lady Foxley can barely stand upright these days, much less chase down two rumbunctious boys and wrestle them into a trunk."

"She wouldn't have to wrestle them anywhere," Daniel replied. "If they thought it was a game—"

"Lady Foxley did not play games with the servants' children," Mrs. Buckley replied. "And the boys were warned not to disturb her."

"And Mr. Chadwick?" Daniel asked. "Did he come in contact with the boys?"

"Not that I know of."

"Mrs. Buckley, I thought I smelled chocolate on the boys' remains," Jason said, phrasing his inquiry in the gentlest way possible. "But Mrs. Powers said they only had pea soup and bread for their lunch."

"Oh, there's a simple explanation for that," Mrs. Buckley said.

"Which is?"

"Sir Lawrence brought me a box of chocolates the last time he went into Brentwood. He knows I have a fondness for sweets. There were two pieces left, and I gave them to the boys since they were complaining about the lack of pudding. Mrs. Powers usually gives them whatever sweet is left over from the night before, but Sir Lawrence and Mr. Chadwick had finished the petit fours Mrs. Powers had made."

"Was there anything pink in or on the chocolates?" Jason asked.

Mrs. Buckley looked startled. "Why, no. It was an orange cream filling."

"And what time did you give the boys chocolate?"

"Just after one o'clock. After they had finished their lunch."

"Would that account for the smell of chocolate?" Daniel asked Jason, eager to rule out the chocolate as the culprit.

"Yes, it would," Jason replied. "Mrs. Buckley, do you keep any remedies in the house?"

"What sort of remedies?"

"The sort any household has on hand for minor cuts, burns, accidents, and ailments. Castor oil, poultices, ointments, ingredients for tisanes."

"Well, yes. We do keep a number of basic remedies."

"Where are they stored?"

"In my office."

"And is your office normally kept locked?"

"No, but there's nothing dangerous in that box."

"Is there laudanum?" Jason asked.

"Well, yes. There is a bottle of laudanum."

"Might someone have helped themselves to its contents?"

"I don't know. Why are you asking me that?" Mrs. Buckley exclaimed. "I thought the children were poisoned."

"Because if someone had added a few drops of laudanum to whatever it was the children had ingested, the boys would have fallen into a stupor and been unable to call for help."

"I'm sure I don't know who'd do such a thing." Mrs. Buckley was looking flustered now, her eyes darting more frequently toward the door. "I really must see to supper. Can I go?"

Daniel nodded. "Thank you. You may."

Chapter 13

"Jason, are you certain this couldn't have been an accident?" Daniel asked again as soon as they were alone. "There's absolutely no evidence that anyone wanted to harm those boys or that there was anything poisonous present in their food."

Jason shook his head. "I really don't think it was, Daniel. If the children had ingested something by accident, they would have run to their mother as soon as they began to feel unwell. That's what children do. No one saw or heard the boys after three o'clock, and then they became ill and died in that trunk without anyone hearing a thing. Someone made certain they went in the trunk before the toxin took effect and during a time when no one would bother to look for them. That feels premeditated to me."

Both men turned toward the door when there was a timid knock.

"Come in," Daniel called.

"Sorry to disturb, but I was told you wished to speak to me," a woman they hadn't yet met said as she peered inside the room.

"Miss Carlin, I presume," Daniel said.

"Yes. I'm just back from the village."

"Please, come in. I'm Inspector Haze, and this is Dr. Redmond."

"Pleasure to meet you both," Miss Carlin said as she advanced into the room.

Helen Carlin appeared to be in her late twenties, maybe even early thirties. With a nose that was a trifle too long and lips that were almost indecently full, she wasn't classically beautiful, but there was something arresting about her face. Her eyes were a soft moss green, and her hair was the color of honey. It was wound into a low knot, but a few curls framed her angular face. Miss Carlin was tall for a woman and well proportioned, with an hourglass figure any woman would be sure to envy. She wore a navy skirt and a high-necked white blouse with a small blue-and-white cameo brooch pinned to the collar.

"Please, sit down, Miss Carlin," Jason invited, and smiled at her in what he hoped was a disarming manner.

Miss Carlin sat in a hardback chair, her back erect, her hands demurely folded in her lap, her feet firmly planted on the floor. There was a watchfulness about her that was probably the result of living in other people's houses and being entirely at their mercy. And Jason could sympathize with any woman who was at the beck and call of Lucinda Foxley.

"How long have you been Lady Foxley's lady's maid?" Daniel asked.

"Just over a year."

"And do you like your job?" Jason asked, giving her his undivided attention.

Miss Carlin appeared surprised to be the object of such scrutiny but didn't seem intimidated in the least. "Lady Foxley has been good to me. She's a kind and generous mistress."

"Generous how?" Jason couldn't see Lucinda being a mistress who was overly concerned with the needs of her maid, but perhaps he was wrong.

"She made me a gift of several gowns she no longer wears and offered to write me a glowing character should I wish to leave her employ."

"*Do* you wish to leave her employ?" Daniel asked.

"Not anymore," Miss Carlin replied cryptically.

"Did you express a desire to leave before?" Jason asked.

"Not in so many words, but Lady Foxley was observant enough to become aware of my unhappiness."

"And why were you unhappy?" Daniel asked.

"I found the country difficult to adjust to," Miss Carlin said. "I've lived in London all my life and this—" She made an expansive gesture toward the window, where all one could see was the lawns and the greening trees in the distance. "This is so…"

She didn't finish the sentence, but Jason took her meaning. To live in an out-of-the-way village was lonely and isolating, especially for a lady's maid since she could hardly fraternize with the other servants or hope to make friends in the village. Miss Carlin was a fish out of water, and she knew it.

"And was Lady Foxley prepared to let you go?" Jason asked.

"She said she understood how lonely I must be. I think she's rather lonely herself."

"Why do you say that?" Daniel inquired.

Miss Carlin sighed. "My lady was happier when we first came to Fox Hollow, even though she missed London. She loves to ride and would go off for hours, just galloping across the fields or walking in the woods. And she accompanied Sir Lawrence when he went hunting or drove into town in his landau. But these last few months, she's been confined to the house on account of her health. She's not the sort of person that can bear being cooped up," Miss Carlin explained. "She has too much spirit."

"That she does," Daniel agreed. "Too much, indeed."

If Miss Carlin was shocked by that observation, she wisely kept her feelings to herself.

"Miss Carlin, can you tell us everything you remember from noon yesterday until the children were found this morning?" Jason invited.

Miss Carlin nodded. "Lady Foxley and Sir Lawrence had luncheon with Mr. Chadwick at noon, then my lady went to lie down. I took my luncheon on a tray in her private sitting room, in case she should need me, and after I finished eating, I took the opportunity to mend some linens. When my lady woke, I helped her get settled in the sitting room and then brought her a pot of chocolate."

"What time was that?" Daniel checked.

"Just after three."

"How many cups of chocolate did Lady Foxley have?" Jason asked.

"Just one. I had one too," Miss Carlin added shyly. "My lady always invites me to join her."

"And how many cups are in the pot?" Daniel asked.

"About three. I always make a little extra, in case my lady should like a second cup."

"What did you do with the leftover chocolate?"

"I left the tray in the corridor for Amy to take away."

"Did you ever offer the leftover chocolate to John and Bertie Powers?" Jason asked.

"No. I didn't have much to do with them."

"Do you know what happened to it?"

Miss Carlin shrugged. "I imagine Amy took it to the kitchen and Dorothy spilled it out and washed the pot."

"So it just went to waste every day?" Daniel quizzed her. "Chocolate is rather expensive."

"I really don't know, Inspector. I never thought about it. Perhaps someone drank it," Miss Carlin replied.

75

"So, what did you do after you set out the tray?" Jason asked.

"My lady and I played cards."

"What game did you play?"

"Old Maid."

"What time did you leave the sitting room?" Daniel asked.

"Around five. My lady wanted to write some letters, so I left her to it and went for a walk. I needed some air after being indoors all day," Miss Carlin confessed. "It was when I returned that I heard that the children were missing."

"Did you see them at all yesterday?"

"I saw them when I came down to make the chocolate. They were in the library. The door was ajar," Miss Carlin explained. "They were playing with the chess set."

"Did you see them after that?"

"No, I didn't."

"How did you spend the remainder of the evening?" Jason asked.

"Sir Lawrence had organized a search party, so almost everyone was out on the estate, looking for the children. My lady was very distressed and wished for my company. She eventually had some soup and went to bed around nine, at which time I went downstairs. The servants had a late supper, on account of the search, and after supper, I went directly to my room."

"Miss Carlin, did Lady Foxley ever talk to you about the children?" Jason asked.

"No, but I know she resented them," Helen Carlin said matter-of-factly.

"How do you know that?"

"I could just tell."

"Why do you think she resented them?" Daniel asked.

Miss Carlin looked deeply uncomfortable and probably wished she hadn't been quite so honest. "She never said as much, but I knew they were Sir Lawrence's children by the cook."

"Was this common knowledge among the staff?" Jason asked.

Miss Carlin nodded. "I think Mrs. Powers was quite proud to be the mother of Sir Lawrence's sons."

"Did anyone else resent the children?" Daniel asked.

"Whom can you mean, Inspector?"

"Mr. Powers, for example."

Miss Carlin appeared shocked by the suggestion. "I don't claim to know how Mr. Powers felt, but from what I saw, he doted on those boys. Everyone did. They were so precious."

"Did anyone that didn't belong there come upstairs yesterday?" Daniel asked.

Miss Carlin sighed with exasperation. "I really wouldn't know, Inspector, seeing as how I was sequestered with her ladyship all day."

"Thank you, Miss Carlin," Daniel said. "You are free to go."

Miss Carlin inclined her head and left the room, her skirts swishing behind her as she swayed her hips.

"Might the poison have been in the chocolate?" Daniel asked, turning to face Jason.

"Miss Carlin made the chocolate as usual, had a cup with Lucinda, then left the tray out in the corridor to be collected by Amy. If someone added poison to the chocolate, it would have to be while the tray was unattended."

"And whoever did it would have no way of knowing that the children would drink it, which suggests that they might not have been the intended victims."

Jason sighed with frustration. "We don't know that there was anything in the chocolate. This is a fairly small household with a distinct hierarchy. Mrs. Buckley is in charge of the domestic servants, while Miss Carlin and Mr. Wiley answer directly to their masters. The staff come together for meals, but everyone knows their place and has a clearly outlined purpose. Unless there's some personal vendetta we have yet to uncover, I can't imagine why someone would want to murder anyone."

"What if we're looking at this all wrong and the intended victim was Doris Powers?" Daniel suggested.

"Why would anyone want to kill the cook? That's like someone in my household deciding to knock off Mrs. Dodson."

"Mrs. Dodson is not the mother of your children," Daniel replied.

"Thank God for small mercies."

Daniel sighed. "Seriously, though. If Doris Powers was the intended victim, the only person who would benefit from her death would be her husband. We have only her word that she was faithful to him throughout their marriage. Perhaps he suspected her of infidelity. And if he's vicious enough, he might have taken that which was most precious to her, her children, rather than killing her outright."

"I hate to admit it, but that makes a horrifying kind of sense," Jason said.

Normally, Jason derived satisfaction from working on a case. He felt deep sympathy for the victims and wanted to see justice done, but he also enjoyed the mental challenge and the exhilaration of fitting the pieces of the puzzle together until they began to form a picture, and the net tightened around the person responsible. This case was making him ill, and he wanted nothing more than to get away from the oppressive atmosphere of Fox Hollow and the memory of those two perfect boys lying dead in a pool of their own vomit and excrement. John's and Bertie's deaths hit too close to home, and the fact that there was nothing more he could do for them broke Jason's heart. He almost wished that their deaths had been a tragic accident. Awful as that would be, at least it would absolve anyone in the house of murdering two small children in cold blood and then joining the search party and pretending to worry about their well-being. Who here was that diabolical and that heartless?

Jason glanced at the carriage clock on the mantel. "I think it's time we were on our way. I'd like to get home in time for dinner."

"Do you think it's safe for us to leave?" Daniel asked, but it was obvious to Jason that he was eager to get away.

"Whoever killed the boys will do nothing to draw attention to themselves," Jason replied. "Their one safety is in carrying on as normal. This case disturbs me, Daniel. More than any case we've investigated before."

"Why?"

"Because it takes a special sort of monster to murder two little boys. In most cases, the victim had wronged others in some way and had harbored secrets, but John and Bertie were innocent of any wrongdoing, and they certainly weren't responsible for their paternity, if that was what was at the heart of this heinous crime."

"Some people don't see their victims. All they see is an obstacle that must be removed."

"I wish I could disagree and say that no human being is that pitiless, but I know I'd be deluding myself," Jason replied.

"What about Lucinda Foxley?" Daniel asked. "Are you happy to leave her unattended?"

"I will return first thing tomorrow. I require supplies, which I'm not likely to find in the village, and Lucinda is safe for the moment. She needs to eat well and rest before she'll be ready to withstand surgery."

"Perhaps we can stay the night in Birch Hill. You can probably find whatever you need in Brentwood, and I sorely miss Charlotte. Once this case is at an end, I will apply myself to finding a new nursemaid. It's time Charlotte came home."

"I agree. As happy as Mrs. Elderman is to have her granddaughter with her, I don't think this should become a permanent arrangement. Charlotte needs her father."

Daniel sighed heavily. "The truth is, I don't trust myself. I made such a hash of things with Rebecca. I know it wasn't my fault Rebecca was murdered, but I still feel responsible. Perhaps if I had been more diligent, more aware of what was really going on, she'd still be alive, living on a cattle ranch in Argentina and enjoying homemade wine on the terrace with her adoring husband, as she had planned."

"Daniel, you made an error in judgment. It happens to the best of us."

"I didn't just make an error in judgment, Jason. I nearly lost my daughter. And now I will have to take a chance on someone new and rely on references that can so easily be forged. Am I to call on every past employer and question them in person to make certain I'm not duped again?"

"You need to trust your instincts."

"That's the problem. I can no longer rely on instinct, Jason. Not where Charlotte is concerned. I can't trust her to a new nursemaid unless I'm one hundred percent certain that my child is in a safe pair of hands."

Jason fixed his gaze on the empty hearth. "There is someone…" he began, but didn't finish the thought.

"Someone?" Daniel prompted.

"Someone who might fit the bill. She's not an experienced nursemaid, but she has a good head on her shoulders and an ability to think on her feet."

"Is this someone you know from your work at the hospital?"

"No."

"Jason, can you kindly elaborate?" Daniel exclaimed.

"I'd like to talk it over with Katherine first, if you don't mind. She knows the person quite well and might not think it a good idea to make an overture."

"Can you at least tell me who it is you have in mind?" Daniel insisted.

"Let's come back to this tomorrow," Jason pushed to his feet. "I really must get home. Would you like me to drop you in Birch Hill?"

"Perhaps it's best if I return to London. Ransome will want a briefing."

"All right, then," Jason replied wearily. "Let's go."

Chapter 14

As Jason looked out over the countryside that was bathed in the dusky light of approaching evening, his thoughts kept returning to John and Bertie. He hoped they had been loved and cherished throughout their brief lives, and he prayed that they hadn't felt too much fear or pain as life had been extinguished, but despite what he'd told their parents, Jason knew better. The boys would have suffered terribly, first with stomach upset and vomiting and then with abdominal pain and respiratory paralysis as the poison took effect. They would have been alive long enough to understand that this wasn't just a normal illness, and they were in serious danger. It was only as they passed that their facial muscles would have relaxed.

Perhaps that was why John had placed an arm around his younger brother and why Bertie had grasped John's lapel, his little fingers searching for something comforting in a world that had suddenly turned excruciatingly painful and unpredictable. They might have called for their mother, but no one heard, or perhaps they had been unable to formulate words and held on for dear life, hoping as children do that everything would be all right in the end.

Whenever Jason saw a child in pain, he longed to hold Lily, to use his skill and knowledge to protect her from any danger or illness she might be exposed to, but he knew he was helpless in the face of chance. Death didn't care who you loved or what you did to safeguard them. When it came, it was brutal, indifferent, and sometimes prolonged. And just because someone lost one child, it didn't mean they wouldn't lose more. There were families that had lost all their children and were left broken and bereft, thinking only of a time when they would be reunited in Heaven.

Jason didn't believe in Heaven any more than he believed in Hell. As a man of science, he thought that people were born and then they died, their brief time on earth the only period when they were truly alive, but sometimes, like today, he fervently hoped that wasn't true. And perhaps it wasn't. Maybe he had allowed his logical nature to override his spiritual needs for too long. After all, he had witnessed a séance and had used the information the medium had provided to track down Rebecca Grainger's killer. And he had heard the voice of Micah's mother and had seen the boy's reaction. That had been no parlor trick, no lie to sell to the bereaved. It had been real.

Skeptical as he was of all things supernatural, Jason believed that Alicia Lysander had a true gift, and if she was able to contact the dead, then they had to be somewhere that wasn't here, a realm where the soul lived on and was aware of those they had left behind. Logically, it didn't make much sense, but neither did nature. The trees shed their leaves in autumn and appeared barren and dead during the winter months, but then the earth began to reawaken in the spring, as it was doing right now, and what appeared to be a husk or a dried-up flower bed bloomed into lush, colorful life once again.

Jason wanted to believe that John and Bertie were out there somewhere, no longer in pain and happy in their new incorporeal form, but he couldn't manage to forget that at this very moment, their bodies were laid out on their bed, the process of decomposition already at work, and their parents planning a funeral.

Rest in peace, boys, wherever you are, Jason thought as Daniel shifted on the seat next to him.

"Any thoughts?" he asked, letting Jason know that he'd been silent too long.

Jason sighed and turned away from the window as London's seedy outskirts replaced the rolling green hills and quaint cottages. "The question I keep returning to is why. Assuming that John and Bertie were the intended victims, why would anyone want to murder two little boys? What possible reason could there be, and who would gain by their deaths? I would be lying if I said that I like or trust Lucinda Foxley, but even Lucinda couldn't be capable of such cruelty. If she resented seeing her husband's children, she could have demanded that the family be moved to the village or forbade the children to come inside the house. But murder? And in her condition?"

"She didn't have to do it herself," Daniel replied. "Lucinda could have easily coerced someone else into doing the deed."

"Who?"

"Her brother was still there when the boys went missing. If I remember correctly, it was Harry that introduced Lucinda to Sir Lawrence, and Harry, as the head of the family, who drew up the terms of the marriage. Perhaps Harry had not known about Sir Lawrence's children and felt duped and humiliated to learn that his sister had been forced to live alongside Lawrence's other family."

"The Chadwicks certainly have a way of courting death, but I can't see Harry resorting to murdering children to make his point," Jason argued. "Besides, even if he is familiar with poisonous plants, how would he have convinced the children to ingest whatever it was they ate and made sure they kept out of sight until the poison took effect? Likewise, John and Bertie had no reason to come into contact with him."

"They were in the library," Daniel pointed out. "Harry could have easily walked in, struck up a conversation, and offered the children a treat. Much as Mrs. Buckley had."

"He would have to have been prepared," Jason argued. "One doesn't walk around with poison-laced goodies in one's pocket."

"No, but he had been at Fox Hollow for several days. Having witnessed his sister's humiliation and angry that Sir Lawrence had betrayed their friendship, he could have easily found a way. He might have even gone into the village and purchased something that could be used to disguise the taste."

"Which would account for the pink particles," Jason mused. "I wonder if there's a baker in the village."

"What are you thinking?" Daniel asked.

"Valentine's Day cookies."

"You mean biscuits?"

"Yes. They're often decorated with pink or red icing and shaped into hearts. Henley actually gifted a box of just such biscuits to Fanny."

"Henley is courting Fanny?" Daniel exclaimed, scandalized.

"It would appear so."

"And is she receptive?"

Jason shrugged. "As I said earlier, it's easier to strike up a relationship with someone who's right under your nose, isn't it?"

"Yes, I suppose it is."

"We need to question Harry Chadwick," Daniel said. "Even if he had nothing to do with the murders, he might have witnessed something while at the house. What about Richard Powers?" he suggested. "Would he murder his wife's children if he found them a nuisance? It's hard to imagine, but if he was constantly reminded of the children's paternity, that would sting."

"It just occurred to me that the crime might have nothing to do with the children and everything to do with Sir Lawrence himself," Jason said.

"How so?"

"Jealousy. Revenge. Or something even more sinister."

"Such as?" Daniel inquired, looking intrigued.

"A threat against Sir Lawrence's legitimate heir."

"What on earth are you suggesting?" Daniel asked, his brows knitting with confusion.

"Perhaps someone wanted to show Sir Lawrence just how easy it is to destroy what he holds most dear."

"But he doesn't even have a legitimate heir yet," Daniel countered. "Lucinda's child could be stillborn, or a girl."

"Children," Jason corrected him. "Lucinda is carrying twins, and one of them could be a boy."

"Still, who would want to harm an infant?"

"Someone who means business and feels no remorse about murdering a child," Jason replied.

"And you think one of the people we met today is capable of that?" Daniel asked.

"We both know that people are capable of anything when they feel threatened or when their pride has been wounded and they feel they're justified."

"Sadly, we do."

"What time should I come for you tomorrow?"

"I'm going to go to Birch Hill," Daniel replied. "I will speak to Harry Chadwick. And see Charlotte," he added.

"I must return to Fox Hollow to monitor Lucinda."

"Then let's reconvene tomorrow," Daniel said. "I know you won't remain idle while at the house."

Jason grinned. "I'll keep my ear to the ground."

"Goodnight, Jason," Daniel said as the brougham drew up before his house in St. John's Wood.

"Goodnight, Daniel."

Chapter 15

Jason had just enough time to have a bath before dinner and hoped to use the time to clear his head, but just as he lay back in the hot water and shut his eyes, Katherine entered the bathroom with a towel folded over her arm. She hung it on the towel rod but didn't leave. Instead, she perched on the marble lip of the bath, her worried gaze fixed on Jason.

"Is everything all right, darlin'?" Jason asked when Katherine didn't say anything.

"You ran past me as if you were being chased by a swarm of bees," Katherine said accusingly.

"Did I?"

Katherine's look was knowing. "You didn't want to tell me about the case."

"And I still don't," Jason replied with a sigh of resignation. If he knew his wife, only one of them could win this battle, and it would be her.

"You know I will imagine the very worst if you don't tell me."

"Katie, I didn't want to upset you."

"Why would this particular case upset me?"

"For one, because you know the people involved. And for another, it involves children."

Katherine's eyes widened. "Now you have to tell me, or I will go mad wondering what happened and imagining every conceivable horror that could befall a child."

"Two small boys were poisoned. They're the natural children of Sir Lawrence Foxley."

"Lucinda Chadwick's husband?" Katherine exclaimed.

"The one and only."

"I didn't know he had children," Katherine said, a tiny line appearing between her brows. It was a sure sign that she was saddened and disappointed, since it wasn't difficult to deduce that the children were illegitimate. "I had thought better of him," she said with a shake of the head.

"If it's any consolation, he seemed to sincerely love them."

"And Lucinda?"

"She didn't love them," Jason said, probably a tad too sarcastically.

"Did they suffer terribly?" Katherine asked quietly. Jason nodded, and Katherine's eyes filled with tears.

"This is precisely why I didn't want to tell you," Jason admonished.

"It's heartbreaking, but I would still rather know."

"Katie, Lily is safe," Jason said, and laid a hand over Katherine's.

She used the towel to dab at her eyes and exhaled heavily, her shoulders sagging with the weight of her sadness. "No one is safe, Jason. You of all people should know that."

"I do, but I need to believe that I have some control over what happens to my family. If I lose that, I won't be able to go on."

"How is Daniel? Is he coping?"

"Daniel is bearing up well, but he's off to see Charlotte tomorrow. I think he needs to be reassured that she's well."

"Is he taking the day off for Easter?" Katherine asked.

"No. He is going to speak to Harry Chadwick. Harry was there when the children went missing. He might have seen something."

Jason decided to leave out the rest of it for now, but Katherine wasn't about to let this go. Now that she felt more composed, she asked the one question that was uppermost in her mind.

"Why?"

"I honestly don't know, Katie. We spoke to nearly everyone who was there yesterday, but no one appears to have a motive, and it seems that no one saw or heard anything."

"What now?"

"I must return to Fox Hollow. Lucinda is pregnant with twins, and I believe her life is in danger."

"From the murderer?" Katherine cried.

"No, from her physician," Jason replied angrily.

"You mean you don't think she will survive the birth?"

"She won't live long enough to go into labor if left untreated. She's extremely weak, and her blood pressure is dangerously elevated. Her heart might give out."

"That poor girl. Is Caroline with her?"

"No. Lucinda feels isolated and afraid."

Katherine's brows knitted again. "Is Sir Lawrence keeping a mistress?"

"Not that I know of."

"How do you intend to treat Lucinda?"

"If I feel she's strong enough, I will perform a cesarean. She's close enough to term that the babies will not be in danger."

Katherine, who had assisted Jason during a cesarean several years ago, looked like she was about to offer to accompany him to Fox Hollow, so Jason hurried to preempt her. "Tell me about your day, Katie. Has Mary said anything to you?"

They knew from the inquiry agent's letter that Mary's husband had got on the wrong side of a Boston gang and had met with a bad end, his actions forcing Mary to flee since she was clearly in fear for her life, but if Mary had offered up any explanation, Jason had not been there to hear it.

"Mary is not herself, Jason. She seems so fragile. Even Micah couldn't get her to talk, and he's been trying all day. He hardly left her side. And she has not mentioned the baby. I can only assume it was a stillbirth."

Jason nodded. Mary had been expecting her second child, who would have been born by now if all had been well.

"And Liam? How does he seem?"

"He's subdued, but he enjoyed playing with Lily's toys and asked me to read him a story. I don't think he remembers any of us. He was too young when Mary took him away."

"Does Mary mean to stay?" Jason asked.

Katherine shrugged. "I don't know. I think she needs time to figure things out, but it's best if we don't press her."

"She's welcome to stay as long as she likes. She knows she always has a home with us."

"I do worry about her, Jason. I think Mary is frightened and lost. She hasn't mentioned her husband, but I got the impression it wasn't a happy marriage."

"Mary and Liam are safe here with us. That's what we need to impress on her."

"She did say she doesn't want to be a burden," Katherine said.

"She's hardly a burden."

"You know how proud Mary can be. She needs to feel useful. She won't take kindly to being a charity case."

"She's hardly that."

"If you're paying her way, then that's how she will feel."

"What are you suggesting?" Jason asked.

"Perhaps she can look after Lily while I attend my charity functions or when we have social engagements. Lily is becoming too much for Fanny to handle, when she has her own work to do."

"If Mary is willing, then I think that's an excellent idea."

"What about Daniel?" Katherine asked.

"What about him?"

"Does he mean to leave Charlotte with Mrs. Elderman?"

"As a matter of fact, we were just talking about that."

"And?"

"And he's ready to hire a new nursemaid and bring Charlotte home."

"I would be happy to help him interview nannies."

"I actually have someone in mind," Jason said. "And I think she might be a good fit."

Katherine stared at Jason, her surprise evident. "Who on earth can you be thinking of?"

"Flora Tarrant."

"Flora? Why would you think she would be open to such a suggestion? She's hardly in need of funds, and her parents would never stand for it."

"I had a letter from her."

"Why would Flora write to you?"

Jason had met Flora Tarrant during the investigation into the murder of Roger Spellman, which had happened at the Tarrants' home, Ardith Hall. Flora had not been present at the séance where Roger Spellman had breathed his last, nor had she been able to shed any light on what had happened, but Jason had liked the outspoken young woman and knew her to be a kindred spirit. Flora was ahead of her time, a young woman stifled by convention and tormented by her parents, who wanted her to marry one of her father's associates and get down to the business of having babies. Katherine was on good terms with the Tarrants and had invited them to dine when they were in London. Flora had asked Jason a number of questions about the hospital where he worked and had inquired about the nursing staff and how one went about obtaining the necessary training.

"Flora asked me for a job."

Jason got out of the tub, reached for the towel Katherine had brought, and dried himself quickly before wrapping the damp towel around his waist. He then walked into the bedroom, Katherine at his heels.

"Why would Flora Tarrant need a job?" Katherine asked. "She never said anything to me."

"Flora wants to relocate to London," Jason said as he shed his towel and began to dress for dinner in the clothes Henley had laid out for him.

"On her own? Her parents will never allow it."

"Which is why I thought of Daniel. Flora would make an excellent nursemaid for Charlotte, and her parents could hardly object to Daniel. They know him and will be comfortable in the knowledge that Flora will not only be safe but treated with courtesy and respect."

Katherine scoffed. "Comfortable? Would you be comfortable if Lily decided to leave us and go work as a nursemaid?"

"If Lily wished to study or decided she would like to work for a living, I would make certain she was happy and safe. We must respect her choices."

"You must be joking. Is that what parents do in America?"

Jason tucked the shirttails into his trousers, then approached his outraged wife and took her face in his hands. "Katie, do you remember how you felt when your father tried to run your life without any regard for what you wanted?"

Katherine's face relaxed ever so slightly, and she nodded.

"Whatever Lily decides to do, we will try to support her. But given that she's not yet two, I think we have time before that happens."

Katherine smiled ruefully. "I know. I just worry so. And seeing the dog's breakfast Mary made of her life—"

"Dog's breakfast?"

"It's no stranger than some of the expressions you come out with," Katherine replied defensively.

"No, I like it," Jason replied, and laughed. "What does a dog have for breakfast? Come to think of it, what's for dinner? I'm famished."

"Soup followed by poached salmon with roasted potatoes and asparagus. I know how you like asparagus," she joked.

"Which I refuse to eat with my hands," Jason replied with a grin. It was an ongoing joke between them, the American versus the British way of eating asparagus and whether it should be served with a bowl for washing one's hands.

"Eat it any way you like," Katherine conceded. "Micah and Mary will."

"We'll make a little savage of you yet, darlin'," Jason said, and lowered his face to kiss his blushing bride.

Chapter 16

It was much later, after Katherine and Micah had retired, that Jason got a chance to speak to Mary. He found her in the library, staring into the dying fire. During dinner, nothing had been said about Mary's sudden reappearance since it was clear that she had no wish to talk about whatever had transpired in Boston. Everyone had carried on as if everything was as it should be, and this was just another family dinner. Micah had told them stories about his school, Katherine had described an excruciating morning visit with a dowager who wanted to quiz her about her American husband, and Jason had scrupulously avoided talking about the case and praised the benefits of country living. He had gone so far as to suggest that they should all spend the summer at Redmond Hall since the children would benefit from the fresh country air and Micah could spend time with his friend Tom Marin. The suggestion had been met with varying degrees of enthusiasm.

Now, in the rosy light of the fire, Mary looked pallid and drawn, her modest gown loose around her waist and noticeably worn at the hem and cuffs. Her bright hair was scraped back from her face, and her eyes seemed larger than they had in the past, probably because she had lost weight and now bordered on gaunt.

Jason was about to press the switch that would turn on the gas lamps, but Mary cried, "Don't. Please."

Jason snatched his hand away as if he'd been burned. He would have left Mary in peace, but he was certain she wished to talk, so he approached slowly and stood before the hearth.

"May I sit with you?" he asked.

"Yes. I was waiting for you."

"So I gathered," Jason said as he settled into the wingchair across from Mary.

Mary's eyes filled with tears, and she quickly looked away, fixing her gaze on the glowing embers. "I'm sorry, Captain," she said softly.

"What are you sorry for?"

"Everything. I was such a fool. I should have listened to you, but I always have to have my own way. My mother always said I had no sense, and she was right."

"Mary, I think you're being too hard on yourself," Jason replied, but Mary shook her head.

"I'm not. I wanted to prove that I don't need your support and could make a life for myself, but I made such a shambles of things."

"Tell me what happened." Jason wanted to take Mary's hand but didn't think she would appreciate the gesture and might even find it patronizing, so he kept his hands to himself.

"I don't want to talk about it. It hurts too much."

"I understand," Jason said soothingly. "Mary, you are safe here with us, and you can stay as long as you like. This is your home, and you needn't feel beholden to me. Ever."

Mary nodded. "Thank you. You are always so kind."

Jason thought he should leave Mary in peace, but he got the feeling she wasn't quite finished, so he sat quietly, his gaze averted from Mary's troubled face.

"He's dead," Mary exclaimed. Tears slid down her cheeks, and her mouth quivered as she tried to rein in her misery.

"Your husband?"

She nodded. "And my girl. Catriona, after my mam. She died aboard the ship, and I had to throw her overboard," Mary wailed. "She didn't even get a proper burial, just a few words from the Anglican minister."

Mary's eyes sparkled with tears as she looked at Jason. "I don't have a single grave to visit, Captain, where I can lay my heart bare and confess my sins to those I once loved. My mother died in Maryland, my father and brother in Georgia, Liam's da is buried Lord knows where, my husband was buried in Boston, and my Catriona's remains are at the bottom of the Atlantic, her tender flesh devoured by fish. Where will my bones rest when my time comes? Where do I belong?" she cried.

"You belong here, with us," Jason replied quietly.

"But I don't, do I? I'm not your flesh and blood, and you owe me nothing."

"Mary, it's never been about paying a debt. I love you, Micah, and Liam. You're my family, and I hope I will always be yours."

Mary sniffed and nodded miserably. "You're a good man, Captain. A generous and fair man, but I don't feel right to impose on you and expect you to raise my son. I must find employment and make my own way in the world."

"And I respect your desire to be independent, but you have suffered a devastating loss, Mary. Give yourself some time to heal, won't you? Spend the summer in Birch Hill, regain your health, and give Liam a chance to flourish. Then, in the autumn, if you still wish to work, I will help you to find respectable employment."

Mary's face brightened. "Will you?"

"I will. How do you feel about working at the hospital?"

"As a cleaning woman?" Mary asked, her eyes narrowing with distaste.

"No, as a nurse. I can see that you receive proper training and get a position on the ward."

"What about Liam?"

"Liam can stay in the nursery with Lily and then share her governess once Lily is old enough to need one. He will need an education, Mary."

Mary nodded, her expression thoughtful. "And until autumn, I will help out with the children. It's the least I can do to repay your kindness and boundless hospitality."

"That sounds like a reasonable plan to me," Jason said. "And perhaps we can arrange a funeral Mass for Catriona whenever you feel ready. Would that help you to feel more at peace?"

"Oh, yes," Mary cried. "It would."

"Then I will see it done. Now, I think you should get to bed. You look exhausted."

"I am," Mary confessed.

They both stood at the same time, and Mary walked into Jason's arms. He held her close, and she rested her head on his chest and wrapped her arms around his waist, pressing herself so close, Jason thought she would have crawled inside him if she could find a way.

"I love you, Captain," Mary whispered into his shoulder. "I would consider myself the luckiest woman alive if I found a man like you to share my life with."

"Just give yourself time, Mary," Jason said gently. "You're still so young. I'm sure life has many wonderful things in store for you."

Mary looked up at him, her face tearstained. "All life has given me thus far is suffering and loss. I can't bear to lose anyone else."

Jason kissed the top of her head but didn't bother to offer any platitudes. He couldn't guarantee that Mary wouldn't lose anyone else. Just because she had lost so many did not mean she wouldn't lose loved ones again. All he could do was look after her and Liam and try to keep them safe. The rest was out of his hands.

"Goodnight, Captain," Mary whispered as she finally pulled away.

"Goodnight, *a stór*," Jason said, recalling the endearment he'd heard Catriona Donovan use to refer to Micah during the séance.

Mary smiled, and then she was gone.

When Jason came upstairs a short while later, he found Micah's door ajar and the light still on. Micah was sitting on his bed, staring morosely into space. A few years ago, Jason would have simply walked in and taken the boy in his arms, but Micah was an adolescent now and might not welcome such a display, so Jason knocked on the jamb and waited to be invited in.

Jason sat on the bed and studied Micah's pinched face. "Want to talk about it?" he asked.

"Will Catriona go to Heaven?" Micah asked without preamble, his eyes pleading with Jason to say yes.

"Why do you think she wouldn't?" Jason asked carefully. He wasn't well versed enough in the Catholic faith to understand all the tenets and didn't want to make a mistake.

"Because she wasn't baptized," Micah replied. "With everything that happened, Mary never got round to it. And Catriona never got last rites or even had a Catholic priest perform the service when her body was consigned to the sea."

"Micah, I think you know that my faith has been sorely tested these last few years, but I still believe that God loves all his children, even when they're less than worthy of the honor, and he would never unjustly punish a newborn baby for circumstances that were beyond her control."

"But what if she'll have to spend eternity in Limbo?" Micah cried. "Then she'll never get to be with Mam and Da and Patrick. And her father," he added as an afterthought. "She'll be all alone. Lost. With no one to love her."

"Surely there must be something we can do," Jason said, hoping Micah would guide him.

"Maybe we can speak to Father McCready," Micah said, his face lighting with hope. "He'll know what to do."

"Then that's what we'll do. And we'll ask Father McCready to hold a funeral Mass."

"Think he'll do that?" Micah asked hopefully.

"I don't see why not."

Micah smiled, his relief evident. "Goodnight, Captain."

"Goodnight."

Jason left the room and closed the door behind him. Lily was still tiny, but some days he felt as if he'd already raised several children and was prepared for anything that was to come.

Chapter 17

Sunday, March 28

"I cannot allocate any manpower to a case in Essex," Superintendent Ransome said wearily. It was barely nine in the morning, but he looked tired and irritable, the points of his moustache drooping, and his hair not as neatly oiled and combed as it usually was. If this were anyone else, Daniel would expect them to be at home with their family on Easter Sunday, but Ransome usually stopped by the Yard on Sundays just to make certain all was well. Judging by his appearance, it wasn't.

"We have a pressing backlog of cases, and a triple homicide was reported in Leicester Square last night. I had to go out there myself since no one was available and spent half the night trying to make heads or tails of what might have happened and who was involved."

"What's the cause of death?" Daniel asked, his curiosity getting the better of him.

Ransome shrugged. "I don't know yet. The deceased were dispatched to Dr. Fenwick, and Mr. Gillespie has yet to deliver the crime scene photos. If we're lucky this will prove to be a murder-suicide pact, and we won't have to waste any resources untangling that particular knot."

"About the case at Fox Hollow—" Daniel began, but Ransome cut across him.

"By your own admission, you found no irrefutable proof that the children were poisoned. Could be they were, and could be they weren't. There's many an accidental death where children are involved. If you believe there's a case to pursue, then perhaps it's time you turned it over to Essex Police. I need you here, Haze."

"Sir, the Foxleys are personally known to me, and they begged for my help. I can't simply walk away, not when the victims are two innocent children," Daniel pleaded.

Ransome gave Daniel a pitying look. "I know you're still haunted by what happened to your daughter, Haze, but you can't make the deaths of two children your personal crusade. They are not your children."

"I know that, sir, but I must see this through."

Superintendent Ransome looked thoughtful. "All right, but only because this case might have a bearing on one of our own."

Daniel was perplexed. "The deaths of John and Bertie Powers are connected to a case in London? How?"

Ransome gave Daniel a wolfish grin. "It just so happens, Haze, that Mr. Plimpton, who called on Sir Lawrence on the day of the alleged murder, is known to me."

"In what capacity?"

"The criminal kind," Ransome replied. "See what you can discover of Sir Lawrence's comings and goings these past few days."

"Are you suggesting that Sir Lawrence murdered his children?"

Ransome sighed with obvious exasperation. "Don't be daft, Haze. I didn't mean that at all."

Daniel was completely at sea as he looked at his superior. Ransome shook his head in dismay, but all the irritation had gone from his expression.

"I have one word for you, Haze. Carmichaels."

"What have the Carmichaels got to do with this?"

"The Carmichaels have expanded their operations in the East End, but they're not bringing their goods into the port of London. What this tells me is that they have a network of well-heeled associates who help them with distribution."

Daniel nodded. "I see. So, you think Sir Lawrence is an associate of Lance Carmichael?"

"Good. I was beginning to think you were going blind. Look into it, Haze. If we're to take down the Carmichaels, we need to hit at their associates as well."

"Yes, sir."

"Bring me something I can use."

"I will do what I can, sir."

Daniel made to stand, but Ransome motioned for him to sit back down. His expression was inscrutable, almost apologetic.

"I have come to a decision about the position of Detective Chief Inspector," Ransome said.

For a second, Daniel's heart soared, but then it occurred to him that if Ransome was going to offer it to him, he'd look considerably less tense.

"I wanted to tell you in person that I have offered the position to Inspector Yates."

Ransome had offered the job to Jason and had begged him to reconsider when Jason had refused, but the news that the promotion had gone to Yates was still a surprise and a disappointment. Daniel had never really expected to be chosen, nor was he sure that he was ready for the added responsibility, but the rejection hurt, nonetheless. He was as qualified as any inspector at the Yard, and certainly as capable as Inspector Yates.

"I understand, sir," Daniel said, and was about to stand again when Ransome forestalled him.

"No, you don't," Ransome said. "Look, Haze, I would have chosen you, were it not for the men."

"I don't understand," Daniel replied. He got on well with the other inspectors and was liked and respected by the constables, as far as he knew.

"There are those who feel that you have an unfair advantage, since they don't have the benefit of Lord Redmond's medical expertise or his valuable input when working a case."

"You've made your regard for Lord Redmond abundantly clear, sir," Daniel said.

He supposed he sounded bitter, but he couldn't hide his true feelings. Jason was undeniably an asset, but in some ways, he was also a detriment, since no one judged Daniel on his own merit. It was always Redmond and Haze, and although Daniel was grateful to Jason for his help, he also knew that there would come a time when he would have to stand on his own two feet if he hoped to get the recognition and the professional benefits that came with it.

"You're a fine detective," Ransome said, and blessed Daniel with one of his rare smiles. "I know you're disappointed, but were I given a choice between a higher rank and a loyal friend who'd lay down his life to help you and yours, I know which I would choose."

Daniel nodded. When put that way, he knew which one he'd choose as well, and he also knew himself to be incredibly blessed. Meeting Jason Redmond had changed his life, and he knew with unwavering certainty that he would never have another friend like Jason.

"You're a lucky man, Haze. Remember that," Ransome said. "There will be other opportunities down the line, and your suitability will be considered and judged impartially. But for now, I must give someone else a shot. Yates has been an inspector longer, and he has an impressive track record."

"I understand, sir. Thank you."

"For what?" Ransome asked.

"For telling me in person and reminding me what's important."

Ransome nodded, and Daniel knew he was free to leave. He found Inspector Yates and offered him his sincere congratulations, then headed out into the overcast spring morning. His anger had dissipated, as had his disappointment, and he found that he was at peace with Ransome's decision. He was right, there would be other opportunities, and when the time came, Daniel would throw his hat in the ring again.

But this morning, all his thoughts were for the case. He would take the train to Brentwood, pay a call on Harry Chadwick, stop in to see Charlotte and Mrs. Elderman, then make inquiries at the Red Stag. The tavern would be closed on Easter Sunday, but Davy lived above the bar and would be in, since there wasn't much else to do in Birch Hill on Sunday. If anyone knew what the Carmichaels were up to, it was Davy Brody, and there was always Moll to supplement Davy's knowledge. Moll had been a fixture at the Red Stag since she was hardly more than a child and was privy to the local gossip. Her easygoing nature and bawdy comments put the men who came to drink at the Stag at ease, and they shared more than they intended to, inadvertently confessing to all their transgressions.

There was also the fact that not so long ago, Moll had fancied herself in love with Tristan Carmichael, and he had seemed to care for her. Lance Carmichael had arranged a more suitable marriage for his only son with the daughter of a trusted associate, but Daniel had a feeling that Moll and Tristan had remained in touch and Moll knew more about Tristan's dealings than his wife did. Whether she would tell Daniel anything was anyone's guess, but it was worth a shot, especially since he would be in Birch Hill already.

Chapter 18

Daniel arrived in Birch Hill just after noon and presented himself at Chadwick Manor after dismissing the cabbie who'd brought him to the village from the station in Brentwood. It was too early to pay a social call on any other day, but the Easter service at St. Catherine's was always held at ten, and Harry wouldn't dare miss it, even if he had to haul himself out of bed at an ungodly hour for a young gentleman. Harry would be at home now, and probably looking forward to a delicious lunch of roast lamb or succulent ham served with roasted potatoes and buttered peas. Daniel's mouth watered, but he pushed the thought of food away. He'd speak to Harry first, then find something to eat later. Llewelyn, the Chadwicks' self-important butler, answered the door and stared at Daniel in obvious surprise that was quickly replaced by disdain.

"To what do we owe the pleasure, Inspector Haze?" he droned. "And on Easter Sunday no less."

"I need to speak to Mr. Chadwick."

"Mr. Chadwick is not at home to visitors."

Daniel sighed with impatience. "We can stand here a little longer and pretend you can keep me out, or I can ask for reinforcements from the Brentwood Constabulary and make considerably more noise."

He hated to throw his weight around, but Llewelyn was the sort of person who only responded to a show of force and gave way when he knew he was either outranked or outnumbered. If Daniel had learned anything from Jason, it was that it was considerably more desirable to outfox rather than outrank, since it allowed the other party to retain something of their pride and the belief that they still had control over the situation.

And noble rank or not, Jason was always entirely, unapologetically himself. Those around him had no choice but to respond to his confidence. There were some who called it brashness or arrogance behind Jason's back and referred to him by unflattering names, but Jason remained unperturbed in the face of their criticism, and he was so much the better for it.

Daniel had yet to achieve such indifference to public opinion, but he had come a long way since leaving the village and knew that he was no longer the same man he'd been before fate or mere chance had so generously put him in the path of his American friend.

"London has changed you," Llewelyn ground out as he finally stepped away from the door to allow Daniel inside.

"And yet you're still exactly the same," Daniel replied. He would have been considerably more polite in the past, but he was no longer a lowly parish constable, and Llewelyn held no power over anything but the front door and his staff. And they both knew it.

"I will tell Mr. Chadwick you're here."

"Do," Daniel replied. "Is Mrs. Chadwick at home?" he called to Llewelyn's retreating back.

The butler turned. "Mrs. Chadwick and Miss Chadwick are currently in London, enjoying a shopping expedition. They're expected back on Wednesday. If you would wait in the parlor, Inspector," Llewellyn said, and walked off without showing Daniel to the parlor as his duties would normally demand.

Daniel made himself comfortable and waited. When Harry Chadwick finally entered the room, Daniel noted a marked change in the young man. Harry had always been handsome in a boyish sort of way, but the man who had returned from his travels was lean and suntanned, and seemed more at ease in his own skin. Perhaps his experiences abroad had helped him shed the guise of obedient son and reluctant husband to a woman he hadn't loved and had not grieved. Harry was wealthy, single, and free to make his own choices, and his newfound independence was evident in his sure step and relaxed grin.

"Inspector Haze, a pleasure to see you. Mrs. Elderman has been regaling me with tales of your exploits in London. Well done, sir. Well done." Harry sat down across from Daniel and crossed his legs.

"Thank you, Mr. Chadwick. And I hear you enjoyed your travels."

"Oh, yes. I must confess that at first I felt lost, like a child suddenly left alone in an unfamiliar place, but after a few weeks, what had seemed like exile from home turned into a wonderful adventure. I met interesting people and visited places I had only read about. It was exhilarating," Harry added, his smile one of absolute delight. "I confess, I didn't really want to come back, but Mother's letters were becoming more insistent."

"What are you plans now you're back?" Daniel asked.

"I expect Mother has a list of eligible young ladies she thinks would make for a suitable bride. It's time I was married again. I do long for a family of my own."

Knowing what Daniel did of Harry's past dalliances, Daniel couldn't begin to guess how Harry pictured his future life, but it was none of Daniel's affair, and he wasn't there to have a pleasant chat about visits to the Parthenon or gondola rides in Venice. Daniel would likely never see any of the places others waxed poetic about but felt no regret at missing out on the world's monuments. He wasn't cut out to be a world traveler. His feet were firmly planted on English soil and would remain so for the rest of his days. The only place he might like to see was America, and only because he'd heard so much about it from Jason. Maybe someday, he thought as he forced his attention back to Harry Chadwick.

"Understandably so," Daniel replied noncommittally.

"So, what brings you to Chadwick Manor, Inspector? Surely, you're not here to hear about my travels."

"I'm afraid it falls to me to be the bearer of bad news. Two little boys were found dead at Fox Hollow yesterday. Lord Redmond is of the opinion that they were poisoned."

"But I just returned from Fox Hollow," Harry replied, looking genuinely shocked. "All was well when I left. What happened?"

"The children's mother raised the alarm after you had departed. They were discovered yesterday morning, in a trunk in one of the unused bedrooms."

"My God, how awful! Whose children were they?"

"The Powers'. Perhaps you met them while you were in residence?"

"Yes, of course, John and Bertie. Charming little boys. What a tragedy."

If Harry Chadwick felt any resentment toward Sir Lawrence or his illegitimate children, he did a fine job of hiding his feelings. He was the picture of sympathy, saying all the right things but clearly not feeling the loss himself or seeing what this news had to do with him or why Daniel would feel the need to personally deliver it.

"I will send a note of condolence," Harry said magnanimously.

It was obvious to Daniel that Harry thought their conversation was at an end and was looking for a way to extricate himself politely, possibly by announcing that he had an engagement elsewhere or was expecting a guest for lunch.

"Mr. Chadwick, did Lady Foxley ever mention the children to you?"

Harry looked abashed. "No. Why would she? We don't generally discuss the children of our servants."

"It seems the boys were Sir Lawrence's progeny."

Harry's reaction was immediate. "They were Larry's sons?" he cried. "No. I don't believe it. I never suspected. Oh, poor Lucinda. She must have been absolutely livid." Harry Chadwick seemed to realize that he had just pointed the finger at his sister and instantly backtracked. "But such things are not uncommon, Inspector. It is a gentlemen's prerogative to bed his servants."

"Is it?"

"Well, yes. What young man hasn't made advances to a parlormaid or comely governess?"

Or a handsome tutor, Daniel's mind supplied.

"Surely you're not suggesting…" Harry's voice trailed away as he waited for Daniel to explain himself.

"Mrs. Powers has accused Lady Foxley."

"Lucinda would never," Harry sputtered. "Besides, she's as big as a house. The poor girl can barely move."

"Nevertheless."

"Nevertheless what? You think Lucinda is capable of murdering two little boys?"

"Mr. Chadwick, what I think is irrelevant. I must follow the evidence."

"And what evidence do you have against my sister?"

"None, but seeing as she's the only newcomer to the house and the existence of the boys served as a constant reminder of her husband's past, she does have a motive, I'm afraid."

"Poppycock!" Harry exclaimed. "Lucinda understands the ways of the world, Mother made sure of that, and those boys were born ages before she even met Larry. Larry dotes on her and wouldn't look at another woman, not even while Lucinda is…well, you know," he added lamely, clearly not wishing to allude to a woman's wifely duties. "Does Lucinda know you suspect her? How is she taking this unfounded accusation?"

"Mr. Chadwick, Lady Foxley is not well. Lord Redmond is on his way to Fox Hollow today to attend on her."

Harry paled. "What are you saying? Is Lucinda in danger?"

"Not if she receives timely medical assistance."

"What does that mean?" Harry asked. "Timely how? What does Lord Redmond mean to do?"

"I believe he is all set to operate."

"Operate? You mean take the baby out before it's due?"

"Babies. Lady Foxley is carrying twins."

"Well, Lucinda never did do anything by halves," Harry replied. "I do hope Lord Redmond knows what he's about."

"I assure you that he does," Daniel replied.

Harry cocked his head to the side, and Daniel could almost see the gears turning in his mind. "If the murder was committed there, why are you here?" he asked at last.

"You departed Fox Hollow right around the time the boys went missing. Did you happen to see or hear anything you might now think of as suspicious?"

Harry made a show of thinking. "Why, no. Larry was very hospitable, and we spent most of our time together since Lucinda hardly got out of bed. I thought she was being terribly rude, to punish me for her unhappiness. I didn't realize she was genuinely ill."

"Why would she punish you?" Daniel asked.

"I fear she's rather disappointed," Harry confessed. "Lucinda was terribly excited at the idea of becoming a baroness, but Larry, being Larry, had made promises he never intended to keep."

"What sort of promises?"

"Lucinda was under the impression that they would spend most of their time in London, riding together in Rotten Row and attending endless balls. She's not one to rusticate. If Fox Hollow were more modern, she might have resigned herself to being the lady of the manor and throwing her considerable energy into entertaining, but the house is old and dreary. It doesn't even have running water or gas lighting, as I'm sure you've noticed. And then there are all those creepy tunnels and secret passages."

"What tunnels?" Daniel asked. No one had mentioned tunnels or passages that might have allowed someone to enter the house unnoticed and offer the boys a treat laced with death.

Harry waved a dismissive hand. "The Foxleys were Papist in centuries past, and like so many other noble families that found themselves on the wrong side of the religion *du jour*, they had to look to their safety. There are at least three priest holes and tunnels that run beneath the house. One leads to St. Luke's and the other somewhere else, I forget where. Larry showed me the tunnels years ago when I visited him during the school holidays."

"Does Lucinda know about the tunnels?" Daniel asked.

"Everyone does. Lucinda said there are strange noises during the night, and she'd even heard voices." Harry shrugged dismissively. "I wouldn't be surprised if the place was haunted. Watched over by the priest who died while in hiding. It's an old family legend. You should ask Sir Lawrence about it. He's quite fond of family history."

"Thank you. I will," Daniel replied. "Were there any visitors to the house while you were in residence?"

"The vicar came by. Dreary old chap. Rather reminds me of the Reverend Talbot. Perhaps they're related."

"I was told a Mr. Plimpton had called by while you were there," Daniel said, watching Harry Chadwick for any sign of recognition.

"Ah, yes. I quite forgot about him. A surly fellow with coarse manners. He and Larry were closeted for a while, so I have no idea what they talked about."

"Had you ever met Mr. Plimpton before?"

"No, I hadn't," Harry replied. "Is he a suspect? What possible reason would he have to harm the boys?"

"I'm only trying to establish who was there when the boys went missing."

"It was mostly just the household staff," Harry replied.

"So, you saw nothing that would give you pause?" Daniel pressed.

"Nothing at all, other than Lucinda's lassitude, but now it makes perfect sense. Should I go back, do you think? To offer my support?"

"I think it's best if you wait a few days. The investigation is ongoing."

"I understand." Harry seemed relieved to be absolved of the responsibility. "You have changed, you know," he observed.

"In what way?"

"I don't know, but London definitely agrees with you. The great cities of the world make one realize just how small our lives in these English villages are. You really must go abroad, Inspector. There's nothing like it."

"I will gladly take your advice as soon as I become a man of independent means," Daniel replied without rancor.

Harry chuckled. "I'm sorry. That was rather thoughtless of me."

"Not at all. We all speak from our own experience."

"Indeed, we do," Harry agreed. "Well, if there's nothing else—"

"I will be on my way," Daniel replied. "I'd actually like to visit my daughter while I'm here."

"I saw her at church with Mrs. Elderman. She's charming." Harry's expression grew somber. "And I'm very sorry about Mrs. Haze. I had always rather liked her."

"Thank you." Daniel pushed to his feet. He felt an overwhelming need to get outside.

He didn't want to talk about Sarah. It was bad enough that everything in the village reminded him of her. They had walked every path, picnicked in every lovely meadow, and kissed in the lane leading to Chadwick Hall. Not for the first time, Daniel reflected that he could never come back, not if he hoped to eventually move forward.

"Llewelyn will see you out," Harry said, and strode off.

Chapter 19

Since it was nearly one in the afternoon, Daniel decided it would be a good idea to stop at the Red Stag first. He had no desire to break bread with his mother-in-law, who always dined at one, while Charlotte had her lunch in the nursery. He'd rather call on them last and maybe take Charlotte for a walk in the woods or sit on the bench in the garden Sarah had so lovingly tended. As much as Daniel admired Harriet and was grateful for her help, it was his daughter he wished to see.

The Red Stag hadn't changed much since the last time Daniel had been there. It still smelled of hops, roasting meat, and the flowery scent Moll Brody always wore. Daniel thought she resorted to dousing herself with perfume to counteract the smell of certain customers, some of whom spent more time at the Stag than they did at home. A few of the regulars were there despite the holiday, occupying their usual tables and nursing tankards of ale. They greeted Daniel and looked all set to interrogate him about London and his most recent cases, so Daniel approached the bar, turning his back on them to discourage conversation.

A different man might enjoy the recognition and spend a happy hour recounting his exploits over a pint, but Daniel wasn't the sort of person who courted attention for its own sake. He had no desire for his life to be fodder for local gossip, which it would be, since there wasn't anything more interesting happening at the moment. Of course, a suspicious death at Fox Hollow would quickly change that since some of the players were familiar to the locals and were always persons of interest.

Davy folded his meaty arms across his chest and blessed Daniel with a lopsided grin. "Well, look what the cat dragged in," he said. "I 'ope ye're 'ere to say 'ow ye do and 'ave a pint, Inspector. Be social-like," he added testily. "It's been a while since ye've blessed our tiny corner of the world with yer exalted presence."

Daniel and Davy Brody had been friends once but had not been on cordial terms in years, since Daniel's choice of profession had not gone down well with a man who made his living by circumventing the law and avoiding the taxman.

"I came in to say hello and have a chat," Daniel replied, returning Davy's insincere grin. "I didn't expect you to be open on Easter Sunday."

It was against the law to open a public house on Sundays, but Daniel didn't think anyone except Reverend Talbot would care to do anything about it. Clearly, Davy felt safe, or he wouldn't risk it.

"I ain't open," Davy said defensively.

Daniel's gaze swept over the patrons, who were all staring into their tankards, clearly not wishing to get involved.

"There's no law 'gainst 'ospitality, is there, Inspector?" Davy demanded. "These 'ere are dear friends who've nowhere else to go. Is it wrong to offer them a drop of ale to wet their whistle if I ain't charging them for the privilege?"

Daniel decided not to engage in an argument. It was no longer his job to police the village, and Davy would simply reopen as soon as Daniel left anyway. He'd learned from Jason that it was wise to pick one's battles.

"Where's Moll?" he asked instead.

"Upstairs. Needed to put her feet up."

"Is she ill?" Daniel asked.

"Nah. She's in the family way. She's married now," Davy said reproachfully, and Daniel realized he had known that but had quite forgotten since Birch Hill news didn't interest him as much as it once had.

"I quite like the fellow," Davy said. "'E's useful and don't talk too much."

"Sounds like the perfect man for Moll," Daniel joked.

He couldn't imagine Moll married to someone who was overly chatty, since he would interfere with her flirting and probably expect her to remain silent while he expounded on his world views. Moll couldn't be quiet if her life depended on it, which was what Daniel had been counting on when he'd decided to stop at the Stag.

"Moll runs circles 'round 'im, and 'e loves 'er all the more for it. The lad is that smitten."

"I'm glad for her," Daniel said, and meant it. Moll enjoyed a questionable reputation where men were concerned and was entirely too forward and outspoken for a woman, but she was a good sort and had the proverbial heart of gold. "Do I know Moll's husband?"

"I doubt it. Bruce Plimpton. Son of Conrad Plimpton."

"Plimpton?"

Davy nodded, his gaze sliding away when a new patron walked through the door and headed toward the bar. Daniel had not made the connection when he'd heard the name from Ransome, but now that Davy had mentioned the man's Christian name, he knew he'd heard it before. Conrad Plimpton, or Limpy as he was known to his mates, had worked alongside Lance Carmichael for decades and owned a tavern in Hullbridge. Located on the River Crouch, Hullbridge was a convenient spot for bringing in smuggled goods. There wasn't much call for French brandy, wine, and lace these days, but that didn't mean the Carmichaels were no longer involved in other forms of illegal trade. They were bringing in opium to supply their dens and probably smuggling in high-duty goods to avoid paying tax. And Daniel could just bet that supplies went out as well, straight to London and into the waiting arms of Tristan Carmichael, who was running the London end of the Carmichael enterprise.

"Does Bruce work with his father?" Daniel asked once Davy had served the customer and turned his attention back to Daniel.

"More or less," Davy replied noncommittally.

"How much more and how much less?"

Davy gave him a look that spoke volumes. He wasn't about to divulge anything that might be viewed as grassing. His livelihood and now Moll's future were directly linked to the Carmichaels, and he would be very foolish indeed to give anything away, especially to a policeman. Daniel no longer had jurisdiction in Essex, but he still had ties to the Essex police and had only to say the word to bring Davy Brody's world crashing down around him.

"I'm not interested in your activities, Davy," Daniel said, "but two children were murdered at Fox Hollow, and a Mr. Plimpton, I can only assume it was Bruce, had paid a call on Sir Lawrence not an hour before they breathed their last."

"Whose children?"

"Doris Powers'. Know her, do you?"

"I know Sir Lawrence, and I know they were 'is boys." Davy looked appropriately shocked. "What would Bruce want with murdering children, Daniel?"

"I don't know. Perhaps it wasn't the children that were meant to die."

"Are you saying 'e were there to kill Sir Lawrence?"

"Was he?"

"Don't be daft. I don't know the details, but I may 'ave 'eard through the grapevine that Sir Lawrence owes Lance a bit of money. Lance don't murder people 'e can profit from. And 'e sure as feck don't kill their children. 'E's got a sense of 'onor, 'e does."

"Right," Daniel said, not bothering to hide his sarcasm. "Honor among thieves."

"There is such a thing, ye know. There must be a code, otherwise, it's anything goes. And that just wouldn't do. Not when there's rival gangs on the move."

Daniel was about to ask Davy another question but paused, what Davy had just said about people's children sinking in.

"Did Lance Carmichael know that the boys were Sir Lawrence's natural children?" he asked.

"Course 'e did," Davy replied. "Lance makes it 'is business to know just who 'e's dealing with and what their weaknesses are."

"Are what are Sir Lawrence's weaknesses?"

Davy shrugged. "Lance doesn't share such things with the likes of me."

"Is there anyone else at Fox Hollow who has dealings with the Carmichaels?"

Davy fixed Daniel with a cynical blue stare.

"What? Everyone?" Daniel asked.

"Well, I wouldn't go so far as to say everyone, but I'd wager that the estate manager is in on whatever it is they're doing up there."

That at least would explain how Richard Powers knew so much about Lucinda's past. Lance Carmichael made it his business to know everything that went on in his corner of Essex, and previous transgressions could be a way to control her husband if he stumbled and fell over his conscience.

"Did Lance Carmichael get his money?"

"Bruce and I don't discuss business," Davy said. "What 'e does for Lance is between 'im and the boss man."

"And how does Moll feel about what her husband is doing?"

Davy smirked. "Ye always did imagine that our Moll 'as loftier ideals than what's fitting for a barmaid."

"She's not just a barmaid, Davy. She's your niece."

"So she is, but she's a grown woman, Daniel. She does what she wants." Giving Daniel a thoughtful look, Davy said, "Bruce makes 'er feel safe, and cherished. 'E's building them a fine 'ouse. Moll will 'ave a good life with Bruce. Prosperous."

"Unless he gets banged up."

"Even if 'e does, Conrad will look after his son's wife and children. That's a comfort to Moll."

"A cold comfort, if you ask me."

"Well, I weren't asking, were I? Now, if ye've no more questions, I'd like to enjoy what's left of my Sunday."

"I'd like to speak to Moll."

Davy shook his head. "Leave 'er be. There's nothing she can tell ye that ye don't already know. She deserves a bit of peace. Now, I can offer you a bowl of stew and a pint of bitter. On the 'ouse," he added, recalling that he wasn't supposed to be doing business.

"You want me gone that badly?"

"I don't want no trouble, Daniel. Ye'll bugger off back to London once this case is done, but I'll still be 'ere, at the mercy of the Carmichaels."

"All right. I'll take you up on your offer."

"And then you'll be on your way."

"Then I'll be on my way," Daniel promised.

Chapter 20

Having spent a delightful hour in the company of Charlotte, who chattered nonstop and had shown Daniel all her newly acquired treasures, ranging from a smooth pink stone to a new picture book her grandmother had ordered for her from Brentwood, Daniel finally found the strength to leave. He was grateful that Charlotte did not ask when she was coming home and seemed happy to remain with her grandmother a little longer. But seeing Charlotte and spending time with her had reminded Daniel just how much he had missed her, and he vowed to find a new nursemaid as soon as the case was solved, and he could turn his attention to domestic matters.

Harriet had offered Daniel the use of her driver and buggy, and Thomas would take Daniel all the way to Fox Hollow. It was a pleasant spring day, and Daniel sat back and enjoyed the ride, grateful that Thomas wasn't in a particularly talkative mood. Perhaps he resented being sent on such a time-consuming errand, but such was the lot of the servant. Some were given the runaround, while others were bedded by their masters. Harry Chadwick had dismissed his friend's dalliance with a servant as typical behavior of the upper classes, but Daniel couldn't help but feel disgusted with men who thought the women in their households were theirs for the taking.

Granted, Mrs. Powers didn't seem bitter about her affair with the master's son and readily admitted to the paternity of her children, but perhaps she had talked herself into seeing the situation as advantageous rather than the blatant abuse of authority it clearly was. Just because Sir Lawrence had been an adolescent at the time didn't mean that Doris hadn't felt threatened or beholden, given her employer's attitude toward the servants. After all, Sir Lawrence's father had sired Richard Powers on a woman who wasn't his wife.

The current baronet seemed to care for his children, but how would his behavior have changed once he had a legitimate child, and the boys became old enough to understand that the master was actually their father? Would Sir Lawrence have acknowledged them then? Would he have provided for their future and seen to their education, or would they have become an embarrassment to him? Daniel supposed it was now a moot point, but Lucinda must have asked herself these questions and found the answers troubling.

Given past events, Daniel was well aware that Lucinda's moral compass did not quite point north, but was she capable of murdering two children, especially in her condition? He didn't suppose giving them something laced with poison would require much effort, but women usually grew more emotional when they were with child, so the murder would be doubly cruel given that Lucinda was about to become a mother herself. But her disillusionment with her husband and living arrangements could have pushed her over the edge, leading to a moral breakdown. Despite Jason's objections, Daniel wasn't quite ready to rule out Lucinda as a suspect.

But now there was another angle to consider, that Sir Lawrence had had business dealings with the Carmichaels and had owed Lance Carmichael money. Davy hadn't said what the money was for, but it had to have been a substantial enough sum to send a heavy to collect it. Bruce Plimpton had arrived at Fox Hollow at around the time the boys went missing, but did his presence have anything to do with their deaths? Daniel couldn't imagine that Limpy would resort to murdering children, especially when Davy had said that Bruce had been able to collect the debt.

Dismissing Bruce Plimpton for the moment, Daniel moved his examination to Harry Chadwick. Although Harry was technically still a suspect, Daniel couldn't see any real reason for Harry to harm the children. He had appeared sincerely surprised to learn that the boys were Sir Lawrence's but hadn't seemed appalled or even particularly angry with his friend. Having seen Harry's newfound contentment and hope for the future, Daniel didn't think Harry cared enough to get involved in his sister's domestic affairs, not when he would be risking not only his freedom but possibly his very life if he chose to avenge his sister's humiliation at the hands of his friend.

Who did that leave, then? None of the servants had a discernable motive, and Richard Powers seemed to care for his stepsons. Daniel had to admit that he was going around in circles and didn't expect a conversation with Sir Lawrence to bring him any closer to the truth.

The gentle sunshine and the motion of the buggy made Daniel drowsy, and he dozed off but came instantly awake when the buggy rolled through the gates of Fox Hollow, the wheels crunching on the gravel drive. The house sat huge and somnolent in the grounds, and the leaded windows reflected the bright afternoon light, but Daniel suddenly got the sense that something wasn't quite right. He wasn't sure what gave him that impression, but after years of witnessing the very worst aspects of human nature, his instinct was alert to any change in atmosphere.

Chapter 21

Daniel thanked Thomas for the ride, handed over a few coins to compensate him for his time, then went inside. The house was silent, the clock ticking ominously on the mantel in the parlor. Even though everyone knew the boys were Sir Lawrence's children, the house was not officially in mourning. The clocks had not been stopped, mirrors had not been covered, and there were no black bows on the door or swaths of black crape inside to indicate mourning. The servants did not wear black armbands, and when Daniel had last seen him, Sir Lawrence had not changed into a suit of unrelieved black.

"Is Dr. Redmond here?" Daniel asked Gwen, who was just coming out of the parlor with a dustpan. No one else seemed to be about.

"He's with her ladyship, Inspector."

Daniel hurried up the stairs and knocked on Lucinda's door. It was opened by Jason, who looked unsurprisingly grim. He wasn't wearing his coat, and his shirtsleeves were rolled up to the elbow. Lucinda was reclining against several lace-edged pillows, her face flushed, her gaze reminiscent of a cornered fox, and her belly swelling beneath the satin counterpane. All her spirit and contrariness seemed to have deserted her, leaving behind a terrified young girl who could see her own end.

Jason stepped outside and shut the door behind him. "Were you able to learn anything from Harry Chadwick and Davy Brody?"

"Harry happened to mention that Fox Hollow has several tunnels and more than one priest hole that date back to medieval times. In itself, that information means little, but given that Bruce Plimpton is an associate of Lance Carmichael and was here only a few days ago, I think it would be prudent to check just what's inside those tunnels."

"You think Sir Lawrence is involved in something illegal?"

"That's very possible. Davy said he owed Lance Carmichael money and Bruce Plimpton was here to collect the debt. Richard Powers is in on it too."

"I can't see how that would lead to the murders of two children."

"Neither can I," Daniel said. "There have always been run-ins between rival gangs and repercussions for those who fell afoul of money lenders, but I've never heard of children being slaughtered as a result. Any leads here?"

Jason shook his head. "Given Lucinda's condition, I can't afford to delay. I will operate as soon as the midwife gets here."

"The midwife?" Daniel had never known Jason to work with a midwife and was surprised that he would rely on one in this instance.

"I need help, especially as there are two babies," Jason explained.

"I could—" Daniel began, but Jason shook his head.

"I need someone who has experience of childbirth and knows how to care for a newborn. But I'm glad you're here, Daniel."

"I think I will take a look at the priest holes and tunnels. If I can find evidence of smuggling, then perhaps Sir Lawrence will be more forthcoming."

"Do you think he knows who murdered the boys?" Jason asked.

"I think he knows more than he's saying. Sir Lawrence is a shrewd man who resides at Fox Hollow nearly all year round. Surely, he must be aware of any undercurrents that flow beneath his noble nose."

Jason looked like he was about to reply when Mrs. Buckley came up the stairs, her expression inscrutable. She approached the two men cautiously, as if bracing for a rebuke.

"Is the midwife here?" Jason asked, his gaze going to the stairs.

"I'm sorry, Doctor, but Mrs. Grimsby has sent word to say she's been delayed. She will be here as soon as she can manage it."

"Will you wait?" Daniel asked.

"Yes," Jason replied. "Another hour or two will not change the outcome, but attempting to perform the surgery on my own will put Lucinda and the twins in danger. I will go tell Lucinda."

"I wager she'll be glad of the reprieve."

"I think she'd rather get the ordeal over with. She's very frightened."

"I can't say I blame her," Daniel said. "A word, Mrs. Buckley," he called after the housekeeper as she turned to leave.

"Of course, Inspector," Mrs. Buckley replied.

Daniel followed her to her office and shut the door.

Chapter 22

"I would like to see the tunnels," Daniel said.

"What tunnels?" Mrs. Buckley asked, her expression one of feigned incomprehension.

"The tunnels beneath the house, Mrs. Buckley. Also, the priest holes."

"I'm sure I don't know what you're talking about, Inspector Haze."

"I think you do," Daniel replied. "I believe contraband is being stored in this house."

Mrs. Buckley gaped at him, her indignation mounting. "Two innocent children are dead, and you want to go on a scavenger hunt?"

"The scavenger hunt pertains to the investigation," Daniel explained patiently.

"How can some Papist hidey-holes have anything to do with the murder of innocents?"

"That's for me to figure out," Daniel replied. He was quickly losing his patience. "I do hope you're not working to obstruct my investigation."

"Goodness me," Mrs. Buckley exclaimed. "Is that what you think?"

"Given that we're still standing here, yes."

"I can show you the priest holes, but I don't know where the tunnels are."

"Now, why don't I believe you?" Daniel demanded.

"The tunnels do not figure into my duties, Inspector. Perhaps you had better ask Sir Lawrence."

"I will. Where might I find him?"

"He's gone out."

"Out where?"

"He doesn't report to me, Inspector Haze."

"Maybe not, but you still know everything that goes on in this house. Does Sir Lawrence have a mistress?"

Mrs. Buckley's mouth fell open. "A mistress?"

"You heard me."

"I think you had better ask him that as well."

"Mrs. Buckley, does Sir Lawrence keep a mistress? It's a simple enough question."

"Not that I know of, Inspector," Mrs. Buckley retorted. "Of course, if a man wishes to see to his baser needs, he doesn't need to keep a mistress, does he? He can very easily visit a house of ill repute or tumble one of the maids."

"And is Sir Lawrence tumbling the maids, madam?" Daniel asked. "And you had better tell me the truth or I will arrest you for obstruction and throw you in jail if you lie to me."

It was an empty threat, but Mrs. Buckley didn't know that. She went pale to the roots of her hair and looked absolutely terrified.

"No," she cried. "Sir Lawrence is not like his father. He loves his wife."

"Does he?" Daniel asked, watching Mrs. Buckley for any evidence of subterfuge.

She nodded. "I think he loves her a lot more than she loves him. He would do anything to make her happy."

"Would he get rid of his natural children to please her?"

"Of course not. Besides, as far as I know, her ladyship has never asked him to. She didn't want the children in the house, but she bore them no ill will."

"And would you know if she had?" Daniel asked.

"In a house such as this, the walls have ears."

"What's that supposed to mean?"

"It means there are few secrets. The walls between the rooms are not as thick as you might imagine, and the keyholes are large."

"Do you listen at keyholes, Mrs. Buckley?"

Mrs. Buckley colored, her discomfiture evident. "I do not, but I hear things from the maids."

"What sort of things?"

"Private things mostly, the sort of things spoken between man and wife. I've warned them time and time again, but Sir Lawrence is a handsome man who likes to make love to his wife in broad daylight. The maids do on occasion sneak a peek. There's little else to keep them entertained in such a remote place."

"So, they spy on their employer and his wife during their most intimate moments?"

Mrs. Buckley shrugged. "The maids see it all, Inspector, whether they want to or not. That's the lot of those who serve."

"Just show me the priest holes," Daniel said.

Mrs. Buckley motioned for Daniel to follow and led him to the library. She walked around the room until she approached a panel in the back wall and pressed on something to make it slide sideways. Inside was a small space, no bigger than a coffin, where one person could stand upright with their arms at their sides. When closed in, it would be completely dark and very tight if the individual were stouter or taller than average.

"Does this lead anywhere?" Daniel asked.

"No. This was used to hide someone on short notice and for a short period of time."

"You mean if there wasn't enough time for them to escape through the tunnels?"

"That is correct."

"Are there more?"

Mrs. Buckley nodded. She led Daniel to the upper floor and opened the door to one of the unused bedrooms. It was two doors down from the room where the boys had died and was decorated in much the same manner, only the bed hangings and linens were blue. Mrs. Buckley walked over to the disused fireplace and opened a panel to the right of the hearth. It creaked open, revealing another dark space. This one was a little bigger than the one in the library, and a thin panel opened to a concealed space in the adjacent room.

"As you can see, Inspector, no one could have used these priest holes to poison the boys. For one, they do not give access to the room where they were found, nor do they offer an escape. These were used to save lives, not take them," she added reproachfully.

"And was anyone's life saved?" Daniel asked.

"Oh, yes. This house was searched many times, but the soldiers never found the hidey-holes. They were too well disguised."

"Are there any more?"

"Not that I know of."

"Where is the entrance to the tunnel?" Daniel asked.

"It's downstairs," Mrs. Buckley admitted, despite claiming ignorance before.

Mrs. Buckley and Daniel returned to the ground floor, where she fetched an oil lamp from a store cupboard and lit the wick before inviting Daniel to follow her. They traversed several narrow passageways and stopped before a room Daniel had not yet seen. It faced the back of the house, and there was a corridor that led to the kitchen. Mrs. Buckley pushed open the door and held the lantern aloft so that Daniel could see inside the room. The chamber had stone walls and a flagstone floor, and the ceiling was fitted with large metal hooks. A surprisingly wide door led to the outside. The room was large and mostly bare, but there was a scarred wooden dresser that held carving knives and bowls of varying sizes, and a long table covered in rust-brown stains.

"The torture chamber?" Daniel inquired as he looked around the windowless space.

"This room was used to butcher game," Mrs. Buckley said. "The carcasses would be brought in through that door and butchered on the table, and the joints hung on the hooks. The stone walls kept in the cold and kept the meat fresh for days. These days, we get our meat from the butcher in the village, and if Sir Lawrence goes hunting, he has the carcass delivered to the butcher with instructions to divide the meat between the tenants."

"He hunts only for sport?"

"Mostly, and he prefers to shoot rabbits. Sir Lawrence enjoys rabbit stew and rabbit poached in wine. He's never been partial to venison."

"I see. So, where is the entrance?" Daniel asked, looking at the bare walls.

Mrs. Buckley approached the dresser, unhooked something with a flick of her fingers, and swung the dresser away from the wall. Behind it was a small, narrow door, just large enough for a person to fit through if they stood bent over double. Daniel could see narrow stone steps descending into the murky darkness below. The air coming from the tunnel beneath was dank, and long, dusty cobwebs fluttered like wings in the draft the opening of the door had created.

"Where does the tunnel lead?"

"To St. Luke's, but it hasn't been used in decades," Mrs. Buckley said.

"Are you certain?" Daniel asked, but given the state of the tunnel, he didn't think anyone had come this way in a very long time, probably in years.

"I am. Now, if you're quite satisfied, Inspector, I will return to my duties."

Daniel cast one last look into the filthy tunnel and turned away. He saw no point in going in since the tunnel was bound to run for at least a mile if it ended at the church. He would remain above ground and check the tunnel on the other side. If Sir Lawrence was using the tunnel to hide illegal goods, he wouldn't be likely to bring them directly to the house, especially if he wasn't the one taking the delivery. It would be much easier to access the tunnel from a public building, especially if the vicar was in on the transaction. Daniel would go to St. Luke's and see what he could discover, but first he needed to ascertain the whereabouts of the baronet.

"Mrs. Buckley, did Sir Lawrence know that Dr. Redmond planned to operate on his wife today?" Daniel asked.

Mrs. Buckley looked nonplussed. "I don't believe so."

"What time did Sir Lawrence leave?"

"Just before Dr. Redmond arrived. He said he needed to clear his head."

"Any ideas where he might have gone?" Daniel asked.

"He might have walked to the village, or maybe he went for a walk in the woods."

"But he definitely left on foot?"

"He did, so he couldn't have gone far. Do you think I should send someone to look for him?" Mrs. Buckley asked.

"Don't bother. I will endeavor to find him myself."

"Very good, Inspector."

Instead of following Mrs. Buckley back to the foyer, Daniel used the door in the butchering chamber to get outside. He could see the square tower of St. Luke's rising above the tree line and headed toward it. If Sir Lawrence wasn't there, then perhaps Daniel could have a word with the vicar. He was sure to know how to access the tunnel.

Chapter 23

Daniel followed a footpath through the woods that brought him directly to St. Luke's. The servants must have used it as a shortcut when they went to church. As Daniel walked through the graveyard to get to the entrance, he spotted a freshly dug grave and wondered if it might be for John and Bertie. Would the children be buried together, to keep each other company for eternity, or would they be buried side by side, laid next to their maternal ancestors instead of occupying the space next to Sir Lawrence's noble kin? Daniel didn't suppose it really mattered since they were well past caring.

He felt a pang of guilt for not visiting Felix's grave while he had been in Birch Hill but pushed his feelings aside. His son was forever in his heart. He didn't need to stand beside his grave to think of him, to miss the little boy he had been or to dwell on the man he would have become. Just as he didn't need to visit Sarah's grave to forgive her, or Rebecca's grave to say goodbye. Regardless of one's own needs and feelings and people's best laid plans, loved ones died, and it served little purpose to remain angry with them or blame them for their mistakes that had led to their untimely end. They were gone, and after a time, the void began to fill.

Daniel still thought of Sarah often and smiled fondly when he recalled the early days of their marriage or the happy years when Felix had been a small boy, but the memories had grown dim, and the pain had dulled. He had no wish to spend the rest of his life alone, nor did he want Charlotte to grow up without a mother. She was still young enough that she would accept a stepmother without question, and as long as the stepmother was gentle and kind, Charlotte would be happy. And Daniel would dearly love to have more children. Perhaps it was time he let go of the past and looked to the future. Katherine Redmond was forever hinting that she could introduce him to women she thought suitable. Perhaps he should let her. He was tired of feeling lonely and envying Jason when he hurried home to his family.

Daniel felt a strange sense of peace descend on him as he entered the church porch and pushed the heavy door open. He was more determined than ever to find John and Bertie's killer, but he had to learn to keep his work separate from his home life if he hoped to protect his sanity and in time create a new family. What he needed to solve this case was cold, incontrovertible logic, and he could hardly achieve that if he allowed himself to be swayed by sympathy or give in to pity for possible suspects.

The interior of the church had that smell particular to country churches. Mustiness, dust, beeswax polish, and candlewax. Gentle sunlight filtered through the stained-glass windows that were set high in the wall and cast colorful beams onto the stone of the nave and the tawny head of Sir Lawrence, who sat in the front pew, his head bowed, his shoulders tense. Sir Lawrence straightened and turned at the sound of Daniel's footsteps, his expression of alarm giving way to relief when he must have realized Daniel wasn't there to impart terrible news and had come to St. Luke's as part of his investigation.

"May I?" Daniel asked as he stopped next to the pew. Sir Lawrence nodded, and Daniel took a seat next to him.

"My mother lost four children," Sir Lawrence said. "There were three boys before me and a girl after I was born. Two boys were stillborn, and the other two children lived only a few months."

"I'm sorry," Daniel said.

It was a story he was all too familiar with. His own mother had lost two children before Daniel, and he knew from Sarah that her parents had lost a son. The boy had lived only two months before passing quietly during the night and leaving his parents to grieve the loss.

"My father said I survived because I was strong," Sir Lawrence said, "but maybe it had nothing to do with strength. I simply got lucky. I got to live. I don't often admit it, but I'm terrified, Inspector Haze. The thought of losing Lucinda and the babies is more than I can bear, especially after John and Bertie just..." Sir Lawrence couldn't finish the sentence, and Daniel saw the glimmer of tears in his limpid eyes. "Life can be so cruel. But you know all about loss, don't you?"

"I do, and you never quite recover, but life does go on, whether you want it to or not."

"What do I do?" Sir Lawrence asked.

"You go home."

"And what if Lucinda is no longer there, and my babies—" Sir Lawrence nearly choked on his words, and Daniel tasted his fear as if he had just swallowed a mouthful himself.

"You face your fate," Daniel said. "There's no other choice."

There was another choice. Sarah had made it after years of battling melancholy and hopelessness, but Sir Lawrence wasn't Sarah. He was strong and resilient, and he would survive no matter what happened today.

Sir Lawrence nodded and pushed to his feet, ready to return home and face the outcome of the surgery. Daniel wanted to ask him about the tunnels, but it seemed awfully callous to question the man when his emotional state was so fragile and his life was about to irrevocably change, either for the better or for the worse.

"Why did you come if not to bring bad news?" Sir Lawrence asked.

"I wanted to ask about the tunnels."

"Ah, the tunnels. Those tunnels are stuff of legend. They were used for storing illegal goods back in the day when entire villages were involved in smuggling. They even used the church. The entrance to one of the tunnels is in the crypt, and the other leads to the tavern. My grandfather made a fortune from illegal trade. If not for him, we probably would have lost the estate. A house built in the fifteenth century requires more upkeep than you can possibly imagine."

"I need to search the tunnels," Daniel said, watching Sir Lawrence for a reaction. He had spoken of smuggling in the past tense, but he was clearly up to something with the Carmichaels, and it had nothing to do with his long-dead grandfather.

"You won't find anything, Inspector," Sir Lawrence remarked. "There's a trapdoor by the eastern wall of the crypt. The tunnel will take you to the house. On any other day, I would be happy to give you a guided tour, but I must get home."

"I will find my way," Daniel said. "God be with you and your family, Sir Lawrence."

"Thank you," the baronet said, and headed for the door.

Daniel found the steps that led down to the crypt and descended into the darkness below.

Chapter 24

Jason was relieved when Mrs. Grimsby finally arrived. She was a stern-looking woman of late middle years and was about as comforting as an avenging angel. She glared at Lucinda as if the young woman had somehow let her down, and then turned to Jason, rearranging her face into an expression of bland subservience.

"Thank you for coming, Mrs. Grimsby," Jason said. "I will be glad of your assistance."

"What will you have me do, Doctor?" Mrs. Grimsby asked. "Her ladyship doesn't appear to be in labor."

"She's not," Jason replied.

He outlined what he intended to do and watched Mrs. Grimsby's eyes widen in shock. She had most likely never witnessed a cesarean section and had no idea what to expect, but she could hardly refuse to help since word would quickly spread that she wasn't as capable and experienced as she would like her patients to believe. The look of uncertainty was quickly replaced by one of speculation. Jason would bet his hat that if the babies lived, Mrs. Grimsby would take the credit and say that it was her expertise that had saved the day, and if they died or if Lucinda did not survive the birth, she would blame it on the jumped-up American doctor who had forced the tragic outcome and clearly wasn't worth his fee.

"Mrs. Grimsby, if you'll wash your hands," Jason said as he unclasped his medical bag.

"What?" the midwife demanded.

"Kindly wash your hands," Jason repeated.

"What on earth for?"

"To reduce the chance of infection."

"Is that some newfangled foreign notion?" Mrs. Grimsby asked as she reluctantly pushed up the cuffs of her gown and reached for the soap on the washstand.

"It is," Jason replied. "And I would ask you not to question my orders during the operation, even if you don't agree with them. Time is of the essence, and we must work in tandem."

"Whatever you say, Doctor," Mrs. Grimsby replied, and dried her hands on the towel.

The midwife and Lucinda both watched in horror as Jason laid out his instruments and prepared the ether mask. Lucinda's skin was flushed and her forehead clammy to the touch. Her hands were shaking, and her breathing was rapid. Jason was sure her blood pressure was dangerously high and offered up a silent prayer that he would save all three Foxleys. Mrs. Grimsby positioned herself next to the bed in readiness, cotton cloths for swabbing and towels at the ready.

"I want my husband," Lucinda cried desperately. She turned toward the door as if expecting Sir Lawrence to walk in.

"You'll see him after it's all over, my lady," Mrs. Grimsby promised.

"No, I need to see him now. There are things I need to say to him. In case I die," she added bravely.

"Lucinda—" Jason began.

"I know what you're going to say, Dr. Redmond, but you cannot guarantee a successful outcome. I need to put my affairs in order."

"What affairs can be so important just now?" Mrs. Grimsby asked. Her annoyance was obvious, and Jason thought she wanted to get the operation over with as much as Lucinda.

"My children are important," Lucinda snapped. "If I die, I want my husband to respect my wishes in regard to the children. And the disposal of my remains."

"My lady," Mrs. Grimsby said irritably.

"Please, bring my husband to me. I will not permit you to operate until I speak to Larry."

"Mrs. Grimsby, if you would be so kind as to see if Sir Lawrence has returned," Jason said.

"Yes, Doctor."

Mrs. Grimsby left the room, and Jason turned to Lucinda. "I know you're frightened, but I have done this before."

"I admire your self-assurance, but surely you know you're not God."

"I never said I was."

Lucinda scoffed. "You think yourself infallible."

"Hardly."

"I envy you, you know," Lucinda said, her tone softening. "You actually like yourself. I don't know too many people who can face themselves in the mirror and say they've always done the right thing."

"I don't always do the right thing, Lucinda, and I question my decisions all the time." That wasn't quite true. Jason did not take decisions lightly, especially when it came to someone's well-being, but once a decision had been made, he generally did not doubt it.

"I think you trust your judgment implicitly," Lucinda replied. "You can't help it. It's just the way you're made." A tear slid down her flushed cheek. "Every decision I have made has cost me dearly."

"Some of those decisions were forced on you by those you trusted."

"Some, but not all. The people around me hold me in such low regard that they would think me capable of murdering two children. They will feel vindicated if my babies never draw breath. They'll see it as a fair exchange."

"I very much doubt that," Jason replied. "Your children are innocent of any wrongdoing, and no one would wish them ill."

"But they would wish ill on me. They want to see me suffer. Please, save my babies, Dr. Redmond. Give them a chance at life."

"I intend to," Jason promised.

"But if you must choose between me and them or between the babies, then save the one you think has a better chance. I need to know that there will be something left of me when I die. Otherwise, it will be as if I had never even lived."

Jason was about to reply when the door opened, and Sir Lawrence strode in. He looked frantic, all his attention on his wife.

"I'm here, Lucy," he exclaimed as he reached for her hand. "I'm here, sweetheart."

"Larry—" Lucinda began, but he cut across her.

"I will wait right outside that door, and as soon as you are awake, I will come in and tell you how much I love you."

"Larry, listen to me," Lucinda pleaded. "I need to know that my babies will be safe should I die."

"I will guard them with my life," Sir Lawrence promised.

"Whoever killed John and Bertie might want to harm our children too."

"Lucy—"

"Someone wants to punish you, Larry. Punish us."

Sir Lawrence sat on the side of the bed and took both Lucinda's hands in his own. "Lucy love, I will do whatever it takes to keep you and our children safe. Whatever," he reiterated.

"Then send Richard Powers away," Lucinda whispered.

Sir Lawrence's face went slack with shock. "You think Richard had something to do with the deaths of the boys?"

Lucinda nodded. "I know you want to do what's right by him, but he resents you, Larry. And he wants you to pay for being the legitimate heir."

"Lucy—" Sir Lawrence tried again, but Lucinda would not be deterred.

"He will bide his time, and then he will murder our babies. Promise me you'll send him away."

Sir Lawrence looked conflicted, but his wife's desperation won out. "I will send him away if it will make you feel safer. You have my word. Now, please calm down and allow Dr. Redmond to bring our children into the world."

Lucinda nodded and reached for her husband, who wrapped her in a fierce hug and held her close, then kissed her chastely on the forehead and pulled away.

"Right outside that door," he said gruffly. "I will be the first person you see when you come around."

"I love you, Larry," Lucinda said softly. "I really do."

"And I love you, my clever little vixen."

"Are you ready, Lucinda?" Jason asked once Sir Lawrence had left.

"I am."

Chapter 25

The trapdoor leading to the tunnel was just where Sir Lawrence had said it would be, and Daniel pulled it up, noting how easily it opened. The hinges did not groan in protest, and the tunnel, or the part he could see at the bottom of the steps, did not appear as spooky as the section he had seen at Fox Hollow. A narrow ledge was hewn into the stone, and there was a thick candle stub in a pewter holder and a box of lucifer matches. The box of matches was more than half full when Daniel opened it.

Daniel lit the candle and made his way down the steps. The tunnel was wider than the entrance at Fox Hollow, but then if the smugglers had used this end to roll barrels and carry crates, it would have to be wide enough to accommodate their cargo. The passage smelled much as one would expect, but there was something beneath the earthy odor that made Daniel scrunch up his nose in disgust. The smell spoke to recent occupation and came from further down, a part of the tunnel Daniel couldn't see, limited as he was to the wavering pool of light from his candle.

He proceeded carefully, illuminating the stretch of tunnel immediately before him before gingerly venturing forward. He was certain that someone was there, lying in wait. The flame came too near a cobweb, and the gossamer lacework caught fire and burned for a few seconds before smoldering into nothingness and leaving behind a curling whiff of smoke. Daniel kicked at a rat that had come too close to his foot, then he continued forward. The tunnel curved, and Daniel sucked in his breath when he saw a pair of legs stretched out on the floor. The legs culminated in scuffed boots and were protruding from around the corner.

"Hello," Daniel called out, but the person didn't reply.

Daniel inched forward, wishing not for the first time that he carried a pistol when involved in an investigation. All he had to hand was the candleholder, and much good it would do him. There was nothing in the tunnel, not even an old crate or a burned-out torch. The man's upper body finally came into view, but Daniel still couldn't see the face. He could make out the right hand, the fingers loosely wrapped around the neck of a bottle. As he drew closer, Daniel smelled the reek of spirits and vomit, and the acrid tang of piss. The man was probably passed out drunk.

"Hello," Daniel called again, but this time he didn't expect an answer.

When Daniel rounded the corner, he was finally able to identify the man. Emmett Doyle sat slumped against the wall, his head lolled to the side, his eyes staring, and his mouth slack. The ropy web of burn scars looked pale in the candlelight and resembled an intricate spider web, Emmett's deformed ear curled like a fat slug. There was a dry puddle of vomit next to the body, and Emmett had clearly pissed himself before he'd passed. The body reeked of spirits, the stench filling the narrow space.

A wooden crate stood within arm's reach, several dusty still-corked bottles of brandy, if that was what it was, clearly all that remained of a long-forgotten shipment. Daniel exhaled and approached the corpse, holding the candle aloft so he could study Emmett's face. He didn't see any signs of violence or evidence of a struggle, but he couldn't say for certain that the death had been natural. He needed Jason to examine the body. Until then, he'd have to reserve judgment.

Daniel pointed the candle into the tunnel but didn't see anything that warranted further investigation. Sir Lawrence had been telling the truth when he'd said the tunnels were no longer in use. Leaving Emmett as he'd found him, Daniel hurried back down the passage, his only thought of emerging into the church and going to fetch Jason.

Chapter 26

Jason's hands were slick with blood as he pulled the silk thread through Lucinda's pale skin for the last time and tied it off just below her navel. He cut the thread, then set the needle aside and washed his hands in the basin Mrs. Grimsby had prepared. He then cleaned the area around the incision, swabbed it with iodine, and affixed a bandage before pulling Lucinda's nightdress over her belly and down to her knees. Jason pulled up the counterpane, smoothed Lucinda's hair back from her forehead, and checked her pulse.

Mrs. Grimsby stood back, watching. She hadn't said much during the operation and had followed Jason's instructions to the letter, which he appreciated since any distraction could have cost him and Lucinda dearly. Jason removed the ether mask from Lucinda's face and set it aside, his gaze never leaving her face. Her skin was no longer flushed but was deathly pale, her face still as marble. Her hand lay atop the coverlet, the nails bluish at the base. It was hard to see her chest rise and fall beneath the thick counterpane.

"Is she…?" Mrs. Grimsby's voice trailed off.

She looked more curious than worried, having never seen anyone anesthetized. Some still saw anesthesia on par with witchcraft and imagined that the person's spirit went someplace dark and unholy. Jason hadn't bothered to explain the process to Mrs. Grimsby. For one, he didn't have the time, and for another, he was sure he'd never see the woman again and the knowledge would serve little purpose since she would never be called upon to use it in her own work.

Jason shook his head. "She's sedated, Mrs. Grimsby. She should start to come around in a minute. The ether wears off quickly once the mask is removed."

"I thought she was dead for sure," Mrs. Grimsby said.

"Lucinda," Jason said softly, and laid his hand over Lucinda's wrist. "Lucinda, wake up."

Lucinda's eyelids fluttered, and she slowly opened her eyes. Her pupils were slightly dilated, and she looked confused, as if she had no idea where she was, until the familiar sight of her bedroom and Jason's presence must have brought it all back. Her hand slid to her belly, and she felt about carefully through the fabric of the counterpane.

"The babies," Lucinda muttered. "I can't hear them cry."

The blank stare of confusion was instantly replaced by sheer panic as she tried to sit up and cried out in pain.

"Lucinda, you must keep still," Jason said. "Your babies are safe and well."

"I need to see them. Larry needs to see them," she croaked.

"Mrs. Grimsby, please ask Sir Lawrence to join us."

Mrs. Grimsby went to the door and asked Sir Lawrence to come inside. When he entered the room, he looked apprehensive, probably unnerved by the silence, which never boded well when it came to childbirth.

"All is well," Jason hurried to reassure him.

"Lucy," Sir Lawrence cried, and rushed to his wife's side. Lucinda gave him a wan smile, and he grabbed her hands and kissed them. "Oh, Lucy, thank God."

"I want to see my children," Lucinda said imperiously. The ether had completely worn off, and she was growing impatient now that she was no longer drowsy or in pain, since Jason had given her a shot of morphine.

Jason walked over to the cot in the corner and carefully lifted out the two sleeping bundles. The babies looked identical, and he could no longer tell which one had come into the world first. Jason handed one baby to Sir Lawrence and the other to his wife.

"Two beautiful baby girls," he said, and watched Sir Lawrence for a reaction.

Jason had been half-expecting disappointment and was relieved to see none. Sir Lawrence looked awed, his finger going to his daughter's rounded cheek. "Oh," was all he said as Lucinda examined the other twin.

"They're exactly the same," she said as she looked from one tiny face to the other.

"Identical twins," Jason confirmed.

"How charming," Sir Lawrence said. "What should we name them, my dear?"

"I don't know. I only thought of boys' names," Lucinda confessed. "But I want names that are synonymous with life, and strength. Dr. Redmond, can you think of any names that mean life?"

"*Vita* means life in Latin."

"Oh, that's perfect," Lucinda cried. "Now we need one more."

"*Valerie* means strength," Sir Lawrence said.

"Life and strength, the two most important things," Lucinda said. "I like it."

"How will we know which one is which?" Sir Lawrence asked practically.

"We will tie different-colored ribbons around their wrists with their names embroidered in silk," Lucinda said. "Oh, I'm so happy, Larry," she gushed, then her gaze turned sober. "You promised me."

"I will have a word with Richard tonight," Sir Lawrence said. "Please, let us enjoy this moment. It's too precious to mar with talk of death."

"I'll give you two a moment," Jason said, and stepped out into the corridor, followed by Mrs. Grimsby, who seemed eager to escape now that everything was well.

He realized he was starving, not having eaten anything since breakfast. Maybe Mrs. Buckley could be prevailed upon to make him a sandwich. And if there was coffee, that would be a bonus. He was just about to ask Mrs. Grimsby to fetch the housekeeper when he heard the pounding of feet on the stairs, followed by the arrival of Daniel.

"Jason, did everything go according to plan?"

"Twin girls. Mother and babies are doing well," Jason replied happily.

"That's good news. Now you must come with me."

"What happened?"

"Emmett Doyle is dead. I found his body in the tunnel."

"Was he murdered?" Jason asked, already hurrying toward the stairs, his need for food momentarily forgotten.

"I can't tell," Daniel replied. "But if he was, then everything we thought so far has to be wrong."

Chapter 27

Daniel held the lantern he'd borrowed from the vicar while Jason sat back on his haunches and studied the body.

"How long has he been dead?" Daniel asked.

"At a guess, twelve to eighteen hours," Jason replied.

"Could this be a natural death?"

Jason didn't reply. Instead, he reached for the bottle Emmett had been drinking from and sniffed. "It has that same musty smell as the children's vomit."

"That bottle has probably been here since the eighteenth century," Daniel pointed out. "I'd be surprised if the contents weren't musty."

Jason straightened and approached the crate. There were three bottles left, all still full, and he uncorked each one and smelled the contents. "These smell as brandy should. Not a hint of mustiness."

"So, you think Emmett Doyle was poisoned?"

"Most likely. May I have the lantern?"

Daniel handed the lantern to Jason, who held it close to the ground and examined the perimeter. He then used his foot to push aside the crate. Two rats lay curled between the wall and the crate, their paws in the air, their teeth bared.

"The brandy spilled when Emmett lowered his arm. It flowed in this direction," Jason said, pointing to a sticky trail that led to the crate. "These rats are proof that the brandy was poisoned."

"So, Emmett Doyle comes down here, helps himself to a bottle of decades-old brandy, and dies. Could this have been suicide?" Daniel asked.

"It could, but I don't think it was," Jason said. "For one, we have two children who died by the same method. For another, if Emmett Doyle came down here routinely, I doubt there'd be any brandy left to poison."

"Might he have poisoned the children, then killed himself?" Daniel tried again.

"What reason would Emmett Doyle have to murder two children, or anyone at Fox Hollow? Rose Doyle said that he rarely comes inside, so his dealings with the Foxleys and the staff would be limited at best."

"Perhaps he held a grudge against someone and tried to poison them but killed the children instead. Filled with remorse, he came down here to die."

"I think that's what someone wants us to believe," Jason said.

He returned to the corpse and looked inside Emmett's mouth before checking his pockets and the area immediately around the body.

"What are you looking for?" Daniel asked.

"If Emmett had decided to end it all, he would have brought the poison with him. There's nothing on his teeth or tongue, which means that he did not chew the leaves before washing the poison down with brandy. And there's no musty smell coming from his mouth."

"The brandy might have washed away any evidence of the poison when he drank it."

Jason shook his head. "The poison is in the brandy. I can smell it. Which means that Emmett would have added it to the bottle before drinking."

"So?" Daniel asked.

"So, there's nothing here that supports that theory. There's no vial, no leaves or flowers, nothing on his hands, and nothing in his pockets. Someone wants us to think this was an accident or a suicide, but I think this was quite deliberate."

"Who would want to murder the gardener?"

"The better question is what has someone to gain by his death?" Jason asked.

"They might have wanted to throw off our investigation."

Jason shook his head once again. "Whoever poisoned Emmett had no way of knowing we would search the tunnels, since you didn't mention the tunnels to me until this morning. If they wanted us to find him, they could have left him in a more obvious place."

"Perhaps someone would have mentioned the tunnels if I didn't bring it up myself," Daniel suggested.

"Yes, that's possible. And then once we found Emmett, we would assume he had killed the children and return to London believing our investigation to be at an end," Jason mused. "If that is the case, then the killer is even craftier than I gave them credit for."

"What strikes me as odd is that no one reported Emmett missing. Surely his wife noticed that he didn't come home last night, or others would have noticed they hadn't seen him today," Daniel said.

"Emmett Doyle was emotionally unstable. Perhaps this wasn't the first time he had failed to come home. He did say that he was so inebriated, he didn't realize he was on fire. And his wife was probably relieved to have a peaceful night."

Daniel nodded. "Mr. Doyle has a history of heavy drinking."

"Which someone decided to use to their advantage," Jason concluded. "I don't think Emmett came down here on his own. Perhaps someone had suggested a meeting, offered Emmett a drink, then waited for him to die and left him down here for us to find."

"But who?" Daniel asked. "If it happened last night, it could have been anyone on the estate."

"Lucinda Foxley thinks Richard Powers murdered the children," Jason said. "She made Sir Lawrence promise to evict him from the estate before allowing me to operate."

"Why would Richard Powers murder the children? To what end?"

"I would say to wound his brother, or his wife, but I find that hard to believe."

"So do I. We need to speak to Richard and Doris Powers again, after we inform Rose Doyle of her husband's death."

"I'll have Sir Lawrence send someone down here to retrieve the body," Jason said.

When they returned to the church, Vicar Hobbs, an elderly man with wispy white hair, was anxiously waiting. "Well? What have you discovered, Doctor? Was Emmett murdered?" he asked, and Daniel saw doubt in his dark eyes.

"We believe so," Jason replied.

"Are you certain? I always did say he would drink himself to death. A lost soul if ever I saw one. I tried to help him. I really did, but some people don't want to be helped, do they?" the vicar prattled on. "I felt sorry for poor Rose. She was always such a sweet girl, so helpful and kind. I would have advised her not to marry Emmett had she sought my counsel, but Rose was in love and wouldn't heed anyone's warning, not even her mother's."

"Did Mrs. Buckley try to warn her off?" Daniel asked.

The vicar nodded. "Emmett didn't start drinking heavily until his discharge from the army, but he was always volatile. Rose saw it as evidence of his passion, but I saw it for what it was—weakness of character."

"Surely he's not the only resident of Fox Hollow who overindulges in drink," Daniel said.

"No, he's not, but he's the only one I know who takes out his anger and frustration on his wife. Most of the men hereabouts are good husbands and loving fathers."

Jason looked dubious but didn't bother to contradict the vicar. The man was entitled to his opinion, and in all fairness, he probably knew most of his parishioners fairly well, having tended to their spiritual needs for decades.

"Vicar, did you see Emmett Doyle yesterday?" Jason asked.

"No, I didn't, but I left directly after Evensong."

"And do you lock the church?" Daniel inquired.

"I've never had reason to. In all my years in Fox Hollow, no one has so much as helped themselves to the collections box much less anything of greater value. And I never imagined that someone would go down into the tunnel. It hasn't been used in years."

"Yet the hinges are well oiled, and there was a candle and matches," Daniel replied.

"Oh, I can explain that. Sir Lawrence paid for a new window recently." Vicar Hobbs pointed toward the beautiful stained-glass window behind the altar. "Lovely, isn't it?"

"It is," Daniel agreed. "But what does it have to do with the tunnel?"

"While we were on the subject of the window, I asked Sir Lawrence to commission a structural evaluation of the building. I thought it prudent to ask while he was in a generous mood. Sir Lawrence agreed, and I called in a well-respected mason from Brentwood to undertake the inspection. He went down into the tunnel to make certain there were no cracks in the ceiling or the walls and the whole thing wasn't going to cave in and undermine the integrity of the structure. He oiled the hinges and cleared away the cobwebs, and I expect he was the one who left the candle and matches behind."

"When was this?" Daniel asked.

"Just before Christmas last year."

"And no one else has gone down there since?"

"If they did, they didn't tell me," Vicar Hobbs replied. "But why would they? There's nothing there."

"There was some brandy," Jason said.

"There were a few cases of brandy left from when the tunnel was used for smuggling, but I never knew about them. Mr. Brown, the mason, told me when he completed his inspection. I told him he was welcome to the lot, but he was a teetotaler and had no interest in spirits."

"Did Emmett Doyle know about the brandy?" Jason asked.

"If he did, he would have sucked it down in one go," the vicar replied.

"Someone must have known the bottles were down there."

"I told Mr. Powers," the vicar replied. "I thought perhaps he'd want to dispose of them, but he didn't seem overly interested. He said they were part of the place, and he was happy to leave them there."

"Might he have told Emmett Doyle?" Daniel asked.

The vicar shook his head. "I very much doubt he would. Mr. Powers disapproved of Emmett's drinking and made it his business to keep an eye on Rose, should she need urgent help. I can't imagine that he would tell Emmett about the brandy."

"Unless he wanted to lure Emmett to the tunnel."

"I can't imagine that he would want to do that," the vicar said, clearly not following the direction of Daniel's thoughts.

"Vicar, would you say that Richard Powers is capable of murder?" Jason asked.

The vicar's eyes nearly popped out of his head. "Richard Powers?" he cried. "Why would you ask me such a thing? Have you any evidence against him?"

"Not as yet, but Lady Foxley seems to suspect him."

The vicar sighed in relief. "Well, that explains it, then."

"Explains what?" Daniel asked.

"Lady Foxley is young and naïve. She doesn't quite understand the ways of men and finds herself shocked and offended by the close relationship between Richard Powers and Sir Lawrence. She would prefer not to be reminded of the illicit relationships that have plagued Fox Hollow for centuries, but the Foxleys have always been a lusty lot, and Sir Lawrence is probably related to at least half the families on his estate. His father in particular was something of a libertine."

"So, you don't believe Richard Powers capable of murder?" Daniel asked, interrupting the vicar's monologue.

"I do not. There's no one at that house that I suspect. They're all good people and devout Christians."

"Thank you, Vicar," Daniel said, and he and Jason headed for the door.

"Lucinda Foxley is not as naïve as the vicar believes her to be, but it's clear he knows nothing about her life before marrying Sir Lawrence," Daniel said.

"But Richard Powers does because he's in contact with someone in Birch Hill. Most likely Bruce Plimpton."

"I would be interested to discover what dealings they have with each other and why Sir Lawrence owed Lance Carmichael money," Daniel said. "He must be up to something."

Jason sighed. "And I would love to find out what it is as soon as I have something to eat."

"Let's stop at the tavern, have a meal, then call on Rose Doyle. If she is not worried about her husband by now, another hour won't make much difference, and you're starting to look peaky," Daniel said.

Jason nodded. "I won't say no to a hot meal and a pint. My hands are shaking."

Daniel hastened his step and was calling out an order to the barkeep before Jason was through the door.

Chapter 28

Less than an hour later, Jason and Daniel approached the Doyles' cottage. Rose was inside, kneading dough on her kitchen table. She beckoned to them through the window, her smile as sunny as if nothing out of the ordinary had occurred the past few days. The door was unlocked, so Jason and Daniel walked in and stopped just inside the kitchen. Once again, there was no sign of Daisy.

"Good afternoon, Mrs. Doyle," Daniel said.

Rose continued to knead, her expression one of mild curiosity. The bruise on her cheekbone had faded somewhat and now resembled a yellow stain, and her belly was pressed against the table as she went about her work.

"How can I help you, gentlemen?" Rose asked when they failed to state their business.

"When was the last time you saw your husband?" Daniel asked.

Rose sighed. "I saw him last night, just before he set off for the pub."

"The pub would have been closed last night on account of Easter," Daniel pointed out. Rose shrugged, as if she didn't really care where her husband had gone.

"And you weren't worried when he didn't come home?" Jason asked.

Rose didn't bother to ask how Jason knew that her husband hadn't come home. She probably assumed that everyone at Fox Hollow knew her business, and she didn't appear to mind.

"Emmett always had a fondness for drink, but since the accident, his drinking went from a few pints with the lads to seeking lasting oblivion. When he gets like that, I prefer that he sleep it off elsewhere, where Daisy doesn't have to see her father in that state. He usually beds down in the stables or the broken-down cottage near the lane. He comes home when he's ready."

It was clear that Rose had not expected her husband to show up for Easter service at St. Luke's and had thought nothing of his absence. He probably missed church quite a bit, sleeping off the drink until well into the afternoon.

Rose's hands stilled when she finally realized that something was wrong, otherwise the gentlemen from Scotland Yard would not be inquiring about Emmett's sleeping arrangements.

"Has something happened?" she whispered.

She went deathly pale and her hands trembled, so she splayed them on the table, bracing for what was to come. Jason thought she had probably been expecting this sort of visit for years but hadn't realized it until that moment.

"Mrs. Doyle, I'm very sorry to tell you, but your husband is dead. I discovered his body in the tunnel that runs beneath the church," Daniel said apologetically.

Rose's hand flew to her mouth, and her eyes swam with tears. "What was he doing down there? I don't understand," she wailed. "How can he be dead? I saw him just yesterday."

"He was drinking," Daniel explained. "We believe he was poisoned."

Rose's gaze turned to Jason, as if he could offer a clearer explanation. "Emmett was poisoned? Like John and Bertie?"

"He was," Jason said. "I don't believe he suffered, Mrs. Doyle. He was too intoxicated to feel anything."

A harsh laugh tore from Rose's chest. "You don't believe he suffered? Have you seen his face? Do you have any idea what he has been through or what his carelessness has done to our marriage? Oh, he suffered, Doctor, and he made me and Daisy suffer. More than you could ever imagine."

"I'm very sorry," Jason said. "I can only imagine what you've been through."

"Can you?" Rose asked, quieter now, as if recalling what she had endured during the intervening years in excruciating detail. Tears ran down her cheeks as she looked at Jason and Daniel imploringly. "Do you know what the strangest thing is? No matter how bad it got, I still loved him, and I still hoped that he would get better and learn to find joy in his life. But some things are lost forever, aren't they? Once you lose that innocence, that belief that you are loved by God, you become frightened, and angry. Emmett lost his faith. He refused to set foot in church, so I can't imagine what he was doing in that tunnel."

"Mrs. Doyle, did you know about the tunnel?" Daniel asked.

Rose nodded. "Everyone knows. The whole village was involved in smuggling in Sir Lawrence's grandfather's day. And everyone benefited." Rose's gaze flew to Daniel, as if she had suddenly realized something. "Where's Emmett, Inspector?"

"He's still in the tunnel. I will have Sir Lawrence send someone to collect his body. Would you like him brought here or to the big house?"

"I don't want him here. It'll frighten Daisy. I don't want her to see her father like that."

"Of course," Daniel said. "I will see to it."

"Thank you. You've been so kind." Rose grasped the back of a chair as another thought seemed to occur to her. "Are we in danger, Inspector? Does someone want to harm us?"

"I don't think you're in danger, Mrs. Doyle," Jason said.

"How can you possibly know that? If someone murdered Emmett, they might want to get us too. Maybe the killer thinks I know something."

"Do you?" Daniel asked.

"What about?"

"Would Emmett have any reason to harm the boys?"

"No!" Rose cried. "He would never hurt a hair on their heads. Emmett loved children. He liked to teach them about plants and talked to them about the wildlife on the estate."

"What wildlife?" Jason asked.

Rose's gaze slid toward him. "The foxes and badgers and rabbits. He loved animals and taught the children that every living thing deserved respect. He hated the fox hunts. He thought they were cruel."

"The fox is a cruel animal," Daniel pointed out. "Feral."

"Emmett said they were just fighting for survival. Same as him."

The gentle man Rose described was difficult to reconcile with the hopeless drunk and wife beater Jason had met, but she clearly needed to talk about her husband and remember him as someone she could mourn, so he bit his tongue and waited for Rose to finish since there were still questions they needed to put to her.

"Mrs. Doyle, was there anyone Emmett didn't get on with?" Daniel asked once there was a pause. "Does anyone benefit from his death?"

"No!" Rose exclaimed. "Who could possibly benefit from Emmett's death? He had nothing and no one except Daisy and me. We were his only family, and the cottage belongs to the estate." She clasped her hands in agitation. "Oh, I do hope Sir Lawrence won't ask us to move out."

"Where would you go?" Jason asked.

"To the big house. There are rooms in the servants' quarters. Sir Lawrence will need a new gardener, and he will need a place to live, especially if he has a family."

Rose swayed on her feet, and Jason caught her under the arm and deftly maneuvered her into a chair. She sank onto the seat and rested her hand on her belly. Her shoulders were hunched, and her chin dipped.

"Mrs. Doyle, are you all right?" Jason asked.

Rose nodded. "Just very sad, Doctor, and more than a bit lost."

Tears slid down her face and dripped onto her apron. Jason poured a cup of cider from a pitcher on the table and handed it to her. Rose accepted the cup, took a sip, then set it aside.

"How am I going to tell Daisy?" she asked. "She's just lost John and Bertie, and now this."

"Where is Daisy?" Jason asked.

"She's at the big house, with my mother. I thought it was all right now that the boys have been taken away." Rose looked from Daniel to Jason, her expression pained. "Please, I need a few moments on my own."

"Of course," Jason said. "Please send for me if you feel unwell."

"Thank you, Doctor. I just need to lie down for a bit and gather my thoughts."

"The poor woman," Daniel said once he and Jason had left the cottage. "It must have been difficult enough living with Emmett after his accident, but now she'll be on her own, and with a child on the way."

"She's better off without that brute. It was just a matter of time before he caused her irreparable harm or raised his fists to the children," Jason said.

"Perhaps she will remarry," Daniel said. "She's still very young, and pretty."

"I think it will take Rose time to learn to trust another man. Once bitten, twice shy."

"Is that one of your American sayings?" Daniel asked with a smile.

Jason nodded but didn't reply.

Chapter 29

"Emmett is dead?" Mrs. Buckley cried. "Are you certain?"

"Yes," Daniel said. "He was poisoned. I found his body in the tunnel."

Mrs. Buckley shook her head. "Poisoned himself more like. He was always threatening to do it. Said he couldn't bear to live looking like he did. Rose deserved better, he'd say, and he'd promise to stop drinking and be a better husband to her, but then he'd get to feeling low again and reach for the bottle. He couldn't stop, not even for Daisy."

"Emmett threatened to commit suicide?" Jason asked.

"All the time. And who'd know how to do it better than him?" Mrs. Buckley replied. "Plenty of options in the country."

"How do you mean?" Daniel asked.

Mrs. Buckley gave him a knowing look. "If a man has a mind to end it all, there are ways to do it. There's the river, the trees, the poisonous plants, and even just a good old shaving razor."

"You don't sound as if you disapprove," Jason remarked.

"Oh, I do, Doctor, but I'd known Emmett since he was a boy, and he was always one for the grand gestures. Probably did it in the tunnel to spare Rose the sight of him. By the time anyone found him, he'd be nothing but teeth and bones."

"That seems an awfully cruel thing to do to someone you love."

Mrs. Buckley nodded. "It is, but also a way to keep them bound to you. No body, no death. No death, no opportunity to start fresh."

"And is that what Rose wants? To start fresh?" Daniel asked.

"No. Rose loved the bones of him, the silly girl. She'll mourn him for the rest of her days," Mrs. Buckley said sadly. "And so will Daisy. She only ever saw the good in him. Girls love their fathers until they see them for the flawed creatures they are."

"Rose said that Daisy was with you," Jason said. He'd seen no sign of the child.

"She's in the nursery. She wanted to play with some of Sir Lawrence's old toys," Mrs. Buckley replied.

"Is she on her own?"

"Heaven forbid. I wouldn't leave her alone, not after what happened. Daisy is with Amy. Sir Lawrence has asked that she prepare the nursery, now that the babies have arrived. And the wetnurse has arrived from the village. She's there as well, settling into her room."

"Mrs. Buckley, who knew about the brandy in the tunnel?" Daniel asked.

"Don't know. I've never been down there myself."

"Did Emmett ever go down there?"

"Not that I know of, but who knew what he got up to when he was in his cups. Maybe he went down there to sleep it off."

"Did Emmett fall out with anyone recently?" Jason asked.

"I don't know. Emmett was an angry drunk. He could have brawled with anyone, for all I know."

"Perhaps you can send someone to collect the body," Jason said. "Rose doesn't want it brought to the cottage."

"I expect we can lay him out in the butchering room. The table's big enough, and no one will have to see him until he's ready to be interred. The sooner Emmett is buried, the better for all involved."

"But who *is* involved?" Jason asked Daniel once they left the kitchen. "If Emmett Doyle was the sole victim, then I could believe that he got on the wrong side of someone in the village, but the fact that the boys were poisoned in this house leads me to believe that the three murders are connected. They must be."

"But how?" Daniel replied. "Emmett had little to do with John and Bertie, and there's no one person who benefits from the deaths of all three. The only theory that makes sense is that the children were poisoned by accident and Emmett Doyle was the intended victim all along."

"Which brings me back to my original question. Why poison a reclusive gardener? Who gains?"

"We need to speak to Sir Lawrence," Daniel said.

Chapter 30

Sir Lawrence was still closeted with Lucinda but joined Jason and Daniel in the parlor when summoned by Mrs. Buckley, who returned to the kitchen, presumably to see to dinner since Doris Powers was at home with her boys.

"Let's drink to my wife and daughters," Sir Lawrence suggested joyfully once he entered the room. "Despite everything, today, I'm a happy man."

"I'm afraid we have some bad news, Sir Lawrence," Daniel said once they had toasted Lucinda and the girls and drunk to the everlasting memory of John and Bertie.

"What now?" Sir Lawrence asked warily.

"The body of Emmett Doyle was found in the tunnel. He was poisoned," Jason said.

Sir Lawrence looked momentarily blank. "Oh, you mean the gardener?"

"Yes. He died sometime last night."

"Poor man. He was never the same after that awful accident. Does Rose know?"

"Yes. We went by the cottage."

"How is she?" Sir Lawrence asked.

"As well as can be expected under the circumstances," Jason replied.

Sir Lawrence nodded and walked over to the sideboard to fetch the half-empty bottle of whisky. He went to pour Jason and Daniel another drink, but they declined, so Sir Lawrence refilled his own glass.

"To Emmett," he said, and tossed back his drink.

"Sir Lawrence, three people are dead by poisoning in as many days," Jason said. "There's a strong possibility that there will be more deaths."

"But who's in danger?" Sir Lawrence cried. "What does the poisoner want?"

"We have yet to figure that out," Daniel said.

"Inspector, with all due respect, you've been here for two days and have spoken to nearly everyone who has access to the house. If you still don't know what's going on, perhaps you never will."

"It's entirely possible that the poison did not come from this house," Jason said.

"Where did it come from, then?" Sir Lawrence asked. "And who would want to poison two small boys and a gardener?"

"Hemlock can be found anywhere, so where it came from is not important. We need to understand why someone would want Emmett Doyle dead."

"Do you think the boys' deaths were accidental?"

"We won't know the answer to that until we figure out the motive for Emmett's murder. His death is key," Jason said.

"Whoever murdered Emmett Doyle was brazen enough to do it with a police inspector on site," Sir Lawrence said, his disgust obvious. "They're either incredibly clever or unbelievably stupid."

"Luring Emmett Doyle to the tunnel was a clever idea," Jason surmised. "If Inspector Haze had not gone down there, the body would not have been found for some time, and by the time it was, no one would make the connection with John's and Bertie's deaths. The assumption would be that Emmett simply drank himself to death."

"There's also another possibility," Daniel said. "Whether found or not, everyone would assume that Emmett Doyle had something to do with the boys' deaths and had either run off to evade justice or had committed suicide. Either way, his death would ensure the safety of the actual killer."

"But why would anyone think that Emmett had poisoned the boys?" Sir Lawrence asked. "He was a bitter, angry man, but I have never seen him lose his patience with the children."

"Perhaps the boys had done something to make him angry. Children can be cruel," Daniel said.

"Emmett lost his patience with his wife. We've seen the bruises," Jason said.

Sir Lawrence gaped at Jason in astonishment. "Are you suggesting that Rose had something to do with his death?"

"Is it at all possible that the child Rose is carrying was not her husband's?"

"Whose child do you think it is?" Sir Lawrence asked. Jason gave Sir Lawrence a meaningful look, and instead of reacting with shock, Sir Lawrence guffawed. "You think I was having my way with Rose?"

"You did have two children with the cook," Jason pointed out.

"The cook wasn't my sister."

"Rose Doyle is your sister?" Daniel exclaimed.

"Half-sister, and a gentler soul you'll never meet. This might be an uncharitable thing to say, but I'm glad Emmett is dead. He was unkind to Rose and would only have got worse as time went on. I asked Rose if she'd like me to throw him off the estate, but she refused. She begged me to give him another chance and try to understand the pain he had endured. Rose loved him, and when he was sober, he was a good father to Daisy. And as far as I know, Rose's child is her husband's. She's not the sort of woman who would betray her wedding vows. For Rose, it was truly for better or for worse."

"Where would Emmett Doyle have gone if you'd asked him to leave?" Jason asked.

Sir Lawrence shrugged. "I really didn't care. I would have given him some money and told him never to return." He seemed to realize how that sounded and hurried to amend his statement. "I did not kill him, Inspector. I can pay someone off if necessary, but I'm not so committed to the outcome as to have someone killed on my say so or do the deed myself."

"We only have your word for that," Jason replied.

"Yes, and you will have to take it, unless you think I also murdered my own sons."

"Do you keep a mistress?"

Sir Lawrence sighed. "I do not. I had an occasional dalliance before Lucinda and I were married, but I have been completely faithful since I made my vows before God. Lucinda can be a spiteful little minx. I freely admit that, but I love her," he added, and smiled dreamily. "She's the only woman for me."

Daniel shot Jason a questioning look, as though he wanted to know if Jason believed the baronet. Jason gave a small nod. He knew genuine feeling when he saw it, and Sir Lawrence was clearly devoted to his bride.

"Lucinda asked you to evict Richard Powers," Jason said. "Why does your wife believe him to be guilty of murder?"

"Lucinda doesn't really believe Richard killed anyone, but she feels threatened by his presence," Sir Lawrence said.

"Why?" Daniel asked.

"I don't have any male relations, Inspector Haze, not even some distant cousin I've never met. With John and Bertie out of the way, Richard would be the only living Foxley descendant left were I to die. And now that I have two daughters, he remains the only one who can make a case for inheriting the title and the estate."

"But he's illegitimate," Daniel pointed out.

Sir Lawrence sighed heavily. "Vicar Hobbs is Richard's uncle on his mother's side. Powers is his wife's maiden name."

"So?" Daniel asked.

"Richard is eight years older than me and was born before my own parents were married. In fact, his mother passed a mere month before my parents were married by Vicar Hobbs, and he and his wife took Richard to live with them. If the vicar were to testify that my father had married Richard's mother in secret, Richard would get the lot."

"Surely it's not that simple," Daniel said. "If the marriage was never recorded in the parish register, then it's as good as never having taken place."

"A clever lawyer could make a case for Richard's inheritance if the vicar were willing to testify to his nephew's legitimacy."

"And would Vicar Hobbs do that?" Jason asked.

"In my experience, people will do whatever it takes to ensure their own prosperity."

"Why did you not mention this before?" Daniel demanded. "This information puts Richard Powers squarely in the frame for murder."

"I didn't mention it because I can't bring myself to believe that Richard would murder my children. I have never seen him treat them with anything less than love and kindness. They were his family. And even if he had decided to clear the way for his very dubious claim, why would he do it before Lucinda had given birth and while I was still alive, unless he had planned to murder us all?"

Sir Lawrence looked from Daniel to Jason. "I know what you're thinking. If he were capable of murdering two children, he'd have no difficulty killing again, but I simply refuse to believe that of Richard."

"Did your father ever acknowledge Richard Powers as his son?" Daniel asked.

Sir Lawrence shook his head. "My father never looked in his direction. He was not a kind man and never took an interest in any of his children. I paid for Richard's education and brought him on to run the estate. I felt I owed him that much. Legitimate or not, he's still my brother."

"Were there other children besides you, Richard, and Rose?" Jason asked.

Sir Lawrence nodded. "No female servant was safe from my father in his younger days. He took what he wanted, whether they were willing or not. There was another sister, born to a barmaid, who died in infancy, and a brother, born to the estate manager's wife, who drowned when he was twelve. I wasn't meant to know they were my siblings, but servants talk, and I made sure to listen."

"So, Rose knows she's your half-sister?" Daniel asked.

"No one knows. Mrs. Buckley married my father's valet when Rose was still an infant, and he put it about that the child was his. Mrs. Buckley did not want Rose to bear the burden of knowing she was illegitimate."

"Did Mrs. Buckley tell you that Rose is your sister?" Jason asked.

"No. My mother told me before she died. She despised my father and wanted me to know the sort of man he was. She told me to look after Rose and Richard."

"Is that why you took such an interest in John and Bertie? Because you didn't want to be like your father?"

Sir Lawrence nodded. "I'm not proud of following in my father's footsteps, but I cared for Doris, and I never neglected my duty to my boys. I would have seen them educated and set up in a business of their choosing. And if they had wished to remain at Fox Hollow, I would have provided them with cottages of their own and a monthly stipend."

"Will you really ask Richard Powers to leave?" Daniel inquired.

"I will have to unless I give in to Lucinda's pleas and take a house in London. She is not happy here, and Richard is not the only reason."

"Look to the safety of your family, Sir Lawrence," Jason said. "I can't help but think that whoever is behind this is not quite finished."

"That's a sobering thought," Sir Lawrence said. "How long until Lucinda can travel?"

"I would give it at least two weeks. Lucinda needs to heal before she can tolerate the jolting of a carriage."

"My poor, dear Lucy," Sir Lawrence said affectionately.

"Lucinda did not suffer any complications during the operation, but she might still develop an infection. I think it best if I remain on hand tonight," Jason said.

"I'll ask Mrs. Buckley to prepare a room for you. Will you stay as well, Inspector?" Sir Lawrence asked.

Daniel hadn't planned on staying the night, but now that it had been suggested, he thought it might be a good idea. If they didn't crack the case within the next twenty-four hours, they would have to admit defeat and return to London, and Daniel couldn't bear to leave the Foxleys and their staff to the mercy of the killer.

"I can take a room at the pub," Daniel said.

"Nonsense. We have plenty of room, and I will sleep better knowing that my wife is under the care of a competent physician and our safety is in the hands of an inspector from Scotland Yard."

"Thank you," Daniel said, but the compliment felt hollow, at least the part that pertained to him. Inspector or not, he felt as clueless as he did helpless to stop another murder.

Sir Lawrence pushed wearily to his feet. "I will see you both at dinner. Now, I'd like to return to Lucinda and the girls."

Chapter 31

"The relationships on this estate border on the incestuous," Daniel said once Sir Lawrence had left the room. "If neither Richard nor Rose knew they are related, they might have had a romantic relationship."

"Are you suggesting that Richard Powers had an affair with Rose Doyle, got her with child, then decided to clear the way for his own inheritance and remarriage by murdering his brother's illegitimate boys and Rose's husband?" Jason asked. "Unless he was going to murder Lucinda's child, Sir Lawrence, and Doris Powers, that plan wouldn't get him anywhere."

Daniel chuckled. "No, it wouldn't. I'm just grasping at straws, since no two pieces of evidence fit together to form even the tiniest bit of a picture. But one thing I do know is that Lucinda has good instincts. If she wants Richard Powers gone, I don't think we should dismiss her concerns."

"All right. Do you have a theory?" Jason asked.

Daniel smiled ruefully. "It's a bit daft, but hear me out. Let us say that Richard Powers is the sort that dreams big and isn't troubled by his conscience. Of all the children, he's the one who is most like his father and feels no remorse about taking what he wants. How difficult would it be to get away with multiple murders if we were never called in?"

Jason considered the question. "John's and Bertie's deaths could be written off as an accident, and no one would question the sudden death of the Foxleys' infant. Babies die all the time. And if Sir Lawrence had succumbed to grief and taken his own life, then Richard would be the only Foxley descendant left standing."

"Precisely," Daniel cried. "He is sure to know about the tunnels and could have been the one to lure Emmett Doyle to his death, which could serve a dual purpose—divert attention from Richard Powers and imply that Emmett Doyle might have been somehow responsible. It would also free Rose from an unhappy marriage, if that was the objective, but we have nothing that would suggest Richard and Rose were in cahoots."

"No, we do not," Jason agreed.

"So, it could work," Daniel insisted.

"I suppose it does make an odd sort of sense, but unless Richard Powers is a consummate actor, I can't see him biding his time all these years and then murdering the boys just before a Foxley heir is to be born. If claiming the title and estate were the objective, then he could have murdered Sir Lawrence before he ever married and tried his luck with the courts. A lot easier to dispose of one man than going on a killing spree and drawing attention to a possible coup," Jason pointed out.

"You're right. And everyone did say that he genuinely cared for those boys. But if not Richard Powers, then who?" Daniel asked, his exasperation mounting.

"I don't know, but there's something bubbling just beneath the surface that we have yet to identify. In fact, we still don't know how Bruce Plimpton and the Carmichaels fit into all this."

"No, we don't. I became distracted with all the interfamilial relationships and forgot to ask Sir Lawrence about his debt to Lance." Daniel sighed heavily. "This case is uncommonly convoluted, Ransome is breathing down my neck. He wants me back in London, which means that our killer only has to bide their time and wait for us to leave."

Jason leaned back in his chair and shut his eyes, suddenly wishing he were anywhere but Fox Hollow. As Daniel had said, this case was convoluted, and Jason was sure they were missing something vital, something that was probably staring them in the face. Just because John and Bertie had died first did not mean they were the intended victims, but if not the children, then it had to be Emmett Doyle because it would make no sense to murder three people and not achieve the desired objective.

"Jason, are you absolutely *certain* these deaths couldn't be accidental?" Daniel asked, interrupting Jason's morbid reverie and voicing the doubt that had been niggling at Jason since the very beginning. "If they were, then that would explain everything."

Jason opened his eyes and sat up. "In theory, any death by poison could be accidental, but when three people die at the same place and in quick succession of what is most likely the same poison, it would be irresponsible to rule out intent."

"Do you have a theory? I'll consider anything, no matter how remote."

"If Emmett Doyle was the intended victim all along, then we're probably looking for a motive in all the wrong places," Jason said.

"But who would gain by his death besides Rose?" Daniel exclaimed.

"Rose is now free," Jason pointed out.

"Free to do what? She's a young widow with one child and another on the way. If every woman that's been roughed up by her husband decided to kill him, the country would be littered with corpses."

"She is free to marry again or to remain single. Sir Lawrence will look after her and Daisy, and she will no longer have to suffer her husband's abuse. And if Sir Lawrence is wrong and the child is not Emmett's, that would give her an added reason to want him dead."

"So, your theory is that Rose tried to poison her husband, but the children somehow got hold of whatever she had prepared and died instead. Refusing to be thwarted, Rose decided to try again?"

"Perhaps the tragic deaths of the boys presented Rose with an opportunity to rid herself of Emmett. If we think that Emmett's death is connected to the deaths of the children, then we won't suspect Rose of wrongdoing."

"You think there are two killers?" Daniel asked, and pushed his glasses up his nose almost violently.

"That's not beyond the realm of possibility."

"Should we search her cottage?"

"If I were Rose, I'd dispose of any incriminating evidence," Jason replied.

"Unless she doesn't think she's a suspect."

"I would really like a word with Daisy," Jason said. "At this point, I'm beginning to doubt her very existence."

"Are you suggesting that everyone has agreed to make up a child that doesn't exist?" Daniel demanded, his eyes wide with disbelief.

"No, but I'm beginning to think that they are intentionally preventing us from speaking with her."

"And do you honestly believe that a five-year-old child can help us solve this case?"

"A five-year-old child whose father and two closest friends are now dead."

"What do you think she knows?"

"Children are very observant, Daniel. They notice things adults sometimes miss."

"If you say so," Daniel grumbled just as the dinner gong sounded. "At this stage, I don't expect any breakthroughs, but I do think you need to rest. It's been a long day, and you look worn out."

Jason nodded and pushed to his feet. "Let's hope for a quiet night and see what tomorrow brings. I do think that we should refrain from discussing the case at dinner. Sir Lawrence has just welcomed twins, and you and I could use a mental break. We'll pick up again tomorrow."

"Agreed," Daniel said. He'd clearly had enough, and the prospect of returning to London was probably not as unappealing as he'd first thought.

A summons from Ransome would absolve Daniel of further responsibility to Sir Lawrence while allowing Daniel to retain his pride and professional reputation. Jason loved his friend, but he had to admit that the past year had changed Daniel in myriad ways. He was no longer the humble parish constable Jason had met in Birch Hill. Daniel was the rising star of Scotland Yard, and if he continued on this career trajectory, he would surely be in the running for superintendent and then maybe even commissioner.

The old Daniel might not have welcomed the responsibility or the attention such a post would bring, but the Daniel that had lost his wife to suicide and had nearly lost his daughter to a criminal family was a changed man. There was the desire for justice and the need to feel that he was making a difference, but now there was also something else. Vanity. After more than a dozen solved cases and frequent mentions in the newspapers, Inspector Haze was gaining notoriety and beginning to believe the hype. He hadn't said so out loud, but Jason got the distinct impression that Daniel was afraid to fail and would rather walk away after proclaiming that the deaths were a series of unfortunate accidents brought about by someone's carelessness. In theory, that wasn't impossible. They had yet to find any solid evidence that someone had set out to poison three people, but Jason had learned to trust his gut instinct and his medical training and couldn't dismiss the deaths as accidental until he had proof that no ill intent had been at play.

Perhaps Daniel was right, and Jason was simply tired. He hadn't slept well last night, partly because he was worried about the upcoming cesarean section and deeply concerned about the well-being of both mother and babies, and partly because he couldn't stop thinking about Mary, and Micah, and their seemingly doomed family. He wanted to protect the Donovan children from further suffering and loss, but although he had every faith in Micah, Mary's judgment gave Jason serious pause. She was the sort of woman who needed to play the savior, be it to her father, her brother, or her husband, and would inevitably find herself on the losing side. Few men wanted to be saved from themselves, and even fewer ever changed for the better.

Mary had fallen for the Confederate soldier she'd rescued in Maryland and then married a man she barely knew only to discover that he was involved in something underhanded and illegal, and her very life had been in danger. Mary might be content to remain in England for a time and take as long as she needed to lick her wounds, but if Jason knew anything of the proud, impetuous woman Mary had become, she would eventually grow restless and find another lost cause. He only hoped that she wouldn't drag Liam along with her and would allow the child to enjoy a happy home life and all the opportunities Jason and Katherine could offer him. He knew only time would tell what Mary would decide, but her flight from Boston and the loss of her baby had left Jason feeling uneasy about the future.

But he would not solve the problem of Mary tonight any more than he would crack the case, so Jason followed Daniel to the dining room and accepted a seat at Sir Lawrence's right.

Chapter 32

The dining room was much like the rest of the house: large, drafty, and dark, the thick velvet panels drawn against the chill of the spring evening, and the heavy carved furniture making Jason feel entombed. A silver candelabra stood on the table, the half-dozen candles casting a mellow pool of light onto the end of the table where the three men had congregated. Jason imagined Lucinda and Sir Lawrence dining in this room each evening and could understand Lucinda's desolation. Jason was a simple man who'd survived in conditions not fit for human habitation, but he would find this a lonely existence as well. A young girl was sure to long for society and amusing company and resent her husband for bringing her to this backwater. Perhaps Lucinda would prevail and the Foxleys would return to London for the Season.

The dinner, when it was finally served, was the sort of fare that might have been offered back in the house's Tudor heyday. Clear broth was followed by boiled beef, potatoes, and vegetables that had been cooked to the point of disintegration. Plain, heavy food that was completely devoid of flavor. If a special meal had been planned for Easter, the menu had been adjusted to utilize whatever was on hand. The wine that was served with dinner soured Jason's stomach, and he refused any refills, citing Lucinda and the twins as his reason for wishing to remain sober. Daniel accepted a second glass and seemed to enjoy his beef, as did Sir Lawrence.

"This is a very impressive house," Jason said when the conversation petered out. "We don't have anything like this in America."

"Consider yourself lucky," Sir Lawrence grumbled. "This house is the root of all our problems. It requires endless repairs. Leaking roof, dry rot, termites, crumbling plaster, ill-fitting windows, you name it. I suppose I should consider myself blessed that the current monarch is not fond of dropping in on her subjects."

"How do you mean?" Jason asked, confused by Sir Lawrence's obvious relief.

Sir Lawrence smiled in understanding. "I forget that you're not familiar with our history, not having grown up here, but I'm sure your ancestors could have told you a tale or two if you had visited them while they were still kicking."

Jason ignored the thoughtless remark and rearranged his face into an expression of polite interest.

"When Queen Elizabeth went on progress in the summer of 1552, she made a stop at Fox Hollow. It was supposed to be a two-day visit, which would have been two days too long if you had asked my Tudor ancestor, Sir Harold, but the heavens opened up and she ended up staying nearly a week. As it happens, she slept in the room where the boys' remains were discovered," Sir Lawrence added morosely.

"I would imagine that a royal visit was considered a great honor," Jason remarked.

"Oh, it was, but a visit from the queen nearly bankrupted Sir Harold Foxley. The house was smaller then, and when he was informed that the queen would be paying him a visit, he had to build an extension."

"For a two-day visit?"

Sir Lawrence sighed. "When the queen traveled, she arrived with hundreds of courtiers and all their servants. The baggage train alone would stretch on for a mile or more. All these people needed accommodation, stabling and feed for their animals, and countless meals. And these weren't just any meals. The queen and her court expected to be wined and dined in lavish style. There would be suckling pig, pheasant, roasted swans, fish, mutton, and everything in between, accompanied by dozens of side dishes, various puddings, and barrels and barrels of wine, ale, and mead.

"Everyone from the village would be expected to help out, since the servants couldn't keep up with the demand for food, drink, and clean linens. And even with the extension, some of the lower servants would be housed in the village and with the families on the estate, who had to see to their needs and feed them for the duration of the stay."

Sir Lawrence shook his head at the memory of this centuries-old royal injustice. "Sir Harold never quite recovered from that visit. He begged and scrimped for the rest of his days just to keep hold of this moldering pile. And the debt he was forced to incur has plagued future generations, since there was nothing to fall back on. And there still isn't. A more recent ancestor, my grandfather Sir Anthony, made a fortune in illegal trade but spent the lot on his two great passions—women and horses."

Sir Lawrence smiled ruefully. "The Foxleys are not known for their restraint or good sense, myself included," he added.

"Lucinda's portion must have come in handy, then," Daniel exclaimed, surprising Jason with his observation.

Daniel wasn't normally so blunt, at least not when it came to money, but he must have had more to drink than Jason had realized. He found that although the English were as concerned with money and other's people's financial affairs as their American counterparts, they avoided speaking about finances in public for fear of being thought vulgar. If Sir Lawrence found the comment offensive, he didn't remark on it, probably because he assumed that the question was part of the investigation.

"Lucinda expected me to use a part of her portion to outfit the house with gas lighting and run water to the kitchen. And she pressed me to install at least one water closet so that we could bathe without having to wait for water to boil and buckets to be brought up to fill the tub, but my first priority was to pay off the most pressing debts."

"And where does Lance Carmichael come into this?" Daniel asked, having clearly forgotten their agreement not to talk about the case at dinner. Or maybe he simply couldn't put the investigation aside, not when his professional reputation was at stake.

Sir Lawrence's jaw tightened with obvious irritation, but he had to have known the question would come sooner or later, and it was probably better to spill his secrets over food and wine than in an interview room at Scotland Yard. He sighed and turned to Daniel.

"The Carmichaels operate a number of gaming establishments, both in London and Brentwood, and I have run up considerable debt. As I said, I'm not known for my good sense."

"Is that why Bruce Plimpton was here the day the boys died?"

"Yes. He wanted money."

"And if you didn't pay up?" Jason asked, abandoning all pretense of having table manners.

"If I didn't pay up, they would make me sorry. Very sorry, indeed," he added.

"By doing what?" Daniel asked.

"By disclosing embarrassing facts about Lucinda and embroiling us in a scandal."

"What things?"

Sir Lawrence nailed Daniel with an angry blue stare. "Don't pretend not to know the truth of Lucinda's paternity, Inspector Haze."

"I do, but I didn't think you'd know," Daniel replied. "That's not the sort of thing one tells a suitor."

"Lucinda didn't tell me. She doesn't know, and I pray she never will."

"So how do you know?" Jason asked.

Sir Lawrence sighed heavily. "Lucinda's grandfather, Colonel Chadwick, was on friendly terms with Lance Carmichael, which is not surprising given that they were both men of questionable moral character and would do anything to attain their goals. It would seem that Colonel Chadwick wasn't above bragging about his exploits."

"What exploits are those?" Daniel asked. He wanted Sir Lawrence to spell it out for him and disclose exactly how much he knew of the Chadwicks' history.

"The colonel didn't hold his son in high regard and found ways to punish him for what he perceived as weakness of character. The colonel routinely forced himself on his daughter-in-law, who had no recourse since her husband wasn't about to challenge his father and allowed the abuse to go on for years. Harry and Arabella's paternity is not known for certain, since it could have been either Chadwick, but by the time Lucinda was conceived, there was no question that she was fathered by the colonel."

"Does Harry Chadwick know that you know?" Jason asked.

"No," Sir Lawrence said. "And neither does Caroline. She would be mortified if anyone knew how she had suffered at the hands of her father-in-law, especially her children. I would pay any amount of interest just to keep this information from getting out."

"But it seems Richard Powers knows, or at least he implied as much."

"Richard has known Bruce Plimpton for years. It's possible that Bruce told him, but Richard would never tell anyone. He'd never hurt me that way."

Wouldn't he? Jason thought. Perhaps he'd threatened Lucinda and that was the true reason she wanted him gone.

"Was that why Harry Chadwick left so suddenly, because you had asked him for money after your meeting with Bruce Plimpton?" Daniel inquired.

Sir Lawrence nodded. "In part. Harry is a decent sort, but he's well aware that I won't be able to repay the debt for some time. Maybe never."

"And why did Bruce Plimpton allude to the church? Your conversation was overheard by Mrs. Buckley," Daniel explained to a surprised Sir Lawrence.

"Because I had recently paid for a new window," the baronet replied. "He said that if I had money to throw away on windows, I had money to pay off my debt."

"So, what did you do?" Jason asked.

Sir Lawrence looked like he was about to cry. "I gave him the necklace."

"What necklace?" Daniel asked.

"I'd acquired a pearl and diamond choker for Lucinda. It was to be a present for her eighteenth birthday. I bought it on credit," Sir Lawrence added. "I felt terrible about it. I really wanted to give her something special."

"Have you ever considered selling Fox Hollow?" Jason asked, and earned himself a look of startled incredulity.

"I could never do that. It's our family seat. The bedrock of our history."

"Of course. Forgive me," Jason said. "Having been raised in America, my attitude toward managing one's finances is somewhat different."

"I wish I had your inherent disregard for family obligations," Sir Lawrence said. "There's something to be said for doing what's best for oneself without suffering pangs of guilt at the sure knowledge that you're betraying not only your ancestors but future generations. There's nothing I would like better than a modest London home equipped with all the latest advances, but I'm afraid I'm chained to this place forever."

"We all have our crosses to bear," Jason replied, and hoped Sir Lawrence had not picked up on his sarcasm since he had no right to judge the man, and to belittle him was unworthy of Jason.

Sir Lawrence's upbringing had been very different than Jason's, and he had to admit that although there was something to be said for having freedom of choice, he might have felt very differently had he been brought up in England. The fact that he had chosen to remain instead of rushing back to New York proved that he felt more of a bond with his family's past than he'd previously cared to admit.

"I'm very sorry, Sir Lawrence, but I had no time to make a pudding," Mrs. Buckley said when she bustled into the dining room, Gwen at her heels.

"That's quite all right, Mrs. Buckley. You've gone above and beyond, and I'm most grateful," Sir Lawrence said.

Mrs. Buckley looked relieved. "Thank you, sir. There might be a jar of fruit compote."

"Let's save it for her ladyship. You know how she likes compote with her breakfast." Sir Lawrence stood, and Jason and Daniel followed suit.

The two women set to clearing the table while the men adjourned to the library for brandy and cigars. Neither Daniel nor Jason accepted the offer of a cigar, but Daniel did have a small brandy. Jason decided to abstain.

"Never did care for brandy," Sir Lawrence said as he poured himself a Scotch. "This is my preferred drink. The elixir of life, the Scots call it. My grandfather swore by it. Said it could cure any ailment. Is such a thing possible, Lord Redmond?"

"I don't know if it can cure what ails you, but it certainly can't hurt," Jason replied. "And the power of the mind is not to be discounted. If you think something can help you, it can, simply by virtue of your faith in it."

"Some would call that self-delusion," Sir Lawrence said.

"Human beings have been practicing self-delusion since the beginning of time," Jason replied. "On the whole, it can be quite helpful."

"How so?"

"If people didn't believe in the impossible, we'd still be living in caves."

"What on earth do you mean?" Daniel exclaimed. "Surely it's not so ambitious to build a house or a church."

Jason smiled. "Men built wooden boats, figured out a way to navigate by the stars, and crossed oceans in their quest for knowledge."

"In their quest for riches, more like," Sir Lawrence scoffed.

"Still, the world is a civilized place compared to what it was even a few hundred years ago. Would you not agree, Sir Lawrence?" Daniel asked. "And there's a new nation where there used to be nothing but forests and rivers, the land inhabited by disparate tribes." Daniel raised his glass to Jason in a toast. "The United States has taught us a thing or two about self-delusion. They took on the might of the British Army and won."

"The greatest military defeat of all time," Sir Lawrence said. "My great-grandfather's older brother was lost in that conflict, as were several cousins. I can thank the War of Independence for my position in life. Had that long-forgotten Foxley lived, I'd be nothing but a poor relation."

"One never can tell what the future holds," Daniel agreed.

"Well, I for one hope my future holds a son," Sir Lawrence replied. "I'm in love with my girls, but I still need an heir."

"Lucinda will need ample time to recover," Jason warned.

"Of course. I completely understand," Sir Lawrence replied, his cheeks turning a deeper pink.

"If you will excuse me, gentlemen, I will check on my patient, then retire," Jason said. "It's been a long day."

"Good night, my lord," Sir Lawrence said with feeling. "Today could have turned out very differently. I owe you everything."

"You owe me nothing, Sir Lawrence," Jason replied modestly, and let himself out.

Chapter 33

Daniel was dismayed to discover that Mrs. Buckley had put him in the room where the children had died. The trunk was gone, and the room had been aired out, but Daniel felt a pang of apprehension as he undressed and eyed the bed. It was unusually high, and the mattress was lumpy and smelled stale and dusty. Daniel couldn't help but wonder who had last occupied this room and what had become of them, then realized he was about to sleep in the same bed as Queen Elizabeth herself. It was a strange turn of events in a murder inquiry, but nothing about this case was straightforward, least of all spending the night in a house full of possible suspects.

Still, it had been a long and stressful day, Daniel was tired, and he'd certainly slept in less comfortable places. He wondered what Jason's room was like and if he would be able to sleep or would worry about Lucinda and check on her periodically throughout the night. Daniel climbed into bed, blew out the candle, pulled up the counterpane, and allowed his thoughts to drift until sleep overtook him.

He had no idea what time it was when he woke. The room was dark, the moonlight unable to penetrate the heavy curtains. Daniel's head was swimming, and his mouth was sour and dry. He tried to swallow but found that his throat was constricted and there was a worrying tightness in his chest. He was desperate for a drink of water and recalled with some relief that Amy had left a pitcher of water on the washstand when she'd turned down the bed.

Daniel went to get out of bed and tumbled to the floor when his legs folded beneath him. He felt as weak as a newborn calf and couldn't seem to find the strength to get to his feet. Daniel lay there for a few moments, his cheek pressed to the cool wood floor, then tried to stand. He would have managed it, but a sharp pain sliced through his belly and his bowels threatened to let go, forcing him to grope for the chamber pot Amy had left beneath the bed. Daniel grabbed the handle and had just enough time to yank the receptacle toward him and pull off the lid before he vomited profusely.

Panting, his face clammy with sweat, Daniel gripped the pot with both hands in case he was going to be sick again. His guts were writhing like snakes, and he felt terrible pressure in his bowels. He thought he might soil his drawers and would have been mortified had he been able to organize his thoughts. They seemed to scatter like billiard balls, rolling in different directions and at different speeds, the bright colors confusing and mesmerizing as they exploded before Daniel's eyes and left him disoriented and reeling with panic. The only thing that felt solid was the floor beneath him, the cool, smooth boards strangely comforting.

Once he was certain he wasn't going to vomit again, Daniel finally let go of the chamber pot and tried to pull himself up by holding onto the mattress, but it began to slide off the bed, and he fell back to the floor.

He tried to formulate a plan, to call for help, but couldn't seem to find his voice. Desperate, Daniel banged his fist on the floor in the hope that someone would hear him and come, but the banging was really no more than dull thuds, the sound too low to penetrate the walls or the thick door that separated him from the corridor. As he lay there, the darkness seemed to condense around him, and he let go, his eyes closing as he lost consciousness.

Chapter 34

Daniel was gasping when he came to. Something long and thick was being forced down his throat, and he gagged, his gullet rebelling against the intrusion and his mouth filling with bile. He couldn't breathe, and it was still too dark to see, but he knew that he was still on the floor, and someone was hulking over him, their shoulders a dense outline against the oppressive darkness.

"Let it out, Daniel," Jason's voice commanded. "It's all right. Let go."

The relentless probe, which turned out to be Jason's fingers, was removed, and Daniel vomited into the chamber pot that Jason held before him, then pressed his forehead to the floor. His stomach continued to heave violently, and the pain in his bowels had returned but wasn't as sharp as before.

"You need to drink." Jason helped Daniel to sit and held a cup of cold water to his lips. "Drink as much as you can."

"I need to…" Daniel began once he'd drained the cup.

Jason nodded and left the room, returning a moment later with an empty chamber pot, probably from his own room. He set the pot on the floor, helped Daniel to his feet, and left him to it. The relief was immense, and once he was finished, Daniel felt almost normal. He covered the pot and pushed it beneath the bed with his foot, then climbed into bed and stretched out beneath the counterpane. It felt good not to be sick, and the warmth of the blanket was cozy and comforting. Daniel exhaled in relief. He was alive, Jason was there, and now all would be well.

Jason knocked on the door, then poked his head in, his worried face illuminated by the flame of the candle he'd brought. Seeing Daniel tucked up in bed, Jason came into the room, set the candle on the bedside table, and pulled up a chair. Peering at Daniel intently, he took hold of Daniel's wrist, presumably to check his pulse, and nodded reassuringly, as though satisfied with the result.

"What happened?" Daniel choked out. The sour taste had gone, and his throat no longer felt raw, but he had yet to regain his normal voice.

"You were poisoned."

"Just me?"

Jason nodded. He was wearing nothing but his trousers, and his upper body and face were gilded by candlelight, his eyes dark, shiny pools that reflected the flame. Looking closer, Daniel noticed the goose pimples on Jason's skin and realized that the room was very cold, the draft from the window diluting the awful smell of severe illness.

"I just saw Sir Lawrence in the corridor. He's fine." Jason stood and refilled the cup, then held it out to Daniel. "Drink some more. We need to flush whatever you ingested from your system."

It took effort to sit up, but Daniel did as he was told and drank the water, this time taking measured sips and enjoying the taste. He handed the empty cup back to Jason and reclined against the lumpy pillows, still lightheaded from his ordeal.

"Why me?" he asked.

Jason glanced toward the door, checking that he had shut it, then turned back to Daniel. "I think it was meant to be me as well."

"What makes you say that?" Daniel was feeling better, but his extremities were cold, his stomach tender and hollow.

"I think the poison was in the brandy, and had I had some, I would have been sick as well."

"The poisoner knew that Sir Lawrence doesn't touch the stuff," Daniel deduced.

"Exactly. They decided to poison us once they learned we were staying the night."

"But who could have done it?"

"Mrs. Buckley told Gwen and the scullery maid that there would be two more for dinner. She also instructed Amy to prepare the rooms. Helen Carlin and Mr. Wylie took supper in their rooms, but they probably knew we were staying the night, since they would have seen Amy getting the rooms ready. Anyone could have slipped into the library while we were at dinner."

"But it wasn't just anyone, was it?" Daniel asked, noting the hard set of Jason's stubbled jaw.

Jason shook his head. "No, it wasn't. In the morning, I want you to arrest Mrs. Buckley," he said, his voice low.

"Mrs. Buckley?" Daniel exclaimed.

Jason nodded and put a finger to his lips. He clearly didn't want Mrs. Buckley to know that she was a suspect and thought someone might be lurking on the other side of the door. "Now, try to get some rest. I'm going to check on Lucinda." He stood and reached for the candleholder.

"Jason," Daniel called after him.

Jason turned, and Daniel saw the lines of tension etched into his tired face. Jason had been scared and was scared still.

"Would I have died had you not found me?"

Jason sighed. "I don't know. Maybe. It depends on how much poison was in the brandy and what the poisoner had intended. Maybe we were only meant to get ill. Or maybe we were both supposed to die tonight."

"Thank you."

"You never need to thank me. Goodnight, Daniel."

"It is now," Daniel muttered.

He lay back against the pillows but knew he wouldn't be able to sleep. Jason seemed convinced that Mrs. Buckley had been the one to tamper with the brandy, but Daniel couldn't fathom why the housekeeper would want to murder two innocent little boys. Perhaps she had wanted to rid her daughter of an abusive husband, but the children had somehow got caught up in her plot, collateral damage of a marriage gone wrong.

But did she really think she could get away with murdering a police inspector and a scion of a noble British family? How would she explain their deaths to the police, for surely Sir Lawrence would call in reinforcements? And Ransome knew where they were and would realize the deaths were the result of foul play. And what if Jason was wrong and it wasn't Mrs. Buckley? There had been a half dozen other people in the house while they were at dinner. Any of them could have poisoned the brandy, even Lucinda, if she had managed to get out of bed long enough to sneak down to the library.

Daniel pulled the counterpane up to his chin but couldn't seem to get warmer. If Daniel and Jason had died tonight, Ransome would have consulted the police surgeon, which almost certainly would have insured that the killer would get away with murder. The surgeon was not well versed in poisons, nor would he have found any evidence by the time he arrived at Fox Hollow. The killer would have removed the contaminated brandy, and Amy would have taken away the chamber pots, leaving no trace of the poison. No one would know who had tried to kill the two men or why. The case would remain unsolved, and the Fox Hollow killer would never be caught. The only thing that made Daniel less afraid was the knowledge that Charlotte would be safe with her grandmother and would want for nothing, even if he were gone.

Chapter 35

Monday, March 29

Morning could not come fast enough, and once the sun was up, Daniel washed, dressed, and hurried downstairs. He still felt nauseated and weak, but the thought of remaining in that bed or that room a moment longer gave him a desperately needed burst of energy. It was only as he was coming down the stairs that he remembered it was Monday and Easter was over. Meals had been a lonely business since Rebecca's death, and Daniel was glad he wasn't home yesterday to dine in solitary splendor. To spend the day with Jason was all he asked, and he thanked God that Jason had been there last night to save him and care for him until he was out of danger.

Daniel was surprised to find Doris Powers in the kitchen. She looked gaunt, and dark circles smudged the skin beneath her eyes, but she moved about with assurance as she prepared breakfast, her movements at odds with her catatonic gaze.

"Good morning, Mrs. Powers," Daniel said. "How are you today?"

The cook gave him a look of such naked misery that Daniel wished he hadn't asked.

"Is there something I can do for you, Inspector?"

"Could I trouble you for some tea?"

"I'll bring it to the dining room."

"I'd like to have it here, if you don't mind."

Mrs. Powers shrugged and went about making the tea while Daniel sat at the pine table and watched her every move. She hadn't seemed surprised to see him, so it stood to reason that she didn't know about the poisoning, but at this point, Daniel didn't trust anyone at Fox Hollow, not even the woman who'd lost two children.

Daniel didn't think he could eat, but the tea was hot and strong and warmed its way down his tortured gullet and soothed his sensitive stomach. It also revived him somewhat. Once he'd had two cups, he thanked Mrs. Powers and went in search of Jason. He found him in his room.

"Daniel, how are you feeling?" Jason asked.

"Angry," Daniel confessed. "Mostly with myself."

"Why is that?"

"Because for the life of me, I can't understand what's going on here, and although I trust your instincts in regard to Mrs. Buckley, I have yet to understand her motives."

"I think her motives will become clear during questioning, but we can't speak to her here. Let's take Mrs. Buckley into custody and bring her to the Brentwood police station."

"And then?"

"And then we'll see where that takes us."

"You must eat," Daniel said, taking in Jason's less-than-sprightly appearance. He looked as hollowed out as Daniel felt. "I won't have you feeling unwell," Daniel added sternly.

Jason smiled. "You should eat something as well. It'll make you feel stronger after last night and absorb any residual bile. We can leave as soon as I've had a word with Sir Lawrence."

"I'm coming with you," Daniel said.

It took Sir Lawrence several minutes to come to the door. He looked bleary-eyed and disheveled, his jaw thick with golden stubble and his hair standing on end. His shirttails hung out of his trousers, and his feet were bare, his toes incongruously pink against the dark wood floor.

"Is it Lucinda?" he cried as soon as he saw the two men. "Did something happen?"

"Lucinda is well. I just checked on her, and she's sleeping peacefully," Jason hurried to assure him. "The girls are sleeping as well."

Sir Lawrence exhaled in obvious relief. "Thank God. I was worried but didn't want to keep checking on Lucinda for fear of disturbing her. She's a light sleeper, and she needs her rest." Sir Lawrence looked from Jason to Daniel. "If Lucinda and the girls are fine, why do you look so grave? Oh, my God," he exclaimed. "Has there been another death?"

"No, but there might have been," Jason replied.

Sir Lawrence listened in stunned silence while Jason explained the situation and outlined his suspicions.

"Mrs. Buckley?" Sir Lawrence cried. "Why would Mrs. Buckley want to poison anyone? She's been employed here since she was fourteen. She's been like a mother to me since my own mother died."

"I have reason to suspect that it was Mrs. Buckley that poisoned Emmett Doyle," Jason said.

"But why would she want to poison the gardener?"

"To free her daughter from a husband who beat her."

Sir Lawrence shook his head in disbelief. "All she had to do was come to me. I would have seen to it."

"You could hardly free Rose from her husband," Daniel said.

"No, but I could have put the fear of God into him."

"Men like Emmett Doyle don't stop being violent just because someone has threatened them," Jason said. "It's a sickness they can't control. A way to release their frustration and feel powerful, if only for a short while. They might experience feelings of remorse later and beg their victim for forgiveness, but they will inevitably hurt them again."

"But why would Mrs. Buckley want to poison you? Did she know you suspect her?" Sir Lawrence asked.

"Inspector Haze and I discussed our suspicions yesterday, and Rose's name came up. Mrs. Buckley must have overheard us."

"Are you sure it was her?"

"No, but she's the only one who'd have motive to kill us," Daniel said. "We would like to take her to the Brentwood police station and interview her formally."

Sir Lawrence looked bewildered. "Did she also…?" He couldn't finish the sentence, but his meaning was clear.

"We have no reason to think that Mrs. Buckley had anything to do with the murders of the children, unless she had made an attempt on her son-in-law's life before and it went horribly wrong," Jason said.

Sir Lawrence shook his head. "I hear what you're telling me, but I don't accept it. Mrs. Buckley would never hurt anyone, not even Emmett. I simply can't believe that of her."

"Do we have your permission to take her in?" Daniel asked.

He didn't really need permission, but he didn't want Sir Lawrence to make a fuss. It would be best for all concerned if they took Mrs. Buckley away quietly, in case they were wrong. And he didn't want to cause Rose any further distress. She was fragile enough already.

"Yes, of course," Sir Lawrence said. "If you think she's responsible, then you must act on your suspicions."

"We will require the use of your carriage," Jason said. He had sent Joe home and had planned to take the train from Brentwood when he was ready to return to London.

"Of course. My carriage is at your disposal. May I have a word with Mrs. Buckley before you take her in?"

"It would be best if you didn't," Daniel replied, and hoped the baronet would accept his decision with good grace.

Sir Lawrence nodded defeatedly. "What do I tell Lucinda?"

"Perhaps you shouldn't tell her anything just yet," Jason said. "She needs to rest and focus on her recovery. You can inform her once we've made an arrest."

"Yes, of course." Sir Lawrence ran a hand through his hair and sighed deeply. "What a train wreck," he muttered, making Jason wince. His parents died in a train wreck, but Sir Lawrence didn't know that, or if he did, had forgotten in his distress.

Mrs. Buckley was white-faced and silent when Jason led her out to the waiting conveyance. He helped her inside and settled in the seat next to her, while Daniel had decided to sit on the box with Sir Lawrence's coachman, Clegg. Daniel needed some air, and the prospect of facing his would-be killer left him angry and confused. He was relieved that Clegg had remained resolutely silent as they drove into Brentwood. Daniel was in no mood to explain why the housekeeper was in police custody. He was also relieved that it was Monday, which meant that the Brentwood Constabulary would be fully staffed. Daniel didn't want to have to deal with Mrs. Buckley any longer than was absolutely necessary.

"Well, look what the cat dragged in," Sergeant Flint growled when Daniel and Jason walked into the Brentwood police station, Mrs. Buckley between them. "And here I thought you two were too grand for the likes of us."

Daniel had no desire to speak to Sergeant Flint or field his barbed comments, but despite the somber occasion, he looked forward to seeing some of the men he'd worked with before moving to London. Constable Pullman, who had often assisted Daniel in his investigations, and Constable Ingleby, who had been shot in the line of duty, looked happy and well as he greeted them.

"Is Detective Inspector Coleridge available?" Daniel asked Sergeant Flint.

"Unless you have an appointment, he won't be able to see you today."

"Is that so?" Daniel asked, wishing he could wipe the smirk off Flint's face.

"'Fraid so," Sergeant Flint drawled.

"Perhaps you can ask him," Daniel suggested, but Flint refused to budge.

The man was spiteful and unpleasant at the best of times, and this was his opportunity to exercise whatever limited power he thought he had. Constable Ingleby looked like he wanted to intervene but kept quiet after casting a questioning look toward the desk sergeant, who glared back, the warning in his gaze unmistakable. Flint would be sure to make things unpleasant for the young man if he undermined his authority, and helpful as he normally was, Constable Ingleby had no desire to get on the wrong side of the sergeant.

"Don't trouble yourself, Sergeant," Jason said, and walked right past Sergeant Flint.

Daniel took Mrs. Buckley by the arm and followed.

"You can't go back there," Flint hollered. "You have no authority here."

Jason ignored him, and Daniel followed suit. Annoying Sergeant Flint might be the only satisfying thing he did today.

"What's all this racket, Sergeant?" DI Coleridge demanded as he stepped out into the corridor. "Inspector Haze. Lord Redmond," he said, his face creasing into a smile of welcome and his generous moustache lifting at the corners. "What an unexpected pleasure."

DI Coleridge looked much as he had before. There was a bit more gray in his dark hair, and the crow's feet around his eyes were deeper and more plentiful, but his air of authority was undiminished, and his booming voice still filled Daniel with confidence.

"Good morning, sir," Daniel said. "It's a pleasure to see you again as well."

"I hear good things about you, Haze. Very good things, indeed. I would like to think that I had a hand in your meteoric rise, but you were always a clever lad. I knew that as soon as I met you. And Lord Redmond. If you ever decide to come back and settle into the life of a country gentlemen, do call on us. We could use the benefit of your expertise."

"Do you not employ a police surgeon?" Jason asked.

"We do, but he's rather a short-sighted fellow. Doesn't like to trouble himself with thinking. Mindless butchery is more his line," DI Coleridge said with disgust. "It's slim pickings around here, I'm afraid, when it comes to willing medical men. Still, he gets the job done."

"I will be sure to let you know if I relocate, Detective Inspector," Jason promised.

"So, how can I help you, gentlemen? Happy as I am to see you, I wouldn't be much of a detective if I failed to deduce that you're here for a reason, and not just to say hello. And I expect this lady has something to do with it."

Mrs. Buckley stared at her feet and kept silent. Daniel couldn't help but wonder what was going through her mind. Surely she would have declared her innocence if she hadn't attempted to poison them, but the housekeeper hadn't said a word, either in her own defense or by way of a confession.

"Inspector, we're here to beg a favor," Daniel said. "Perhaps we can speak in private."

"Of course," DI Coleridge said.

"You go on," Jason said. "I'll wait out here."

Daniel followed DI Coleridge into his office and shut the door. "I'm afraid we're outside our jurisdiction, but the woman you saw attempted to murder me and Lord Redmond last night. We also believe she might be responsible for three other deaths," Daniel said once they were both seated.

"What would you have me do?"

"We would like the use of an interview room, and then, if a charge is warranted, we would like you to arrest her and send her down to await trial."

"In that case, I would like one of my men to sit in on the interview."

"I have no objection," Daniel said.

Inspector Coleridge grinned. "I daresay you would prefer to keep Sergeant Flint precisely where he is, so I will ask Inspector Pullman to join you."

"Constable Pullman made inspector?" Daniel asked.

"Indeed, he has. He still has much to learn, but we were short-handed after you left us."

"I am sorry about that."

DI Coleridge shook his head. "Never apologize for seizing an opportunity, Daniel. There are few chances in life to improve one's circumstances, and a place with Scotland Yard is something to be proud of. I'm genuinely happy for you, and I think you're finally where you belong."

"Thank you, sir."

Daniel wasn't sure if DI Coleridge knew about Sarah's death and chose not to bring it up. His personal pain had nothing to do with the case, and although he liked and respected DI Coleridge, the two men were hardly friends.

"Don't leave without saying goodbye," DI Coleridge said when Daniel stood and turned to leave.

"I won't."

"And if you ever decide you've had enough of London, there will always be a place here for you, Daniel."

"Thank you, sir."

"Go on, then," DI Coleridge said, giving Daniel leave to get started.

Daniel saw Jason and Mrs. Buckley to an interview room, then went to find Inspector Pullman.

Chapter 36

"It's good to see you, Inspector Haze," Inspector Pullman said with a smile. "I owe you a thank you. If not for you leaving us, I'd still be in uniform."

"I doubt that," Daniel replied. "You were always going to achieve great things."

Inspector Pullman clapped Daniel on the shoulder. "You always were kind. That's what I liked about you. I just hope you're not planning a triumphant return to Essex. I rather enjoy being the rising star," he joked.

"I'm not coming back. This is a one-time occurrence."

"Good," Inspector Pullman said, his relief obvious. "Shall we get started, then?"

Inspector Pullman brought in an extra chair and sat in the corner, while Daniel and Jason settled across from Mrs. Buckley. Now that a reckoning was upon her, she looked frightened, especially once her gaze swept over the iron ring used for chaining cuffed suspects to the table. Mrs. Buckley wasn't a flight risk, nor did she appear bent on violence, so there was no reason to put her in cuffs, but the interview room was a stark reminder of things to come if she was charged.

"Mrs. Buckley, Inspector Haze was very ill last night. Based on his symptoms, I am of the opinion that he was poisoned," Jason said. "The only thing he had consumed that neither I nor Sir Lawrence had was the brandy. I removed the decanter, but I expect you had disposed of the contaminated brandy and replaced it with fresh stores before you went to bed last night."

Mrs. Buckley remained silent, her gaze glued to the iron ring.

"Your son-in-law was poisoned with brandy the night before," Jason said. "Was that a coincidence?"

Mrs. Buckley shrugged but refused to be drawn.

"The way I see it, only one person had reason to poison Emmett Doyle—your daughter," Jason said.

"We will be questioning Rose next," Daniel said.

"Rose is innocent," Mrs. Buckley cried.

"So was Emmett," Daniel said, hoping to get a reaction. He didn't have long to wait.

"Innocent?" Mrs. Buckley cried. "There was nothing innocent about Emmett. I begged Rose not to marry him. Even before his accident, Emmett had a cruel streak, but she refused to see it. Whenever he got angry, Rose blamed herself. 'What husband doesn't occasionally chastise his wife?' she'd say. 'It's not so bad,'" Mrs. Buckley recalled. "He'd mostly slap her across the face when he wasn't happy, but after the accident, things changed. He hit her with a closed fist and even took a belt to her. And this last time, he punched her in the stomach."

"There should be laws against spousal abuse," Jason said. "But as there aren't any, it often falls to the woman's family to intervene. Did you murder your daughter's husband to stop the abuse?"

Mrs. Buckley didn't reply.

"Mrs. Buckley, why did you not ask Sir Lawrence for help? He would have been glad to help his sister."

Mrs. Buckley's surprise was evident. "He told you, did he?"

"He did," Jason said. "And he made it clear that he would have done anything to help Rose."

Mrs. Buckley's gaze slid toward the high window, her shoulders slumping. She eventually turned back to face the men. "I didn't want to involve Sir Lawrence. If he had interfered in Rose's marriage, Lady Foxley might have thought there was something between them and the child Rose was carrying was Sir Lawrence's. She might have demanded that he throw Rose off the estate. Lucinda is a jealous, willful woman, and knowing that her husband had fathered two children with the cook didn't calm her fears."

"So, you thought it would be more prudent to murder your daughter's husband?" Daniel asked.

"I didn't kill Emmett, and neither did Rose. I'd stake my life on that, but you don't care to find out the truth. You need someone to pin the murders on so you can go back to London and congratulate yourselves on a job well done. I was afraid you'd choose Rose to be your scapegoat."

Having made her statement, Mrs. Buckley hunched her shoulders and pulled in her head, as if trying to disappear.

"What was in the brandy?" Jason asked.

"Arsenic. That's all I had to hand."

"Just to be clear," Daniel said, "you're admitting to the attempted murder of myself and Dr. Redmond, but you claim that you did not kill Emmett Doyle."

"That's correct, but I will confess to murdering Emmett if you go after Rose. I will not have her suffer any more than she already has."

"Mrs. Buckley, it is not our intention to charge just anyone. We must get to the truth. If you didn't kill Emmett as you claim, then who besides your daughter would have reason to want him out of the way?"

"I don't know," Mrs. Buckley cried. "I've thought of nothing else since I heard he was dead, but I don't know. Emmett was of no consequence. Who'd wish to kill him?"

"Did he owe money to anyone?" Daniel asked.

Mrs. Buckley shook her head. "No one in their right mind would lend Emmett money. They knew he'd spend it at the tavern."

"Was there any connection between Emmett Doyle and the Powers children?" Jason asked.

"Not that I know of, but those children were the only thing keeping Doris and Richard together. They weren't happy, and the deaths of the boys will tear them further apart."

"Why weren't they happy?" Jason asked, his ears pricking like a dog that had just picked up the scent of its prey.

"Because Doris was always a schemer, even when she was a girl. She seduced Sir Lawrence when he was hardly more than a boy, and then did it again when she wanted another child. The boys were her ticket to a better life."

"In what way?" Daniel asked.

"Sir Lawrence always said he would settle money on his boys once they came of age. Between Richard's wages and the boys' portion from Sir Lawrence, Doris would be sitting pretty. The baronet has his faults, but he honors his commitments. He loved those children, and he would have seen right by them, and by their mother."

Daniel looked at Jason, who gave a barely perceptible shrug. None of these revelations explained why the children had been murdered or what relevance their deaths had to the murder of Emmett Doyle, but at least it was now clear who'd tried to poison Daniel and Jason. Mrs. Buckley would not face a murder charge, but she would most likely spend the rest of her life in prison, a sentence that could be worse than death, especially for a woman.

Turning to Inspector Pullman, Daniel said, "She's all yours, Inspector."

Inspector Pullman pushed to his feet and approached the table. "Ann Buckley, you are hereby charged with the attempted murder of Inspector Haze and Dr. Redmond. Please come with me."

"Where are you taking me?" Mrs. Buckley asked fearfully.

"You will be sent to jail to await trial."

"And when will that be?"

"At the next assizes court, I imagine. Come now."

"I'm sorry," Mrs. Buckley cried. "I never meant either of you harm. I was just protecting my daughter."

"You could have just talked to us," Jason said, and walked out.

Chapter 37

Jason and Daniel adjourned to the Three Bells, a tavern the men from the constabulary frequented due to its proximity to the police station. It was too early for luncheon, but the owner was happy to provide a plate of bread and cheese and pull a few pints. He remembered Daniel well and was eager to hear about life in London and his work at Scotland Yard, and would have happily joined them for a pint had Daniel not explained that they were working a case and needed to speak privately.

Daniel reached for a piece of bread and helped himself to cheese, glad to put something into his empty stomach at long last. He felt queasy and lightheaded, and wondered how long the aftereffects of the arsenic would last. The bread helped, as did the ale, but mostly, Daniel was glad of Jason's presence. He didn't seem overly concerned with Daniel's symptoms, which meant that he was going to be just fine.

"Did you believe her?" Daniel asked Jason, who hadn't touched the food and sat staring fixedly out the window.

"I do," Jason said, reluctantly returning his attention to Daniel.

"But if she truly believed her daughter was innocent, why would she try to poison us?"

"Because she was afraid we'd fit Rose up for murder."

"Not without evidence, we wouldn't," Daniel protested.

"There are some coppers who don't need evidence. All they need is a convenient suspect, and Rose had good reason to want Emmett dead. If Mrs. Buckley's gamble had paid off, no one would be the wiser and you and I would be dead, our demise pointing to whoever killed John and Bertie."

Daniel shook his head. "I don't know about that, Jason. The fact that Mrs. Buckley didn't hesitate leads me to believe that she had reason to fear. Perhaps she really did think that Rose killed Emmett."

"Perhaps," Jason agreed. "Everyone has their breaking point. If she thought that Rose had reached hers, she was willing to do anything to protect her."

"You sound as if you sympathize with her."

"I sympathize with her dilemma, not her actions," Jason replied. "What would you do if Charlotte's husband was beating her?"

"Kill the man."

"Precisely," Jason said. "And maybe she did but doesn't want to admit to it. John's and Bertie's deaths handed Mrs. Buckley an opportunity, but even when faced with life in prison, she doesn't want her daughter to think she had murdered her husband and the father of her children."

Daniel nodded. "Yes, I suppose that's possible. Then she tried to kill again when she realized she had unwittingly framed her daughter."

"Which doesn't bring us any closer to figuring out who murdered John and Bertie," Jason said tiredly.

"Could it have been Mrs. Buckley?"

"What would Mrs. Buckley have to gain by the deaths of the children?"

"I don't know, but she did admit to giving them chocolates. If the chocolates were laced with poison, then the children would have died shortly after. It fits."

Jason reached for a piece of bread but made no move to take a bite. "Yes, it does, but I'm not sold on the idea that Mrs. Buckley is our killer."

"Then who is?"

"There's someone in that house who's watching and waiting, and I have a very bad feeling, Daniel."

"What sort of feeling?"

"I think there will be another death."

"Today?" Daniel cried.

Jason looked thoughtful as he considered the possibility. "The killer will not risk murdering anyone else as long as Mrs. Buckley is in custody. If they do, they will be showing their hand. They will wait until they deem it safe."

"Safe to do what?" Daniel wasn't sure he understood where Jason was going with this.

"To accomplish whatever it is they had set out to do."

"So, what do we do now?" Daniel asked.

"We should go back."

Chapter 38

When they returned to Fox Hollow, the household was in complete disarray. Rose was hysterical, saying over and over that her mother couldn't have done what she stood accused of and it was all a terrible misunderstanding. Doris Powers was calling for Mrs. Buckley to be strung up from the nearest tree because she had to have murdered her babies. Sir Lawrence appeared to be in shock, and Lucinda was furiously demanding that they leave Fox Hollow immediately. Only Richard Powers seemed grimly determined to keep everyone calm and had convinced Gwen and Amy to put something together for luncheon, since no one had eaten.

The only two people who seemed relatively unaffected were Helen Carlin and Bruno Wiley. Helen was in the kitchen, assembling tea, toast, and a bowl of fruit compote for her mistress, while Bruno was in Sir Lawrence's dressing room, taking an inventory of his shirts.

"Do I need to get my family away?" Sir Lawrence demanded. "I must keep Lucinda and the girls safe."

"Perhaps it would be best for all concerned if you were to spend a few days at Chadwick Manor," Jason said. "Just to be on the safe side. I will make sure Lucinda's bandage is firmly in place and give her something for the pain. The journey will be uncomfortable for her, and she must go straight to bed once she gets there."

"I will instruct Carlin and Wiley to pack our trunks. What will you do?" Sir Lawrence asked, rather belligerently. "Three people have died, and you two are only alive by the grace of God."

"We will continue to interview the servants," Jason replied. "Someone always knows something, even if they don't realize it's germane."

"You've already interviewed the servants," Sir Lawrence pointed out. "And you've learned nothing. Mrs. Buckley had you fooled," he added sadly. "She had us all fooled. The audacity—" Sir Lawrence shook his head at the thought. "I knew she was a strong woman, but to try to murder a detective from Scotland Yard takes a special kind of strength."

"Or desperation," Jason replied. "I think she truly believed she had to kill us to protect her daughter from prosecution."

"I would happily murder the wretch that took my boys from me," Sir Lawrence said. "With my bare hands."

He held up his hands, which were large and capable, and would probably choke the breath from anyone in mere moments.

Amy, who'd overheard him, scurried toward the dining room, her face ashen, the plate of sliced ham in her hands shaking precariously.

"Perhaps the servants will be more forthcoming with you and Lady Foxley out of the way," Daniel said.

"You think they're afraid to tell you the truth for fear of repercussions?" Sir Lawrence asked.

"It's possible," Jason replied. "Especially if they fear for their lives."

Sir Lawrence stared at Jason. "Are you suggesting that someone else might die?"

"I am."

"Carlin," Sir Lawrence roared. "We'll be leaving within the hour. See to your mistress."

"Yes, Sir Lawrence," Helen Carlin replied from the top of the stairs. "I will pack while her ladyship eats her breakfast."

"Address all your requests to Richard Powers when I'm not here," Sir Lawrence said, and sprinted up the stairs.

Chapter 39

Sir Lawrence and his family departed soon after, with Lucinda ensconced in a carriage with Helen Carlin and surrounded by pillows to minimize any jolting or swaying, and the wetnurse and the babies following with Sir Lawrence. Wiley rode on the bench of Lucinda's carriage, armed with a pistol, should any unforeseen threat arise. Once the family had departed, the servants scattered. Richard and Doris Powers had gone home to say a final goodbye to their children before they were buried tomorrow, and Rose had retreated to her cottage to try to make sense of her mother's actions. The rest of them crept about the house in obvious fear, probably feeling as if they had been abandoned to their fate.

"What now?" Daniel asked as he watched Gwen clear away the remainder of Sir Lawrence's meal.

"Now that Rose has had some time to calm down, I think it's time we paid her a visit," Jason said.

"I don't know what more she can tell us."

"Me neither, but her husband is dead, and her mother is in custody. Rose has been thrown off balance, so she might let something slip."

"Such as?" Daniel asked pessimistically.

"Do you have a better suggestion?" Jason replied. "I don't think the servants know anything. Amy and Gwen look terrified, and the scullery maid hasn't left the kitchen."

"I hate to say it, Jason, but I think we might have to abandon our investigation. Ransome expects me back tomorrow, and we're no closer to figuring out who killed John and Bertie than we were on Saturday. We have to accept the fact that not every case gets solved."

Jason didn't look overly surprised by Daniel's suggestion. "If we've made no progress by the end of the day, then we will return to London."

They left the house and walked across the park to the row of cottages that looked as desolate as the big house. No smoke rose from the chimneys, and no laundry hung in the back gardens. There was no smell of cooking or the laughter of playing children carried on the wind. The windows reflected the midday sun, and the birds squawked in the trees, but there were no signs of human habitation, the occupants hunkering indoors, closeted with their fear and grief.

The door to the Doyle's cottage stood partially open, but Jason knocked on the doorjamb, so as not to frighten Rose. She sat at the kitchen table, her hands folded before her, her gaze blank. She looked up when they entered, but there was no welcome this time, only resentment.

"Please leave," Rose said. "I have nothing more to say to you."

"We need to ask you a few more questions," Daniel said.

Rose's eyes welled with tears. "I want my mother," she wailed. "She was only trying to protect me."

"Rose, your mother tried to murder us. We can't simply dismiss the charges against her."

"She was scared," Rose cried.

"She must have had good reason to think you'd be arrested. Did you murder your husband?"

Rose shook her head. "I didn't kill Emmett."

"But your mother thought you did. Had something changed recently?" Jason asked.

Rose nodded miserably. "I didn't care if Emmett took out his anger on me. I could take it as long as I knew he was sorry afterwards and wanted to make it up to me. He was always so sweet after he'd hit me, so contrite. He was like the old Emmett, the one I fell in love with, and I talked myself into forgiving him. I made excuses," she admitted.

"But then you got with child," Jason said.

Rose nodded again. "When I told him, he flew into a rage and kicked me in the stomach. I thought I'd lose the baby for sure."

"Why didn't he want the child?" Daniel asked.

"It wasn't that he didn't want the child; it was the pregnancy that upset him. It took me a long time to recover from Daisy's birth, and she was a fussy baby. I was always tired and had no time for Emmett and his needs. He wanted my attention and got it by tormenting me. He liked to see my fear and hear me beg for forgiveness. He said he only hurt me to teach me to be a better wife." Rose drew in a quivering breath. "And then he started to take his anger out on Daisy. I was afraid for her and told her to hide whenever Emmett came home until I told her it was safe to come out."

"Is that where Daisy has been? Hiding?" Jason asked, his voice shaking with anger.

"She's afraid."

"Surely she knows that not all men are like her father," Daniel said.

Rose smiled sadly. "Daisy loves Richard Powers. She knows she can trust him. Richard never raised a hand to John and Bertie, no matter how badly they behaved sometimes. He just said they were little boys, and it was natural for them to act out. And Daisy adores Sir Lawrence. He is always kind to her. Never a cross word."

"So, if you didn't kill your husband and you don't believe your mother murdered him, whom do you suspect?" Daniel asked.

"I don't know," Rose cried. "I've thought of nothing else since you found him in that tunnel, and I still don't know. No one cared about Emmett. His existence made no difference to a living soul."

"It made a difference to someone," Jason replied. "They clearly wanted him out of the way." He reached for Rose's hand and squeezed it gently. "Rose, is there someone else?"

"Someone else?" she repeated, her expression one of utter incomprehension.

"Were you seeing someone else?" Jason asked, his gaze traveling to Rose's rounded belly.

"No. Emmett would have killed me if he thought I was unfaithful to him. He watched me all the time, except when he was dead to the world with drink."

"Might someone have wanted to free you?"

"You think someone would commit murder for me?" Rose asked, her mouth twisting with the absurdity of the suggestion.

"Did you speak to anyone about Emmett? Ask anyone for help?" Daniel pressed.

"I asked Richard to help me. He paid Emmett's wages directly to me, but that made Emmett even angrier. The last time Richard paid me, Emmett beat me black and blue and threw Daisy against the wall. That was when Richard suggested that Daisy and I move into the big house."

"Why didn't you?"

"Because it wouldn't keep me safe. I was still Emmett's wife in the eyes of God and man. Where I slept made no difference."

"You are free now," Jason said.

"And I would thank God for it if my mother wasn't in jail. If she's taken from me, I will be all alone in the world."

"You're not alone, Rose. Sir Lawrence will look after you and Daisy."

Rose nodded. "I suppose, but that's not the same as having a family of one's own."

"No, it isn't," Jason agreed. "Will you be all right on your own?"

"I'll have to be, won't I?" Rose replied. She looked utterly depleted. "I'm sorry, but I need to lie down."

Jason helped Rose to bed, and he and Daniel left the cottage, stepping outside into the gentle sunshine of the spring afternoon.

"We keep going around in circles," Daniel said wearily.

"Maybe not," Jason replied. "Rose said she spoke to Richard Powers about her troubles, and he withheld Emmett's wages and paid them to her instead. Emmett was livid and felt humiliated to be curtailed in that manner. Could it be that Emmett Doyle decided to revenge himself on Richard Powers by murdering John and Bertie?"

"And could it be that Richard Powers murdered him in turn? He knew about the tunnels and would probably think it a safe place to leave Emmett's corpse. He wouldn't want Rose or Daisy to stumble upon Emmett's remains." Daniel permitted himself a smile. "I think you've cracked it, Jason. At last, we have a motive for both murders."

"Let's go have a word with Richard Powers," Jason replied.

Chapter 40

The Powers' cottage was next door, the two properties divided by a low stone stile. There didn't appear to be anything on the other side of the divide, but Emmett Doyle had planted flowers on his side, the row of rosebushes interrupted by a stone bench beneath a white-painted arbor. It created a shady oasis in the summer, but just then, the alcove was clearly visible. A small girl sat on the bench, a well-loved doll clutched in her arms. She looked at the men shyly, and Jason immediately knew who she was. Like John and Bertie, Daisy resembled Sir Lawrence enough to mark her as a relation.

"Hello," Jason said as he approached the child. "You must be Daisy."

The little girl nodded. She seemed frightened and lonely, and was probably very confused by all the recent happenings at Fox Hollow.

"I'm Jason Redmond and this is Daniel Haze. We're guests of Sir Lawrence."

"I know," Daisy muttered. "You're the gentlemen from London."

"That's right," Jason replied. "We're looking into what happened to John and Bertie."

"And my father?" Daisy asked, fixing Jason with a worried stare.

"And your father. Are you all right, Daisy?" Jason asked.

"I want my mum to stop crying," Daisy said. "And I want John and Bertie to come back."

"I'm sorry," Jason said, "but John and Bertie are with God now."

"Are they really, or did you say that to make me feel less sad?"

"Did it help?"

"I suppose," Daisy replied.

"They really are with God, Daisy. And they wouldn't want you to be sad," Jason said.

"I don't want my father to come back. He frightens me."

"He won't trouble you again," Jason promised.

"My nan has gone away too. Will she be back soon?" Daisy asked, looking up at Jason with absolute trust.

"I don't know. But even if she's not, you must find ways to be happy."

Daisy looked dubious, then brightened. "I am to go to school in the village next year. I'll make new friends then. John was going to go too, but Bertie was too young. He'd have to wait two years." She smiled sadly. "This was going to be our last summer before school. I'm sad that the boys will not be there to play with me."

"What was your favorite game?" Jason asked.

"Hide-and-go-seek. That's what they were playing the day they died."

"Just the two of them?" Daniel asked.

Daisy nodded.

"But they were both in the trunk. Who were they hiding from?" Jason asked.

The child's smile was surprisingly bitter. "They were hiding from Miss Carlin."

"Why?"

"They were making too much noise, and Miss Carlin said they should go hide and she'd find them. She just wanted to keep them quite because Lady Foxley needed her rest."

"Did Miss Carlin play this game with you often?" Daniel asked.

"No, only sometimes. When we got too rowdy."

"And John and Bertie always agreed to play?"

"Most times. But sometimes, if we didn't want to play, Miss Carlin would give us a biscuit from her pretty tin. We would hide just to get the biscuits."

"What kind of biscuits were they?" Jason asked.

"They came from a shop in London," Daisy said dreamily. "Some were shortbread, and some were chocolate."

Jason and Daniel exchanged looks, then Jason turned back to Daisy. "Did Miss Carlin give the boys biscuits the day they died?"

Daisy nodded again. "I wanted a biscuit too, but I had to help Mum in the dairy, so I couldn't play. Mum said that we were going to bake a cake for Mrs. Powers, and I could lick the spoon, so I went."

"Did Miss Carlin know you were going to help your mum?" Daniel asked.

"She said I should be a good girl and run along and she'd give me a biscuit next time."

"Did Miss Carlin give you anything to drink?" Jason asked.

"No. Like what?"

"Like leftover chocolate."

Daisy shook her head. "No, but she gave some to John and Bertie. She said it was their secret and not to tell Mrs. Powers."

"Did she give them chocolate all the time?" Jason asked.

"No, just that day, because her ladyship wasn't well, and the boys had to keep quiet."

"Thank you, Daisy," Jason said. "Maybe you should go inside and sit with your mum for a little while. She'll be less sad with you there."

"All right," Daisy said, and slid off the bench. "Or maybe we'll just be sad together."

Chapter 41

"Don't you want to speak to Richard Powers?" Daniel asked when Jason began to walk toward the big house. He felt a sudden urgency to get back and knew Daniel would follow.

"Jason?" Daniel called.

"We can speak to Richard Powers later," Jason tossed over his shoulder. "There's something I'd like to do first. Let's get back to the house."

"But there's hardly anyone left," Daniel protested as he hurried after him.

"No matter."

Once they were back at Fox Hollow, Jason asked Amy where he could find Helen Carlin's room and hurried upstairs, Daniel right behind him. The room was on the uppermost floor, a tiny gabled closet with a narrow bed, a chest of drawers, and a chair. A tiny window was the only source of light and air, but at least Helen Carlin had a room to herself, unlike Gwen, Amy, and Dorothy, who had to share. Mr. Wylie had his own room as well, and Mr. Clegg and the second groom shared a room. Mrs. Buckley's bedroom was downstairs. The servants' rooms were kept unlocked at all times, so Jason and Daniel didn't need a key to enter.

"What are you hoping to find?" Daniel asked. He had remained just inside the doorway, since there wasn't enough space for two people inside the room.

"I'll know it when I see it," Jason replied.

He opened the drawers, but they were half-empty. Helen Carlin had taken nearly everything she owned to Chadwick Manor, leaving behind a spare collar, woolen stockings, and a lawn nightdress. There was also a muslin dress and a straw bonnet with a pale blue ribbon. Jason looked around the room, but there was little of Helen inside the mean little space. It was utilitarian and devoid of any decoration or personality. There were no photos or books, not even a cheerful picture or a sampler on the wall. The only thing that belonged to Helen was a lap desk that stood atop the drawers, her initials etched into the small brass plaque screwed to the top. It was a polished wooden box with a sloped top that held paper, pens, ink, and the owner's correspondence. Jason thought it must have been a gift from someone who'd loved Helen enough to engrave her initials into the lid, or maybe she had bought it for herself, a small concession to vanity for a woman who took her correspondence seriously. Most lap desks didn't lock, but Helen's desk was equipped with a lock, and Jason was certain she had taken the key with her.

"I need to see what's inside," Jason said as he lifted the desk to test its weight. It was heavier than one would expect a writing desk to be.

"What do you hope to find? Do you think Miss Carlin keeps a journal?" Daniel asked.

"Maybe."

Daniel left and returned a few minutes later with a hairpin. "This might work. Step aside."

He fiddled with the lock, but the hairpin proved useless. One would need a special lockpick to open the box.

"Can you find me a knife?" Jason asked.

He could see that Daniel was perplexed by his desire to examine the contents of the box and was hoping for an explanation, but Jason couldn't offer him one, at least not yet. All he knew was that he had to follow his hunch. According to Daisy, Helen Carlin had given the children both the biscuits and the remainder of the chocolate and had told them to go hide. Perhaps there was nothing to it and it had been just an innocent game designed to keep the children quiet, or perhaps the game had been meant to serve a purpose. Poison the children and send them to hide in a trunk, where they would die and remain undiscovered for hours, effectively removing Helen Carlin from suspicion, since no one would think to blame Lady Foxley's maid when they found the bodies much later.

The chocolate could be the culprit, but until Jason could pin down the motive, he wasn't going to accuse Miss Carlin of murder. And the only way he could discover her motive was to pry into her most secret place, the box she kept locked in her room. Perhaps she did keep a journal, or maybe there were letters inside that would explain her motives. It was also entirely possible that Helen Carlin had nothing whatsoever to do with the deaths of John and Bertie, and Daisy's revelations were of no account. After all, Helen had given the children biscuits before, and no one had become ill or died. Perhaps it did make more sense that Emmett Doyle had murdered the children to get back at Richard Powers, and Richard had got his revenge by poisoning the one thing Emmett loved most in the world, his brandy.

Jason supposed it would be poetic justice, but the one thing that didn't make sense was Emmett's choice of victim. Why murder Richard's stepsons when he could murder the man himself? It seemed unnecessarily cruel, even for a man who was violent toward his wife and child. Emmett's bouts of anger had been sporadic and spontaneous, but the murder of the boys had to have been planned. Emmett would have to have had the poison ready and presented it to the boys in edible form. He would have to have bided his time until the perfect opportunity presented itself and made sure his daughter wasn't there. Jason hadn't known Emmett Doyle well, but such patience and planning seemed beyond a man who had been ruled by his need for strong drink.

When Daniel returned with a small paring knife, Jason fitted the tip into one of the screws that held the lid in place and deftly unscrewed it. Eight screws later, he was able to lift the lid from the back without damaging the lock. The space was too narrow to take anything out, but it was enough to see what was inside the box and to slide two fingers through the opening.

"Anything interesting?" Daniel inquired. He seemed perplexed by Jason's determination to read Miss Carlin's correspondence but didn't question him. He knew Jason well enough to trust his instincts.

Jason pushed his fingers deeper into the box and touched the objects that were stored inside, then drew his fingers back, surprised by what he thought he'd found. He had little choice but to pry the lid off, breaking the lock in the process and splintering the front panel, but if his hunch was correct, a broken box would be the least of Helen Carlin's problems.

"What is that?" Daniel asked. He peered over Jason's shoulder as Jason took out a thick glass tube with a metal nozzle and sniffed the opening.

"This is a douching syringe," Jason replied. "And there are traces of condensation on the glass as well as a hint of vinegar, which suggests that it was used recently, then washed out and hidden away."

"Why would a respectable unmarried woman need a douching syringe?" Daniel asked.

"To avoid unwanted pregnancy and venereal disease. If she used it shortly after sexual congress, she would be able to flush out her lover's seed and disinfect the area. A strong solution of vinegar and water would do the job."

Jason looked around and spotted a bottle on the washstand. He pulled out the cork and sniffed. "Vinegar," he said. "Miss Carlin could easily explain the presence of vinegar in her room, since it's frequently used to get out stubborn stains, but she clearly had other uses for it."

"Did you know that was going to be there?" Daniel asked.

"No, I didn't, but knowing that Miss Carlin was having an affair gives her a solid motive."

"You think the children knew about her trysts?"

"It's possible. They might have seen something and threatened to tell, or maybe they unwittingly said something and made Miss Carlin realize she was in imminent danger of being dismissed without a reference."

Jason returned to the box and lifted out a pretty flowered tin. There were only two biscuits left, and they were a thing of beauty, pink-frosted hearts decorated with a delicate red-and-white pattern. There was no doubt that the biscuits were meant to commemorate St. Valentine's Day and had most likely been given to Helen Carlin by her lover.

Jason lifted out a biscuit and held it up for Daniel to see. "This hard pink shell would account for the particles I found in the boys' vomit. They had eaten the biscuits just before they died, or the sugar would have had time to dissolve."

"Which puts Helen Carlin square in the frame."

"Perhaps Emmett Doyle knew something as well and blackmailed Miss Carlin, which would explain why he also had to die."

"Do you think she was having a relationship with Sir Lawrence?"

"It's possible, but given that she has left the syringe behind, I don't think she is. Her lover is here, at Fox Hollow," Jason said. "She knew she wouldn't need it until she returned."

He turned his attention back to the desk. There were several rectangular compartments that contained writing paper, a bottle of ink, and two pens. A thin stack of letters tied with a pink ribbon was hidden in the bottommost compartment, a small envelope containing a valentine at the very top. Jason pulled out the card and opened it. It read:

If only...

Yours R

"There's only one man here with the initial R," Jason said. "Richard Powers."

"And, as they say, the proof is in the pudding," Daniel said, taking hold of the card and stuffing it into his breast pocket.

"Let's have that word with Richard Powers now," Jason said. He didn't bother to replace the items in the writing box. It was highly unlikely that Helen Carlin would be returning to her room.

Chapter 42

After checking at the cottage, they tracked Richard Powers to his office, his vacant gaze fixed on the wall opposite his desk, fingers drumming on the armrest of the chair. He quickly rearranged his expression into one of polite interest when Daniel and Jason entered the office, then looked over his desk, which was covered with ledgers, stacks of invoices, and hastily scribbled lists, judging by the impatient scroll coupled with erratically crossed-out items. Closing the ledger before him, he smiled politely.

"Gentlemen."

"Back to work so soon?" Daniel asked.

"I couldn't remain at home. Seeing the boys…" He shook his head. "It's more than I could bear."

"Mr. Powers, if we might ask you a few more questions," Daniel said, and settled into a guest chair, Jason taking the chair next to him.

"Of course," Richard Powers replied warily. "Although I see that your investigation appears to have stalled."

"On the contrary. We're very close to making an arrest."

"An arrest won't bring John and Bertie back." Richard choked up, then forced himself to continue. "Until a few days ago, we were a family. Now Doris and I are two people who don't have much to say to each other or a future to look forward to."

"Perhaps you can comfort each other in your grief," Jason said.

"Doris doesn't care to be comforted. At least not by me."

"Why is that?" Daniel inquired.

"Because she doesn't believe that my grief can match hers." Richard's eyes sparkled with tears. "I was the only father those boys had ever known, and they were the only children I was likely to have. They loved me, and I loved them. Is that not enough?"

"It is," Jason said. "Or it should be."

"So, whom do you suspect?" Richard Powers asked.

"How well do you know Miss Carlin?"

Richard's reaction was instantaneous. His eyes widened in disbelief, his face paled, and he gripped the armrest of his chair but immediately let go in a failed attempt to appear nonchalant.

"Not well. Miss Carlin keeps mostly to the house."

Jason's gaze slid toward the back room, which was furnished with several cabinets and a narrow cot.

Richard's gaze followed Jason's. "I kip in the office sometimes."

Jason walked into the back room and looked around, then opened a bottle that stood on a shelf and sniffed. He replaced the bottle on the shelf and reached for the second bottle, which he carried back into the office and set on Richard's desk.

"It's an odd thing to keep a bottle of vinegar in one's office."

"I use it to clean the windows," Richard Powers replied, but a deep red flush spread across his cheeks.

"Do you indeed?" Daniel asked, nailing the man with his gaze.

"Or perhaps your lover used it after your trysts. I expect she brought the douching syringe with her, so as not to take any chances," Jason said.

"My lover?" Richard muttered.

Daniel pulled out the Valentine's Day card and pushed it across the desk. Richard Powers didn't need to open the envelope. He knew what it contained just as surely as he knew that he had been found out.

"I was lonely," he exclaimed. "And Helen was so…"

"So what?" Jason asked. "Trusting? Vulnerable? Willing?"

"Adoring," Richard replied at last. "She made me feel like I was interesting and worthy of love. Doris has barely looked at me these past few years."

"Why? You're a handsome man who holds a respectable position. What was it that made your wife turn away from you?"

"She turned away from me because I'm not Larry," Richard cried, his pain right there in his eyes. "Doris tried to love me, but the heart wants what it wants, and what Doris wants is not me."

"And Helen wanted you?" Daniel asked.

Richard nodded. "She said we should run away together. Start a new life in a place where no one knows us. We could pretend to be married, and no one would know different."

"And what did you say, Mr. Powers?"

"I told her it was a lovely dream, but I couldn't do that to the boys. I would never leave them behind."

"And was that the real reason you turned her down?" Jason asked. He was studying Richard Powers, his head tilted to the side, but Daniel couldn't tell if he felt sympathy for the man or wanted to thump him.

"Yes and no," Richard said. "I enjoyed spending time with Helen, but what we had was enough. The truth is that I love Doris. I always have. And I loved being a father. Helen didn't want to have children, but she did want marriage, so our ruse wouldn't be enough for her in the end." Richard paused and then added, "And to be honest, I didn't want to leave Fox Hollow. I hold a respectable position, and even though Sir Lawrence can never openly acknowledge me as his brother, we have a good relationship, and I value that."

"And how did Helen take your refusal?" Jason asked. He was still watching Richard Powers intently, as if trying to figure out if the man was really that obtuse or that innocent of the events he'd set in motion.

"She was disappointed but said she understood." Richard smiled ruefully. "She said she loved me all the more because my devotion to the boys proved I had a sense of honor and would never shirk my duty. She's a remarkable woman."

"Yes, she is," Jason agreed. "Will you continue the affair when she returns to Fox Hollow?"

"If she's amenable," Richard replied. "I know it's wrong, but if we're both willing, what's the harm?"

"What harm, indeed?" Daniel muttered under his breath.

"Thank you, Mr. Powers. You've been most helpful," Jason said, and stood.

"Wait, why did you ask about Helen?" Richard exclaimed, the realization that the affair wasn't all he had to worry about finally sinking in.

"We believe Helen Carlin was the one who poisoned the boys," Daniel said.

"But why?" Richard cried. He seemed genuinely horrified, and Daniel actually felt sympathy for the man.

Many a man had an affair, but few paid with the lives of the children they loved and the stability of their marriage. Once the truth came out, Doris would never take her husband back, no matter how ardently he proclaimed his innocence of the plot. Richard's affair with Helen Carlin had robbed Doris of her children, and she would never forget or forgive.

"I expect Miss Carlin wanted more than sordid trysts in a back room," Daniel said.

"But even if we ran away together, it'd still be sordid. I'm married. Lying doesn't change that." Richard went even paler as he met Jason's piercing gaze and understanding finally dawned. "She was going to murder Doris," he whispered.

"Most likely," Jason said. "Maybe not right away and not using the same method, but I think it's safe to say that your wife wouldn't be long for this world."

"Helen could never," Richard sputtered, but the horror in his eyes told a different story. "Could she?" he muttered. "Did she really murder two innocent children to set me free?"

"There's a fine line between adoration and obsession," Jason said, his voice uncharacteristically flat. He'd clearly had enough of this case and the selfish people whose singlemindedness had resulted in the deaths of two children.

"What will happen to Helen?"

"If found guilty of murder, she will hang."

"Dear God," Richard moaned. "What have I done?"

"You had no way of knowing that your lover would resort to murder," Daniel said. He wasn't sure why he was trying to comfort the man, but the weight of guilt they had just draped over his shoulders was sure to crush him. Daniel didn't think he deserved that.

"I allowed Helen to believe that I loved her and that things would be different if I were free. I gave her a motive," Richard cried. He was sobbing now, spittle flying from his mouth as he bawled unashamedly. "And Doris… Dear God, what will I tell Doris?"

"Mr. Powers, you were unfaithful and deceitful, but you didn't murder those boys," Jason said. "You need to remember that."

Richard did not reply. He was lost in his misery and hardly seemed to notice when Jason and Daniel left.

"We need to get to Brentwood," Daniel said as soon as they were outside. "But the Foxleys have taken both carriages."

"So we travel on horseback," Jason said. "There are sure to be horses in the stable." He took out his pocket watch and consulted the time. "We had better hurry if we hope to take Helen Carlin into custody tonight."

Chapter 43

They arrived at Chadwick Manor not long after the family since the Foxleys' progress had been laboriously slow, the carriages hampered by the rain that had begun to fall and turned into a downpour by mid-afternoon. The rain had all but stopped by the time Daniel and Jason left Brentwood Constabulary, DI Coleridge's borrowed brougham followed by the police wagon driven by Inspector Pullman and Constable Ingleby. Llewelyn shot Jason and Daniel a filthy look but invited them into the drawing room, where a warm fire blazed in the grate and Sir Lawrence and Harry Chadwick sat in tufted wingchairs, enjoying a restorative drink.

"Lord Redmond. Inspector Haze," Sir Lawrence exclaimed. "Has something happened? I wasn't expecting to see you again today." His gaze traveled to the two policemen who'd taken up a position in the foyer but were clearly visible through the open door of the drawing room.

"I'm afraid there have been some new developments," Daniel replied.

"Sir Lawrence was just telling me about the housekeeper," Harry Chadwick said excitedly. "Terrible business. I'm relieved to see you're both well."

"This is not about Mrs. Buckley, is it?" Sir Lawrence asked, his jaw stiffening with tension as the implication of their presence must have dawned on him. He gripped the armrests of his chair, his shoulders flexing. One word from Daniel and he would be on the move, ready to place himself between his defenseless family and any danger they might be in.

Harry looked from Daniel to Jason, his gaze searching. "Have you made another arrest?" he exclaimed, obviously failing to make the connection between the extra men and the reason they were in his home. "Is that what you've come to tell us?"

"Not quite, Mr. Chadwick," Jason said. "But we're close."

Apparently noting Jason's calm demeanor, Sir Lawrence relaxed somewhat, seemingly inferring that there was no immediate threat to Lucinda and the girls.

"Sir Lawrence, we'd like a word with Miss Carlin," Daniel explained.

"Miss Carlin is unpacking Lucinda." Sir Lawrence looked disappointed and confused, his initial alarm replaced by an air of resignation. "I thought you'd spoken to her already."

"We have," Daniel said. "But there are a few more questions we'd like to put to her. Mr. Chadwick, if you would instruct Llewelyn to ask Miss Carlin to join us."

"We would appreciate the use of the library, Mr. Chadwick. We need to speak to the lady in private," Jason added.

Both Harry and Sir Lawrence appeared perplexed, since Daniel had made no move to arrest anyone despite bringing reinforcements and seemed only to want to clarify a few points, but Daniel wasn't ready to explain himself. The policemen were there as a precaution, close by if needed but not so close that Miss Carlin would spot them. The library faced the back of the house, and snob that Llewelyn was, he would almost certainly insist that Miss Carlin use the servants' stairs.

"Of course. The library is at your disposal, gentlemen. Would you care for a drink while you wait?" Harry asked politely.

On any other day, Daniel would have refused, but his clothes were damp, he hadn't eaten in hours, and the prospect of finally bringing this case to its conclusion had made him jittery.

"Why not?" he said, and turned to Jason, who nodded. He seemed outwardly composed, but Daniel thought Jason was feeling just as anxious, his need to bring the children's killer to justice bubbling just beneath the surface.

Harry walked over to the wall and yanked on the bellpull. A parlormaid Daniel hadn't seen before appeared as if by magic. She made her expression deliberately bland as she passed through the door, but Daniel had noticed her shock when she'd spotted the policemen. She had to be wondering what was afoot but could hardly inquire and would have to wait for Llewelyn to address the staff later on.

"Sir," she said by way of greeting, her gaze fixed on Harry Chadwick since her loyalty was to him.

"Tell Llewelyn to fetch Miss Carlin and bring her directly to the library. She's with Lady Foxley. Say only that Sir Lawrence wishes to see her," Harry added, having finally caught on that it was best to avoid any unpleasantness.

"Yes, sir."

"Whisky all right?" Harry asked once the parlormaid had departed.

"Fine," Jason replied.

Harry walked over to the drinks cabinet, poured four large whiskies, and handed them around. The men drank in silence, each lost in his own thoughts.

"If you will excuse us, gentlemen," Jason said once they finished their drinks. "Inspector Haze and I have an interview to conduct."

"Of course," Harry said. "If there's anything you require—"

"We'll be sure to let you know," Jason replied. "Thank you."

The fire in the library had not been lit and the room was cold and dark, the bare branches swaying ominously beyond the window and nearly obscuring the darkening sky. The parlormaid they had seen earlier hurried in after them, smiled apologetically, and turned on the gas lamps before lighting the fire that had been laid in the grate. She cast a curious glance toward the men, then left as quickly as she had arrived, shutting the door behind her. It would take time for the room to warm, but the gaslight and the glowing flames made it feel more welcoming, the setting perfect for a private conversation.

Daniel moved a chair as close to the flames as safety would permit and sank into its tufted embrace. The wool of his trousers steamed, and he held out his cold hands to the flames. Jason remained standing, his hands clasped behind his back, his gaze fixed on the door. He looked tired and tense but also determined to get a result.

"Miss Carlin," Llewelyn announced gravely as he threw open the door.

Miss Carlin balked at the sight of the two investigators but managed to put on a small smile as she entered the room.

"Good afternoon, gentlemen. How can I be of service?"

She looked as bland and meek as the parlormaid and probably assumed, or more likely hoped, that their inquiry had something to do with her mistress and she would return upstairs in a matter of minutes. Jason smiled at Miss Carlin politely and invited her to sit down. She took the chair across from Daniel and folded her hands in her lap, her demeanor as prim and proper as if she were a schoolgirl.

"Miss Carlin, we know all about your relationship with Richard Powers and your plans to run away together," Daniel said, watching Miss Carlin intently for any change in expression.

Her eyes widened in feigned surprise, her demeanor becoming haughty and defensive. "I'm sure I don't know what you mean, Inspector."

"There's no use denying the allegation. Mr. Powers admitted to the affair," Daniel replied.

Helen Carlin tilted her head to the side, her gaze challenging Daniel. "All right. Yes, Richard Powers and I had a romantic relationship. It might be a sin in the eyes of God, but last I checked, a liaison between consenting parties was not a crime."

"No, but murder is," Jason stated flatly.

"I didn't murder anyone, Dr. Redmond," Helen Carlin snapped.

"You gave John and Bertie biscuits, and chocolate laced with poison, then told them to go hide, knowing all along that they would die alone and in agony," Jason ground out. "The pink glaze was present in their vomit, as was chocolate residue."

Daniel thought that Jason would gladly throttle the woman if he could square it with his conscience, but all he could do was prove her guilt and leave the punishment to the law.

Miss Carlin shrugged, her indifference maddening. "I gave them biscuits from time to time. What of it? Why would I wish to poison two little boys?"

"Because as long as John and Bertie were alive, your lover would never consent to leave Fox Hollow," Daniel replied.

Helen scoffed. "You have no proof of any wrongdoing. I gave the children a biscuit each, and I allowed them to finish the chocolate. I freely admit that. But I do not admit to poisoning them."

"You don't need to," Jason replied. He withdrew a small packet from his pocket. "I found this in your writing desk."

Helen Carlin paled, and her hands began to tremble. "You searched my writing desk?" she choked out, her disbelief almost comical after the bravura performance of innocence.

"We did, and a revelation it was too," Jason said, allowing his words to sink in.

Helen Carlin looked positively ill.

"Dried water hemlock," Jason said as he held up the packet. "I expect you picked the flowers months ago and kept them on hand."

Helen remained mute, her expression mutinous.

"All parts of the plant are poisonous, but the seeds are especially deadly," Jason continued. "All you had to do was mix a few flowerheads into the chocolate, and the children wouldn't have noticed. The chocolate is thick and sweet and would mask any bitter taste, and the petals would have dissolved in the liquid, leaving no trace."

"That's hardly proof," Helen sputtered at last. "I kept the packet safely locked in my writing desk, and as you have just pointed out, there was no trace of poison in the chocolate. Your accusation is based on nothing but supposition."

"What did you intend to do with the poison, then?" Jason asked conversationally.

Helen looked away, seemingly ashamed. "It was for me," she said.

"Were you thinking of taking your own life?"

"There was a time when I was deeply unhappy," Helen admitted softly. "There were moments when an easy out seemed preferable to a life of bitter disappointment. But then I met Richard. I should have thrown the poison away. I don't know why I didn't, but the children had no access to it, and you can't prove I gave it to them," she stated in a firm voice.

"But we can, Miss Carlin," Jason replied. "In themselves the items might appear harmless, but when taken together, they paint a clear picture."

"And what picture will you be painting, Dr. Redmond?" Helen demanded hotly.

"We have the valentine signed by Richard Powers, the biscuits decorated with the pink glaze I found in the boys' vomit, the douching syringe you used to prevent pregnancy, and the packet of hemlock, all hidden away in your writing desk. And most damning of all, we have Richard's admission that you were sexually involved and had discussed a possible future to tie it all together. Did you really think he would forgive you for murdering his children?"

"They weren't even his," Helen said, then remembered herself and went quiet before she further incriminated herself.

"Mr. Powers had no plans to leave Fox Hollow, Miss Carlin," Daniel said.

"He said he loved me and wanted to make a life with me," Helen countered. "He said he wished he'd met me first." This admission only pointed to her guilt, but her wounded pride seemed to get the better of her, and she felt the need to set the record straight.

"So, the plan was to dispose of the children, then murder Doris Powers a few months later? A grieving mother taking her own life," Jason mused. "All perfectly natural. Richard Powers would be free to marry, and you could move into the cottage and leave Lady Foxley's employ. I daresay she ran you ragged and was sure to become even more demanding once the babies were born."

"Is it so wrong to long for a life of one's own?" Helen cried, her eyes brimming with tears. "Do you have any idea what it's like to always be at the mercy of someone else? I had to wait hand and foot on that spoiled brat, wait like a faithful dog to be summoned to Richard's office, and all the while try to keep clear of Sir Lawrence and Mrs. Buckley, in case they began to suspect that I was up to something. It wasn't easy, but that doesn't mean I was bent on murder."

"Weren't you?" Jason taunted. "Why did you poison Emmett Doyle? What was his role in your plan? Or was he simply a decoy meant to throw us off the scent?"

"Emmett Doyle was a horrid man, much like my father, who used me as a punching bag whenever life disappointed him, but I didn't kill him. Why would I? I had nothing to gain from Emmett's death."

"You used Emmett's death to confuse our investigation," Daniel replied.

"Have you considered the possibility that someone else might have used John's and Bertie's deaths to their advantage?" Helen challenged him.

"Like who?" Jason asked, even though both he and Daniel knew precisely who Helen Carlin was referring to.

"Like Rose Doyle. Emmett made her life a misery. Anyone with eyes in their head could see that. I wouldn't be surprised if she finally snapped. Clearly her mother thought the same thing, or she wouldn't have tried to poison you."

"There's no evidence that Rose Doyle poisoned her husband," Daniel said. "And Mrs. Buckley will spend the rest of her life in prison because of what she did."

Helen Carlin smiled mirthlessly, the grin making her look unexpectedly ugly. "Mrs. Buckley is a fool. Had she done nothing, you two would have given up and left."

"Now there you're wrong, Miss Carlin," Jason replied. "Few people are clever enough to commit the perfect crime. There's always something or someone that gives them away. In your case, it was a comment made by a five-year-old girl."

Helen's grin slipped off her face. "Daisy?" she whispered.

"That's right. It was Daisy who told us you sometimes gave the boys biscuits and asked them to go hide."

"I'm surprised you were willing to waste such a lovely token from your lover on children you despised," Daniel mused.

"I usually gave them biscuits from Lady Foxley's tin, but it was empty. The boys were making too much noise in the corridor, so I gave them my Valentine's Day biscuits to keep them quiet," Helen rushed to explain.

"And lucky for us that you did," Jason said. "If not for the pink glaze, we might have never made the connection."

"It's not a crime to give children a treat," Helen exclaimed.

"No, it isn't, but you had motive, means, and opportunity. You saw the chance for a better life, and you took it," Daniel said. "But it seems your plan backfired."

Helen's face twisted with derision. "You can't prove any of this, Inspector."

"Richard Powers' testimony will go a long way toward proving your guilt."

"Richard will never testify against me, and without his testimony, you have nothing but a string of unrelated events."

It was true that Richard Powers' testimony would make or break the case since the affair alone or the possession of poison that was kept under lock and key would be viewed as circumstantial. It was Richard's refusal to leave the boys that had provided Helen Carlin with a motive, but there was no telling whether Richard Powers would testify. He might want to save his lover from the gallows or more likely choose to absolve himself of guilt. To admit that he had given Helen a motive would make him feel as guilty of the boys' deaths as if he had poisoned them himself. It would be up to the court to make a case against Helen Carlin, but Daniel wasn't about to be tricked into letting her go. If there was such a thing as a copper's instinct, he felt it then. He was certain that Helen Carlin was guilty, and he saw the same conviction in Jason's eyes.

Daniel stood and faced the suspect. "Helen Carlin, I hereby charge you with three counts of murder," he said, and slipped the cuffs he'd pulled from his pocket onto her wrists.

"What happens now?" Helen asked. She seemed calm once more. Either she was trying to mask her feelings, or she truly believed that Richard Powers would never testify against her and the case would be dismissed due to lack of evidence.

"Inspector Pullman will take you into custody. You will be tried here in Essex."

Miss Carlin lifted her chin and stared them down. "Mark my words, Inspector, I will be found innocent."

"Your punishment is a matter for the law," Daniel said. "And your conscience is something you must live with, whether you are convicted of murder or not."

"May I fetch my coat and hat?"

"I will accompany you." Daniel wasn't about to give this woman a chance to escape justice or to poison herself. It would be just like her to die on her own terms and cheat John and Bertie's parents of seeing justice done.

"I will inform Sir Lawrence we've made an arrest," Jason said as he followed Daniel and Miss Carlin from the library.

"Do you think Miss Carlin might be right?" Daniel asked once he and Jason were finally on their way back to London. "Could she really go free?"

"I think that all depends on her counsel. A clever lawyer can endeavor to convince the court that there's no physical proof that Helen Carlin poisoned either the boys or Emmett Doyle."

"Is there nothing we can do to obtain a confession?"

"Helen Carlin is too clever to offer proof of her guilt, especially now that she knows precisely what we have on her," Jason said. "If she maintains that she gave the children the biscuits and chocolate but didn't poison them, she might be found innocent. After all, no one saw her add the poison, and there was nothing left of the chocolate. The proof went down the drain. If Richard

Powers refuses to testify, there's no compelling motive for the murders. And no one saw Miss Carlin with Emmett Doyle."

Daniel shook his head. "I have a bad feeling about this, Jason."

"So do I, but the rest is up to the law. And Richard Powers."

"I'm sorry you missed Easter with your family," Daniel said. "I hope Katherine won't be too angry with me."

Jason checked his watch. "We can still enjoy a late supper. I bet Mrs. Dodson made enough food to feed an army and there is plenty left. And once we've eaten, I will write to Flora Tarrant and invite her to come to London for an interview, but only if you want me to."

"Will her parents not object?"

"I think Flora will do what she wants, and her parents will feel safer in the knowledge that Flora is under the protection of a policeman."

"Need I remind you that Rebecca resided under my roof when she was murdered?" Daniel pointed out morosely.

"Rebecca's death is not on you, Daniel. The die had been cast long before you met. Things will be different with Flora, if you choose to give her a chance."

Daniel smiled for the first time that day. "Okay, let's do it."

"Glad to see you're adopting my American lingo," Jason replied, and grinned. "I think you two will make a good team."

"What makes you so certain that Flora is right for the job?"

"You need a strong, capable woman in your life who could also become a trusted friend."

"Amen to that," Daniel said with feeling. "And one without a secret history."

"As far as I know, Flora is a clean slate, at least where romantic entanglements are concerned. I can't say the same for her opinions."

"Opinions I can deal with. Ex-lovers bent on revenge is an entirely different matter."

Chapter 44

June 1869

Daniel came downstairs early and settled at the dining room table. He liked to read the paper in peace while enjoying his breakfast. Flora Tarrant was an absolute gem, as she was bound to be when hand-picked by Jason, but unlike Sarah and Rebecca, who had both been somewhat reticent in their opinions, Flora loved to debate. She had an opinion on everything and wasn't shy about sharing it with Daniel. At times he almost felt as if he worked for her and not the other way around. Flora had filled the house with her gregarious presence, and Daniel found that he was no longer mired in grief, and to his utter surprise, he laughed more often and actually looked forward to his verbal duels with Flora.

Charlotte adored Flora and had blossomed in her care, and for the first time in years, Daniel felt as if he was once again part of a family. Flora planned outings for his days off, and the three of them explored London's parks, zoological gardens, and any attraction suitable for a child of three. Those were happy days filled with harmony and joy, and Daniel prayed that they would last forever.

"Ah, there you are, Inspector," Flora said as she walked into the dining room and settled in her usual seat. "Just toast please, Grace. And some of that wonderful marmalade you made last week. I swear, you are a marvel in the kitchen. Isn't she, Inspector? That marmalade is ambrosia. Just the right balance of sweet and tangy."

"Of course, Miss Tarrant." Grace beamed and hurried to the kitchen to prepare Flora's breakfast. Daniel suspected that Grace would walk over hot coals for Flora and never notice the heat.

"So, did I give you long enough to read your dreary paper?" Flora teased.

"You did, and I thank you," Daniel replied with a smile.

"Anything you care to share?"

"There's a short article about the trial of Helen Carlin, compliments of Superintendent Ransome. He made certain to point out that Scotland Yard was responsible for the arrest."

"It's important to give credit where credit is due, and justice for two little boys is the sort of thing that sells papers. Ransome knows that."

"It feels wrong to profit from their deaths," Daniel said.

He had attended the funeral along with Jason and had been embarrassed to cry until he noticed Jason crying freely, unashamed to show emotion. Giving vent to his pent-up feelings wouldn't bring the boys back, but it had brought Daniel some relief.

"People need to feel reassured that the monsters are consigned to hell, where they belong," Flora said. "Thank God Helen Carlin wasn't found innocent."

Daniel decided not to tell Flora that just such an outcome had nearly come to pass. He and Jason had attended the trial and by the third day had been certain that Helen Carlin would be exonerated since Richard Powers had declined to testify. Despite the judge's obvious disapproval of Helen's lascivious behavior and her willingness to lead a married man astray, there simply hadn't been enough evidence to conclusively prove that she had murdered the children or Emmett Doyle. Helen's lawyer had looked smug, Helen herself practically crowing with delight at the prosecution's lack of a solid case.

But all that had changed when Richard Powers entered the courtroom. He had aged noticeably since Daniel had seen him at the funeral. His face was very thin, his cheekbones angular and sharp, and his nose more hooked in a face that was nearly devoid of flesh. But what had shocked Daniel most was the dead-eyed stare that told him everything he needed to know. He'd seen that stare many times before, in individuals who were technically still alive but were already gone, their desire to go on eradicated by whatever tragedy had robbed them of hope. Richard Powers had wrestled with his conscience and had admitted his culpability to himself. And having done that, he was now ready to have his say.

Richard Powers took the stand, and when he spoke, his voice was low, his eyes suddenly blazing, and his gaze fixed on Helen's pallid face as if he could set her alight with the sheer force of his resolve. Everyone had grown quiet, their rapt attention fixed on the drama playing out before them. The observers were like vultures anticipating fresh carrion.

"I never loved you, Helen," Richard said. "Not for a second. You were a distraction, a tool I used to assuage my loneliness. The more time I spent with you, the more I realized how much I loved my wife and how desperately I wanted to win back her love and repair our family. I only told you I couldn't leave Doris and the boys to spare your feelings, but even though I knew from the first that you were a callous bitch, I never took you for someone capable of cold-blooded murder. Did you really think that any future happiness could be bought with the lives of two children?" Richard cried, his voice shaking with anger. "Did you imagine I'd thank you for setting me free?"

Helen was trembling, her lips quivering as she tried to hold back tears. The space between her and Richard was charged, the air vibrating with something so powerful, everyone in that courtroom could undoubtedly feel it and held their breath to see what would happen next. There wasn't a sound, not a cough or a sigh, not the rustling of a newspaper or an urgent whisper. Everyone was mesmerized, riveted by this two-actor play.

"If you have any decency, own up to what you have done," Richard said at last. "It's not too late to redeem yourself and save your soul."

Perhaps if anyone had made a sound or had done something to break the tension, Helen would have come to her senses and brazened out Richard's challenge, but she couldn't bear the weight of Richard's scorn. She shut her eyes and nodded slowly, as if in a trance. The words were barely audible when she spoke.

"I did it because I loved you, and now I confess for the same reason, to bring you peace." Helen's head shot up, and she fixed the prosecutor with an unflinching gaze. "I'm guilty of the murders of John and Albert Powers."

The courtroom erupted, but everyone quieted down when the judge brought down his gavel and banged it repeatedly to get their attention.

"I will have silence," he roared. He waited until the uproar had subsided, then placed the all-too-familiar black square atop his wig. Someone in the courtroom gasped, but most people nodded with approval, believing this to be the only acceptable outcome.

"Helen Carlin, I find you guilty of the murders of John and Albert Powers. You will be taken to a place of execution, whence you shall be hanged by the neck until you are dead."

"I'm dead already," Helen said, and walked out of the courtroom toward the waiting police wagon that would take her back to prison.

It was an outcome Daniel and Jason had hoped for, but Daniel was still shaken when he exited the courtroom, amazed that a woman of Helen Carlin's will had been persuaded to admit her guilt. Perhaps she really had loved Richard Powers, or perhaps in those final moments, she had come to realize she would never find peace or the life she craved and needed to make things right with God. Whatever her reasons, she had made her choice, and Richard Powers had made his. His body was found the following day by Mr. Clegg. Richard had hanged himself in his office, the suicide note he'd left begging Doris for forgiveness and urging her to start again.

Helen Carlin's execution was scheduled for next week. Neither Daniel nor Jason would attend, but Daniel was sure that Doris Powers would be there, front and center. She would want her face to be the last thing Helen saw before she died and for her to know that she wasn't forgiven. Daniel couldn't say he blamed her. Helen had cost Doris not only her children but her husband and whatever future they might have had together, and although Doris probably hoped that Helen Carlin would go straight to hell, Doris was in a hell of her own. Perhaps someday she would find peace, but that day wouldn't come for a long while yet. Maybe never.

Daniel set aside the paper and turned to Flora. He was ready to put the murders at Fox Hollow behind him and focus on his own little family. He was just about to ask Flora what she had planned for them that week when there was a knock at the door. Daniel and Flora exchanged looks before Daniel pushed back his chair and got to his feet.

"Constable Putney for you, sir," Grace said as she entered the room with a rack of toast and a dish of marmalade.

"Thank you, Grace."

Daniel went out into the foyer to find Constable Putney stepping from foot to foot. The young man looked apologetic, as much about the earliness of the hour as about the news he had no doubt brought with him.

"I'm sorry to disturb you on your day off, Inspector Haze, but Superintendent Ransome sent me to fetch you."

"What's happened, Constable?"

"A possible murder, sir."

"Possible?"

"I don't believe there's a body."

"Where did this hypothetical murder take place?" Daniel asked.

Constable Putney clearly didn't know what hypothetical meant but got the gist of the question.

"I really don't know, sir. Superintendent Ransome said he will explain the situation in person. He's sent Constable Ramsey to get Lord Redmond. The superintendent wants him on this case."

"Do you know anything at all of what has transpired, Constable Putney?" Daniel asked, annoyed to be kept in the dark.

The young man smiled ruefully. "It's all very hush hush, Inspector Haze," he said. "Not even Sergeant Meadows knows the details."

"All right. Just give me a moment."

"Take as long as you need, sir. I don't think there's any real urgency," Constable Putney replied. "On account of there being no body, you understand."

Daniel didn't understand, but it made no sense to grill the young man. He clearly didn't know anything. Daniel returned to the dining room, hastily finished his breakfast, then said goodbye to Flora and rejoined Constable Putney in the foyer, where Grace was already waiting with his coat and hat, her eyes twinkling with curiosity. Daniel had to admit that he was quite intrigued himself. He was eager to hear the details and discuss the case with Jason once they were on their way to the crime scene, if there even was one. As he walked down the steps and approached the waiting cab, Daniel felt a tingle of anticipation. A new case was about to begin.

Epilogue

Lucinda Foxley smiled at her babies and handed them off to the wetnurse, who took them away for their feeding. Reclining against the pillows, she gazed toward the window, glad to see that the rain had stopped, and the sun was shining. She would have her breakfast, then go for a walk. Or maybe even a ride. The incision had healed cleanly, and she felt more herself than she had in months. Perhaps Larry would come with her. His grief over the boys' deaths had abated somewhat, and life at Fox Hollow was running smoothly once again now that the trial was behind them.

Lucinda heard footsteps and turned toward the door, assuming it was her new lady's maid come to bring her breakfast, but it was Rose Doyle, who'd taken over as housekeeper. Rose was near her time, her belly entering the room before she did. Rose missed her mother and still carried guilt over her incarceration, but like Lawrence, she was starting to come around to the new normal that life had handed them.

"I thought you might want to see this, my lady," Rose said, and handed Lucinda a folded newspaper.

Lawrence did not permit Lucinda to read the papers, but he often left them lying around, and the servants used them when lighting a fire in the hearth or to line the floor when they cleaned out the ashes.

Lucinda opened the paper and scanned the headlines, stopping at the one that had caught Rose's attention.

Fox Hollow Seductress to

Hang Next Week

"Seductress," Lucinda scoffed. "Doesn't take much for a lonely man to get his prick out."

"No, ma'am," Rose agreed.

"Foolish woman," Lucinda said with disgust. "If she wanted Richard Powers to marry her, all she had to do was poison Doris. Richard Powers would be looking for a mother for those boys in no time. Instead, she murdered two innocent children and brought the wrath of Dr. Redmond upon herself."

"You don't think it was Inspector Haze that solved the case?" Rose asked.

"Pfft," Lucinda said with a dismissive wave of her hand. "That man couldn't find his own backside with both hands." She refolded the paper and set it aside, her eyes narrowed as she fixed Rose with a speculative gaze. "It was you, wasn't it?"

"I beg your pardon, my lady?"

"That fire that maimed your husband was no accident, was it, Rose?" Lucinda nailed Rose with her gaze, their eyes locked in a moment of spiritual communion. "That's why your mother did what she did. She knew it and thought you'd tried again. And I don't think she got it wrong."

Rose went white to the roots of her hair, but Lucinda smiled at her kindly. "Your secret is safe with me, Rose. We must protect ourselves from the cruelty of men when the law won't."

"Yes, ma'am," Rose mumbled.

"Emmett Doyle got what he so richly deserved."

And so did I, Lucinda added silently. Sorry as she was about John and Bertie, she was also glad that her daughters would not be growing up alongside their father's by-blows or their bastard uncle. Richard Powers was gone, and they'd see Doris Powers off by the end of the month. She couldn't bear to remain in a place where she'd lost her entire family and would be moving to London to take up a position with one of Larry's bachelor friends.

And Helen Carlin would be meeting her Maker next week. Lucinda had no sympathy to spare for that woman, but she couldn't help but wonder if Helen might have got away with murder if Jason Redmond had not been called to the scene and the deaths had been either labeled accidental or investigated by the clodhoppers that were the Essex Police.

Lucinda sighed and smiled sadly, permitting herself a rare moment of self-pity. She loved Larry as much as she was capable of loving any man, but if Jason Redmond had so much as looked at her when he'd first arrived in England, she would have followed him to the ends of the earth. Even to America, which was just as far where Lucinda was concerned. If there was ever a match for her, it was that infuriating, brilliant, unconventional doctor whose values would not be compromised and whose love had to burn hotter than a housefire. She still couldn't see what he'd found to love in Katherine Talbot. Surely that mouse of a woman couldn't manage to hold his attention for long, but for now he seemed content, happy even.

But perhaps their paths would cross again someday…

The End

Please turn the page for an excerpt from

Murder of a Medium, A Redmond and Haze Mystery Book 15

Prologue

It had been a pleasant evening, warm and fragrant with the scents of flowers and cut grass, but tendrils of thick yellow fog had begun to drift from the river after the sun had set, turning the air thick and soupy, and very cold. Neil Lacky couldn't wait to return to Bermondsey and leave his hansom at the cab yard so he could finally go home, rest by a warm fire, and enjoy a good supper and a pint of lager. Maybe two.

He had just dropped off his previous fare in North Audley Street and had turned into Upper Brook Street when he saw her. The woman emerged from the fog like a vengeful apparition, all swirls of black silk and wild hair. Her face was bone-white, and her eyes resembled dark caves. Pale lips were compressed into a thin line as if she were making a supreme effort to contain a scream.

The woman raised a quivering hand to get Neil's attention, but he wasn't interested in picking up some drunken doxy. The last time he'd made that mistake, his hansom had reeked of vomit for a week. But something about the woman gave him pause as she stumbled into a pool of shimmering light cast by a streetlamp. Now that he could see her more clearly, Neil realized she was no streetwalker. Her silk gown was fashionable and well made, a jeweled brooch was pinned to the high lace collar, and she wore earbobs that sparkled like diamonds in the gaslight. The woman carried a beaded reticule, and the ring she wore over her black glove looked like the real thing, not a paste bauble.

"Please, stop," the woman moaned, and Neil took pity on her.

She had difficulty getting into the hansom, so Neil climbed off his perch and gave her a hand. The woman gripped his wrist and stared into his eyes. Her gaze was unfocused, and her speech was slurred, but she didn't smell of spirits, nor did the folds of her gown release the sickly sweet aroma of opium. The woman let go of his wrist and held up one finger, then unclasped her reticule and fumbled inside until she found what she was looking for. She pushed a card into his hand and slumped back against the seat, closing her eyes, and resting her head against the side.

Neil looked at the address on the card, then pushed it into his pocket. One last fare, and then he was off home.

Chapter 1

Friday, June 18, 1869

Inspector Daniel Haze hurried up the steps and pushed open the heavy door. The duty room at Scotland Yard was pleasantly quiet in the morning, when most miscreants were still abed. The action picked up throughout the day and built to a crescendo after sunset, when the constables hauled in brawling drunks, weeping prostitutes, and underage pickpockets who loudly proclaimed their innocence despite their bulging pockets.

Sergeant Meadows sat behind the desk, perusing last week's edition of *The Illustrated London News*. The *News* was published weekly and was a favorite with the men, not only because they enjoyed the pictorials but also because sometimes their names were mentioned and their likenesses captured in the drawings that depicted violent criminals being arrested by the brave and dedicated constables of the Metropolitan Police. Sergeant Meadows set the newspaper aside and smiled in greeting.

"Good morning, Inspector Haze. Beautiful day."

"So it is," Daniel agreed.

"Might take the missus out for a stroll once I go off duty."

"I'm sure she'd like that."

"The superintendent is expecting you," Sergeant Meadows said, now that the pleasantries were out of the way, and they could move on to the business at hand.

Although Daniel wasn't quite sure what that business was. He had been summoned by Superintendent Ransome, but the message had been cryptic at best, and Daniel wasn't quite sure if a crime had taken place, and neither was Constable Putney, who'd come to fetch him. The constable had assured Daniel that Jason Redmond had also been sent for, which usually implied that a postmortem was called for, but the constable had said that there was no body, which was puzzling in the extreme.

"Do you know anything about the case, Sergeant?" Daniel asked before moving along to Ransome's office.

"Nah. He's playing it close to the chest with this one," Sergeant Meadows said. "And you know what that means."

Daniel nodded. If Ransome was keeping the details from his men, then whoever was involved was an important personage whose name was best kept out of the mouths of the constables, whose penchant for a good gossip could rival that of any fishwife. Taking off his bowler, Daniel crossed the duty room and strode down the corridor toward Ransome's office. Ransome had been in a good mood these past few weeks, but Daniel had a feeling that was about to change, and this case would bring out his less amiable qualities. The door was firmly shut, so Daniel knocked and waited until he was bidden to enter.

Ransome sat behind his desk, but whereas he was usually applying himself to a never-diminishing pile of paperwork, the desk was clean, the pot of ink, blotter, and pen neatly arranged in the right corner. Ransome appeared to be staring into space, his shoulders drooping with either resignation or fatigue, despite the early hour.

"Good morning, sir," Daniel said.

"Nothing good about it," Ransome snapped. "Shut the door and take a seat, Haze."

Daniel settled in one of the guest chairs and waited for Ransome to explain himself. Asking questions would only irritate the superintendent, and he would share the details with Daniel in his own time. Ransome sighed so heavily, Daniel felt a gust of warm air hit his face.

"What's happened, sir?" he couldn't help but ask.

"Constantine Moore was waiting for me when I arrived this morning. Remember him, do you?"

Daniel nodded. Constantine Moore was the assistant and paramour of Alicia Lysander, the famed medium, whose ability to commune with the dead had reached mythical proportions in recent years. Members of the ton were willing to pay any amount, no matter how exorbitant, to lure Alicia to their homes, where she conducted private séances and somehow managed never to disappoint those who were desperate to contact their dearly departed.

Daniel had been skeptical of Alicia Lysander's ability and had believed her to be a charlatan of the highest order until Alicia had helped him locate his missing daughter at Jason's behest. If not for Alicia, Daniel might have never seen his darling Charlotte again, and Daniel's gratitude was boundless. He would move heaven and earth to help Alicia if she were in trouble, and by extension Constantine Moore, who had to have come to see Ransome on Alicia's behalf.

"What did Moore want?" Daniel asked.

"He was worried about Mrs. Lysander," Ransome replied. "She had been invited to conduct a séance at the home of the Earl of Ongar last night. They had agreed that Mr. Moore would collect her at ten o'clock, once the séance had finished, but when he arrived, Mr. Moore was informed by the earl's butler that Mrs. Lysander had already departed." Ransome sighed again. "This was unusual, but not overly alarming. Mr. Moore thought that perhaps the séance had not gone as planned, or that maybe someone had become distressed and wished to call an end to the proceedings. He assumed that he would meet Mrs. Lysander at home. When he arrived, there was no sign of her, and as of this morning, she had not returned."

"I see," Daniel said, but he was certain he wasn't looking at the whole picture.

It was concerning that Alicia Lysander had not returned, but as of now, there was no indication that anything untoward had befallen her. And why the secrecy and such obvious concern on Ransome's part? If Alicia Lysander had left the séance of her own free will, what possible reason would Ransome have to worry about the earl's involvement?

"The Earl of Ongar is a very important man, Haze," Ransome said, as if he had read Daniel's thoughts. "He's quite close with the commissioner and has the ear of the prime minister. His Grace and Mr. Gladstone dine together at least once a month, and I hear Mrs. Gladstone has taken Ongar's young countess under her wing. The earl has a reputation for having a short temper and a long memory. If we handle this incident in a manner he finds offensive, he could ruin all our careers and begin a campaign of attrition that could affect the police service as a whole."

"You mean he can ensure that our budget is cut?" Daniel asked.

Despite the stellar work of the Metropolitan Police and the superhuman efforts the public seemed to expect of the thinly stretched and underpaid policemen, there were always those who advocated to defund the police or at the very least cut the funding significantly since they believed the Met's efforts to be useless and a waste of valuable resources. The commissioner was always fighting their cause, and Ransome, who had been an experienced copper before his promotion, spent most of his time trying to figure out how to stretch the budget to pay the men a decent wage and hire enough bobbies to patrol the more turbulent areas of London, where one man with a truncheon and a whistle was about as effective as a slingshot against a cannon.

"Among other things," Ransome said. "We need to handle this very carefully."

"Do you think the earl is somehow involved in Mrs. Lysander's disappearance?"

"I don't know, but she was last seen leaving his house in Grosvenor Square, so that is where we need to begin our inquiries."

"I see no need to involve the earl," Daniel said. "I can question the staff, then try to ascertain which way Mrs. Lysander went after leaving the earl's residence."

"Good man," Ransome said. "I have sent for Lord Redmond. He's on good terms with Mrs. Lysander and has the trust of Mr. Moore. Perhaps this is a case of domestic discord and Mrs. Lysander and Mr. Moore have simply had a falling out."

Ransome looked like he hoped for just such an outcome, but if Alicia Lysander did not appear unharmed within the next twenty-four hours, they would have no choice but to involve the earl and his family, since they had been the ones to host the séance and the earl's servants had been the last people to see Alicia Lysander alive.

"Do you know who was present at the séance, sir?"

"I don't have the names of the attendees, but I'm sure anyone the earl associates with will not appreciate being interrogated by the police."

Daniel was about to ask another question when there was a knock at the door.

"Come," Ransome called.

Daniel was pleased to see Jason, who nodded silently to both men as he walked in and sank into a vacant chair with the relief of a man who'd been on his feet for hours. Jason looked unusually tired for so early in the morning and wore an expression that was too grave to be explained away by carriage traffic or some minor domestic incident.

"Thank you for coming, my lord," Ransome said. "I was just explaining to Inspector Haze that we have a rather delicate situation on our hands. Yesterday evening, Alicia Lysander conducted a séance at the home of the Earl of Ongar. She left the earl's residence before ten o'clock but never returned home. I expect she and Mr. Moore had a lovers' tiff and she simply decided to put some space between them, but until we can be certain that no one in the earl's household was involved in the lady's disappearance, we must tread very, very carefully. With any luck, Mrs. Lysander will turn up today and we'll say no more about it."

"Mrs. Lysander has turned up already," Jason replied gruffly. He did not look like a bearer of happy news, but his somber expression seemed to be lost on Ransome.

"Splendid," Ransome exclaimed. "I'd rather deal with ten run-of-the-mill murders than investigate a case where a high-ranking member of the nobility is involved, especially someone as highly esteemed as the Earl of Ongar."

Jason's expression became even grimmer, and Daniel strongly suspected that he was about to deliver a blow that would thoroughly ruin Ransome's day.

"Superintendent, last night, around half past ten, Alicia Lysander hailed a cab in Upper Brook Street. She gave the driver my address. By the time she arrived in Kensington, Alicia Lysander was dead."

"Dead?" Ransome sputtered. "Where is she now?"

"Downstairs, in the mortuary."

"You brought her with you?"

"I don't have the means or the inclination to perform a postmortem at my home."

"Yes. Of course," Ransome said under his breath. "What was the cause of death?"

"I cannot say for certain until I open her up, but I think she was attacked."

"That's it," Ransome said. "She must have been set upon in the street. A random mugging."

"Mrs. Lysander still had her reticule and was wearing several pieces of jewelry. As far as I could tell, nothing was taken."

Ransome nodded. "Then I suggest we hold off questioning the earl's staff until we're sure about the cause of death."

"I agree," Jason said. "Shall we reconvene in say three hours?"

Ransome checked his watch. "I'll see you at one o'clock."

Chapter 2

Shutting the door to the mortuary behind him, Jason stood still, his gaze on the woman laid out on the table. Alicia was fully dressed, her hair, which had come free of its pins, rippling down the sides like the dark water of the Atlantic on a stormy day. Her skin was chalky, her lips parted in what must have been a final cry. Jason had closed Alicia's eyes, but they had been open when he'd come out to fetch her from the cab, her pupils dilated with either pain or a drug she might have taken shortly before death, her skin still warm. Her body had felt light in his arms, even though a dead body always weighed more than a living one, and her limbs had been pliable, rigor mortis not having set in.

Some part of Jason had hoped that Alicia was still alive and he would be able to bring her around despite the lack of a pulse or the absence of breath, but deep down he had known it was too late. Alicia had passed away on her way to him. Perhaps she'd had something she'd needed to tell him, a final message she couldn't take to her grave, or the more likely answer was that she had hoped he'd be able to save her. Jason hadn't noticed any wounds when he'd laid her down on the settee and had gone through the ritual of confirming death, but Alicia must have known that she was dying, and her final living act had been to give the cabbie Jason's address.

The cabbie had looked shocked as he stood with his hat in his hands, watching Jason lift Alicia out of the cab and carry her inside. He had been able to answer a few basic questions and had shown Jason the card Alicia had given him, but didn't seem to know anything else, only that the woman had been alone and unsteady on her feet, clearly unwell but still alive. The cabbie had fled before Jason could ask for his name and address or fetch money to pay him. He had been understandably terrified that he would be accused of hurting a passenger, but Jason was certain that the man had had nothing to do with Alicia's death. Whatever had occurred had happened shortly before Alicia had got into his cab.

Worried that someone would come downstairs and see the dead woman in the drawing room, Jason had asked his surly butler to guard the body while he roused his coachman, who preferred to sleep in a loft above the carriage house. Together, Jason and Joe had hidden the body in Jason's brougham until he could deliver it to Scotland Yard in the morning. Joe had gone back to bed, but Jason had remained in the carriage house, watching over Alicia until the first rays of the morning sun painted the sky salmon pink and Alicia's still face melted out of the darkness.

Only then had Jason returned to the house. He'd washed and dressed, explained what had happened to a sleepy Katherine, and returned to the carriage house. As he sat next to Alicia in the brougham, he'd reached for her hand, and even though he knew she was gone and couldn't hear him, he had promised that he would discover what had happened to her. He wasn't a religious man. He had lost his faith after the horrors he'd witnessed during the American Civil War, but he now believed that a person's spirit lived on, some kernel of consciousness surviving death and decay and passing to some other realm, where it dwelled for eternity. Alicia had been able to tell him about his parents' final moments, and more important, she had been instrumental in getting Charlotte back after she had been abducted. Jason wouldn't call Alicia a friend, but he had liked and respected her, and he owed her this one last service.

Approaching the table, Jason studied Alicia's frozen features. Had she known what was going to happen to her? Had she foreseen her own death? Was that why she had carried his card in her reticule when they hadn't been in contact for months? Jason's arms felt leaden as he removed his coat and hung it on a hook, then put on the leather apron and tied the strings behind his back. He pushed his hair beneath the linen cap and set out the instruments he would need for the dissection. Ready at last, he took a deep breath and laid a gentle hand on Alicia's cheek.

"Forgive me," he said.

Jason didn't expect an answer, but something in the air shifted, and although no sound had passed Alicia's lips, not even an exhalation of gas that was already beginning to build up in the lungs, Jason could have sworn he heard Alicia's voice in his mind.

"I trust you, Jason."

"I won't fail you," Jason said, and carefully turned the body over, ready to undo the buttons that ran down the back of Alicia's gown and begin the postmortem.

Chapter 3

Normally, Jason needed to eat after a postmortem, since he never breakfasted before starting on a body, but today he had no appetite. He felt worn out and nauseated as he ascended the steps and paused before the door to Ransome's office. He didn't want to talk about Alicia as if she were nothing more than a body. To him, she was still a person, an intelligent, vibrant woman who had been like no one he'd ever met, but the tang of her blood was still in Jason's nostrils, and even though he'd scrubbed with carbolic soap, his hands didn't feel clean, reminding him that she was now a cadaver. Sadness tugged at his heart, and his limbs felt heavy and sluggish. He wished he could take a short rest, but given what he'd learned, he realized that his day was just beginning, and he had to find a way to tap into his reserves of energy if he were to be useful.

"Come in," Ransome called once Jason knocked. "Where's Haze?"

"Right here," Daniel said as he strode down the corridor.

The two men resumed their seats, as if the hours in between had not happened. Daniel looked expectant, but Ransome's expression was strained, his lips compressed into a thin line as he studied Jason across the expanse of his desk. He probably hoped Jason would tell him that Alicia Lysander had died of natural causes and there was no need for an inquiry. Jason wished that were the case. He would be sad and angry that Alicia's life had been cut short, but he would accept her passing and hold on to the memory of the woman she had been. The only thing he would remember now was her eviscerated body, the glistening organs, and the weight of her brain in his bloodstained hands.

"Well?" Ransome asked when Jason failed to speak. "What's the cause of death?"

"Alicia Lysander died of a cerebral hemorrhage that was the direct result of blunt force trauma that fractured her skull."

"And yet she still managed to find a cab and get to your house," Ransome said confusedly.

"Death is rarely instantaneous when there's a slow bleed on the brain," Jason explained. "The person might have a headache and suffer from disorientation, blurry vision, and slurred speech, but they're still able to formulate thoughts and move about, although their coordination might be impaired. Had Alicia lived another few minutes, she might have been able to tell me what had happened to her, but she slipped away shortly before she arrived. I would like to think that her passing was peaceful, but given that someone had fractured her skull, she was likely in great pain."

"She may have fallen and hit her head," Ransome offered.

Jason shook his head. "I don't think that's likely."

"Based on what?"

"Based on my examination of the contusion. The fracture is at the top of the parietal lobe." Jason pointed to the top of his head for the benefit of Daniel and Ransome. "If Alicia had fallen, the fracture would be lower, whether she fell backward and landed on the ground or hit her head against something hard while still upright. No debris was caught in the hair or had adhered to the skin. Had she fallen to the ground, there would be dirt and grit, and if her head was smashed against the wall, there would be residue from the bricks. However, there was mud on her skirts and dirt on her palms. I think she went down on her knees after she was struck and balanced herself on her hands before pushing to her feet."

"Can you tell anything about the object used to hit her?" Daniel asked.

"I think it was heavy, round, and made of metal, since there were no splinters or bits of stone."

"Would she have seen her attacker?" Ransome asked.

Jason shook his head. "There are no defensive wounds. It is my belief that someone came up behind her and hit her hard."

"Would the person have to be taller than the victim to strike her at that angle?" Ransome asked.

"Alicia was tall for a woman, so they would have to be at least as tall as she was."

"And were there any health concerns that would have hastened her demise?"

"Alicia Lysander was in good health at the time of her death," Jason said.

"Was she hit repeatedly?" Daniel asked.

"I saw no evidence of multiple blows," Jason said. "Perhaps her assailant saw her go down, assumed she was dead, and ran. Had they looked back, they might have seen her rise, but the darkness and the thick fog would have hidden her from view as soon as her assailant was a few feet away. I don't know how long she was down, but eventually, she rose and was able to stumble to the road, where she stopped a cab."

"So attempted murder, then?" Ransome asked, now all business.

"Attempted and accomplished," Jason replied. "Alicia died of her injuries."

"Are you able to estimate the time of the attack?" Ransome asked.

"If Alicia was due to leave the séance at ten but departed early and was delivered to my door just before eleven, then she was probably attacked between nine thirty and ten thirty, after she had left the earl's house."

"Grosvenor Square is not known for violent attacks on respectable women," Daniel pointed out.

"Mrs. Lysander's respectability was questionable at best, but you're right, Haze. This sounds premeditated. We need to fill in that missing hour if we're to find out what happened."

"Which means we must start with the earl and his household," Daniel replied.

Ransome glared at him. "Well, get to it, then. And remember, kid gloves, Haze."

"Yes, sir," Daniel replied, and pushed to his feet.

Jason stood as well. The sleepless night and lack of food had finally caught up with him, and he swayed on his feet, but he quickly caught himself on the back of the chair and followed Daniel out of Ransome's office. He had every intention of accompanying Daniel to Grosvenor Square.

Printed in Great Britain
by Amazon